# Privileged Spectatorship

# Privileged Spectatorship

*Theatrical Interventions in White Supremacy*

✦

Dani Snyder-Young

NORTHWESTERN UNIVERSITY PRESS
EVANSTON, ILLINOIS

Northwestern University Press
www.nupress.northwestern.edu



Printed in the United States of America

10 9 8 7 6 5 4 3 2 1

Library of Congress Cataloging-in-Publication Data

Names: Snyder-Young, Dani, 1977– author.
Title: Privileged spectatorship : theatrical interventions in White supremacy | Dani Snyder-Young.
Description: Evanston, Illinois : Northwestern University Press, 2020. | Includes index.
Identifiers: LCCN 2020020312 | ISBN 9780810142510 (paperback) | ISBN 9780810142527 (cloth) | ISBN 9780810142534 (ebook)
Subjects: LCSH: Theater and society. | Race in the theater. | Theater—Political aspects. | Theater audiences—United States—Psychological aspects. | Whites—Race identity—United States.
Classification: LCC PN2049 .S63 2020 | DDC 306.4848—dc23
LC record available at https://lccn.loc.gov/2020020312

Whiteness has to be acknowledged as something that is performative, something that does something in the world, or at least in the moment of its engagement. It has to be something that is linked with access, the social construction of power, worth and value—that leads to the (dare I say it) practice of privilege.

—Bryant Keith Alexander, "Black Skin/White Masks"

White liberalism generally doesn't aim to end white domination. Quite the opposite: it aims to render it more tolerable, both to its beneficiaries and its victims, and so to perpetuate itself indefinitely—an aim it shares with its "enemy" white supremacy.

—Shannon Sullivan, *Good White People*

CONTENTS

## LIST OF ILLUSTRATIONS

# ACKNOWLEDGMENTS

Thank you to Trevor Perri, Gianna Mosser, and everyone at Northwestern University Press for all your support throughout the writing and publication process.

This work would not have been possible without the collaboration of artists and artistic leaders who welcomed me into their praxis, spoke with me about their work, and gave me feedback on early drafts of chapters: Robert Duffley, Brenna Nicely, Keith Wallace, James Scruggs, Mark Rayment, Charlotte Meehan, Michael Bryan, Tony Adams, and Jenn Adams.

This book is deeply indebted to the many research assistants who not only helped me collect and analyze data but also helped me understand their lived experiences of the theatrical events we studied together. Thank you to Pablo Hernandez Basulto, Liam Hofmeister, Amos Nasongo, Ilyssa Kosova, Jamie Kreppein, and Chloe Bluml, as well as the many collaborators collecting and analyzing data at Halcyon Theatre: Jenn Adams, Hayana Kim, Maggie Patchett, Victoria Apodaca, DeZane Rouse, Gelyssa Rankin, and participating artists Isabel Quintero, Valeria Rosero, Isaly Viana, Tamika Lechee Morales, Noe Jara, and Arik Vega. Sarah Menke's work on Halcyon's pilot study did not make it into this volume, but the research methodology we developed is indebted to her insights and assistance.

My work on this project spans two institutions, and it has been made possible by generous support at both Illinois Wesleyan University and Northeastern University. When I began work on this book, Illinois Wesleyan University's Artistic and Scholarly Development Grant program provided funding for me to develop the foundational theoretic framework. I completed work on this project as a faculty member at Northeastern University, where course releases gave me time to complete this manuscript and a College of Arts, Media and Design 2025 Research Collaborative Grant through the Design + Human Experience working group funded my work on *The White Card*. In addition, the Arts Work Fund for Organizational Development provided generous funding for the two-year-long audience research study I conducted with Halcyon Theatre.

Thank you to many colleagues for valuable feedback and inspiration as I developed portions of this book in working groups, roundtables, and symposia. The foundational framework for the book was developed through the 2016 ASTR working group Transverting Whiteness, convened by Megan Lewis and Shannon Walsh. Chapter 1 benefited from rich conversation at

IDIERI in 2018 with Kelly Freebody, Michael Balfour, Matt Omasta, and Monica Prendergast and the assembled body of colleagues who attended our session "Perspective Change, How Are We to Know It?" and the 2018 ATHE panel "Talk Back: Engaging Audiences beyond the Theatrical Event" with Brenna Nicely, Julia Listengarten, and Kevin Becerra. Colleagues at Northeastern University's College of Arts, Media and Design provided valuable feedback on chapter 2 at a 2017 lunch talk. Sections of chapter 4 were developed through the ASTR working group Feeling Extra Ordinary: Populist Activism and Performance convened by John Fletcher and Sonja Kuftinec in 2017, who were joined by Suzanne Shawyer and Andrew Friedman in giving feedback on a draft of this chapter as part of the ATHE 2019 roundtable "Confronting Polarized Scenes in Activist Performance: Bridge-Building, Bridge-Burning, and Beyond."

Chapter 5 includes material adapted from previously published essays and reviews, the editors of which assisted me not only in developing these pieces but also in working through the foundational questions at the heart of the book. It includes material originally published under Creative Commons license on HowlRound in my reviews "Gentrification and the American Dream" (November 14, 2013), "Race and Real Estate in Next Theatre's *Luck of the Irish* by Kirsten Greenidge" (March 25, 2014), and "Broken Public Schools and Community Dialogue at Collaboraction" (December 4, 2014). These pieces benefited from the keen editorial eyes of P. Carl, Jamie Gahlon, and Srila Nayak. Tamara Underiner and Stephani Etheridge Woodson provided valuable feedback on "Despite artists' intentions, emancipated spectatorship reinforces audience members' existing attitudes and beliefs," in their edited collection *Theatre, Performance and Theories of Change* (2018), reproduced with permission of Palgrave Macmillan. "The Promise and Pitfalls of the Real," published in *Theatre Survey* 57, no. 3 (August 2016), and reprinted with permission from Cambridge University Press, was developed through the symposium on Theatre and Social Change convened by Harvey Young and Dassia Posner at Northwestern University in 2016.

Thank you to my colleagues at Northeastern University: chair Scott Edmiston and colleagues Janet Bobcean, Jonathan Carr, Jesse Hinson, Frances Nelson McSherry, Antonio Ocampo-Guzman, Oliver Watson, Darren Evans, and Marti McIntosh. I am particularly grateful for Nancy Kindelan's mentorship; she has extended herself to support me and my work on this book in many ways, and I appreciate her guidance and attention. At Illinois Wesleyan University, early work on this project was made possible by the support of provost Jonathan Green and colleagues Curtis Trout, Nancy Loitz, Jean McFarland Kerr, Scott Susong, David Stoughton, Thomas Quinn, Saundra DeAthos-Meers, Sheri Marley, Chris Connelly, Armie Thompson, and Kelly Ullom.

Sociologist Meghan A. Burke introduced me to critical whiteness studies, and the writing group that she, economist Adrienne Ohler, and I shared for eight years in Illinois was a source of much support. She started me asking the questions that fueled this study. As an undergraduate, Raven Stubbs spent many hours in my office trying to get me to understand her experiences as a working-class student of color at a predominantly white institution; over many years she has taught me much about white racialized performances (including my own). Matt Omasta has been a backbone of support in the trenches of academia.

We tend to underplay the relationship between domestic and professional labor, but for me, they are deeply entwined. I began work on this project in the antepartum ward of Prentice Women's Hospital, where I lived for eight weeks while my daughter Parker Marie Young thankfully remained safely in my womb. So thank you, Parker, for staying put through the winter of 2015. Since she was born, my research and writing have been made possible by a small army of childcare providers including Erin Daly, Chloe Bluml, Lee-Anna Studt, and Bridget McConaville, among others. Jeanne "Nana" Young's generosity and assistance was essential to my ability to do much of the field research at the heart of this book, and she continues to be an ongoing source of support. None of my work would be possible without the encouragement and early material support of my parents, Bill and Phyllis Snyder. And last but certainly not least, my number one husband Dan Young provides unconditional love and support.

# Introduction

✦

# Mainstream Theater and Privileged Spectatorship

In a breakout discussion group following the 2018 world premiere of Claudia Rankine's *The White Card*, two Latinx men in their early twenties and a white man in his sixties discuss what they connected to in the production. Produced by American Repertory Theater and presented by ArtsEmerson, *The White Card* is a dinner-party play about the commodification of black art, turning focus to the white people who consume and commodify black suffering with antiracist intentions but ultimately reassert a collective imagination in which to be black is to suffer. The affluent, politically progressive white characters in the play perform unrecognized biases as they fetishize black suffering, failing to recognize the damage they wreak on the successful black artist they have invited to dinner. The play's activist aim is to make whiteness visible to the predominantly white, affluent, older spectators frequenting large institutional theaters. The theatrical event is structured in two parts: Act 1 is a traditional performance, which audience members sit and watch. Act 2 is a facilitated post-performance discussion session in which trained facilitators ask audience members to discuss the play with one another in low-focus breakout groups and then come together for a facilitated high-focus discussion. It is designed to help them draw connections between the play and their own lived experiences and is framed as an integral part of the production.

On this evening, an African American cofacilitator foregrounds act 2 in her commitment that Black Lives Matter. The assembled audience consisting mostly of white spectators sits in silence for a beat until a single audience member breaks the silence, affirming her commitment with applause. Once the applause begins, the rest of the audience joins in. They perform for one another and for the facilitator their participation in a collective valuing black life. A white cofacilitator describes her belief in the power of theater to provoke change. The audience again applauds, this time with less hesitation. With their applause, spectators signal a desire for the antiracist play they have just seen to intervene in the problems it depicts. The facilitators ask the audience to get into groups of three or four people they do not know and discuss the questions, "What did you connect with?" and "What did you find challenging?" in the play.

In this breakout group, the white man responds to the question "What did you connect with?" that he found the characters "cartoonish"; "I suppose some people are like that, but . . ." he says, "the play was not realistic." Throughout the run of *The White Card*, audience members of color frequently affirm how the play reflects their lived experiences circulating in the corridors of power. In contrast, white audience members routinely distance themselves from the problematic performances of whiteness on display in the production, responding to them as exaggerated, unrealistic, and unrepresentative of how educated, progressive white people behave.

One of the young Latinx men pushes the white man to probe a little deeper, again asking, "but what did you connect with?"

The white man stumbles for a moment and then responds, "Well, I don't like the thing about Black Lives Matter. All lives matter. Your lives matter, my life matters."

The young man who has not spoken takes a sharp intake of breath.

The other young man does not allow the white man to continue. He replies, "I connected to Charlotte [the protagonist, the acclaimed black artist], who spent the play trying to get the white characters to understand the oppression and colonialism present in the sentiment 'all lives matter.' I am trying to figure out how to communicate that concept in a way white people will understand because clearly this [the play] did not work."[1]

Many professional theater artists want to use live performances in formal theater spaces to disrupt racism and create a more equitable society. This book examines evidence of the impact of such projects on their audiences, looking at how and why they do and do not work to intervene in white supremacy. It looks at audience responses to a range of theatrical events produced at mainstream not-for-profit professional theaters in large US cities from 2013 to 2018, all of which focus on race-related conflict or racial identity in the contemporary United States. Many of these productions explicitly intervene in antiblack racism within the context of the larger Black Lives Matter movement, which developed and grew through this period.[2] The audiences for these performances reflect dominant patterns of theater attendance—the majority of participants in these theatrical events are older, affluent, white people who describe themselves as politically progressive. Most of the case studies in this book rely on qualitative data collected through participant observation of audience behavior at theatrical events, contextualized with data from interviews with artists; one chapter focuses on social media comments from audience members and published reviews from professional critics. This book is about the ways white audience members consume the stories of racialized others, analyzing how particular artistic, organizational, and programmatic strategies can (or cannot) mitigate white privilege.

These case studies straddle a particular nodal point in recent US history: the presidential election of 2016. This event shook many politically progressive white people—including me—out of a space of complacent comfort, leading many to ask urgent questions about our own complicity in oppressive power structures. I am learning that, at best, theatrical events can be pedagogical spaces in which audience members can productively grapple with these questions and strategize ways to make real change in the world—and at worst, they can be spaces in which these same audience members' urgent desire to make change can be diffused into a smug confirmation that they are what moral philosopher Shannon Sullivan terms *good white people*, reinforcing class hierarchies by displacing racism as a problem perpetuated by an imagined, verboten other.[3] This project examines the specific tactics artists, institutional leaders, and program facilitators use that seem to create pedagogical spaces rather than spaces of complacency and elitism. Many of its most practice-focused learnings orient toward the work of production dramaturgs, community engagement staff, and theater critics, emphasizing the ways in which audience members' understandings and actions are shaped by an ensemble of discourses and structures surrounding theatrical production.

Qualitative research relies on the trustworthiness and transparency of researchers, and I make no pretense of disembodied, neutral objectivity. I am a white scholar-artist specializing in theater and social change: a teacher, critic, applied theater facilitator, dramaturg, and director. My graduate training is in educational theater, and as such I am interested in the intentional and unintended lessons theatrical events teach. I needed to write this book because I struggle with my own complicity in oppressive systems of power and am driven to learn how to better dismantle them. I feel tremendous responsibility that my students—young people who want to do right in the world—model their own engagement with their privileges after the ways in which I structure my language, demonstrate a capacity to tolerate discomfort, disengage or make excuses, displace or accept responsibility for the role I play in sustaining oppressive systems of power, and visibly grapple with the messiness of my unearned advantages. Many of my students are, like me, white, able-bodied, cisgender US citizens from relatively affluent households of origin. I see more awareness of the nonneutrality of these subject positions in recent years, and with this awareness comes a kind of paralysis. I sympathize; I spent my first year of graduate school mired in guilt and fear grappling with my unearned advantages. With the aid of some particularly patient mentors and collaborators, I pushed past the paralysis to accept that avoiding tough conversations would only uphold an unjust status quo, but I will not pretend I do not still feel uncomfortable broaching these topics. Through this book, I include moments in which I responded in imperfect ways—moments in which I shied away from necessary discomfort, distanced myself from culpability, performed unconscious bias, chose the wrong words. I use the terms "we" and "us" to describe white people throughout the book, including myself in the white racialized collective. For I, too, am a privileged spectator of theatrical events, performing my whiteness, part of the target audience for the artistic interventions I study.

## The Haunting Whiteness of Mainstream Theatrical Events

"Who are we trying to reach when work is made, and to what end, and by what means?" Caridad Svich asks, framing the key question for audience engagement.[4] When artists make plays in formal theater spaces, we make them for the audiences who will come to those spaces. Alan Brown found that in the United States, "white Americans use purpose-built arts facilities at several times the rate that Hispanics and African-Americans use them. In contrast, populations of color report using places of worship and informal settings at several times the rate of whites."[5] The audience attending plays in purpose-built theater spaces is predominantly white and college educated. The richer the institution—the more resources for the art—the more exclusive the space feels. This situation is incredibly frustrating for artists and institutional leaders, and it is the source of much conversation regarding equity, diversity, inclusion, and community engagement within the theater industry. Tammie Kennedy, Joyce Irene Middleton, and Krista Ratcliffe use the term *haunting whiteness* to describe the cultural spaces in which, absent a racial signifier, whiteness "functions as an unstated norm."[6] Most mainstream theaters are hauntingly white.

The majority of mainstream theatergoers in the United States are middle-class white people. The National Endowment for the Arts (NEA) reports that, demographically, the people in the United States most likely to attend arts events are college-educated white women between the ages of fifty-five and seventy-four with household incomes greater than $150,000.[7] The theatrical events I describe in this book would be considered "nonmusical plays," whose audience nationally breaks down as about 59 percent female, 80 percent white, 61 percent college educated.[8] Subjective social class identity in the United States is notoriously slippery, as concrete educational attainment and income levels intertwine with people's understanding of their own position in relation to that of others. Statistically, the more education and household income, the more likely an individual is to go see a theatrical event, and the NEA found that "individuals who self-identify as middle or upper class are significantly more likely to attend the arts, compared with those who identify as working class," even when household income is similar.[9] Patterns of arts attendance in the United States reinforce Pierre Bourdieu's findings that arts attendance reflects and builds the kinds of cultural capital valued by the upper classes—and the upper middle class in the United States is 75 percent white.[10]

Carmen Morgan articulates a commitment echoed throughout broad swaths of the US not-for-profit theater community that "theater that is rich in diversity and fully inclusive will create work that will inspire us to be agents of change—work that will ultimately change the world."[11] This commitment does not erase the way in which mainstream theater is haunted by a pervasive link to the habitus of the upper classes—cultural scripts that, as I discuss in this book, are coded "white" regardless of the races of the bodies performing them. Marvin Carlson in *The Haunted Stage* articulates, "The expectations an audience brings to a new reception experience are the residue of memory of previous such experiences."[12] This residue certainly includes prior theater experiences in general, but also prior experiences with specific details and textures present in the theatrical event. Audience members who have had many positive experiences in which they have felt welcome in cultural spaces with spotless, lushly carpeted lobbies, high ceilings, and dramatic chandeliers (or for that matter, basement studios with black walls and risers crammed with folding chairs) are likely to feel welcome in theater spaces with these architectural features. An audience member whose past experiences in such spaces include being misrecognized as custodial staff or followed by security officers carries that memory into such a theater, regardless of whether that experience took place in some other theater space or a different kind of cultural institution all together. As Melissa Hillman points out, a young, working-class audience member of color might come to a theater once, but "he knows he's a tourist in someone else's world" and won't stay if the space isn't really his.[13]

Audience members do not just go to the theater; they go, as Carlson highlights, "to the particular part of the city where the theater is located, and the memories and associations [connected with] that part of the city help to provide a reception context for any performance seen there."[14] In chapter 2, I will describe how Keith Wallace subtly invokes the racialized violence implicit in the locations of many mainstream theater buildings. The institutional theaters in which he often performs are located in affluent neighborhoods in which black bodies like his are in danger of being misrecognized as criminal and subjected to state-sanctioned violence. Many of the locations and spaces that feel *safe* to the predominantly affluent, white audiences dominating mainstream theatrical events are haunted by legacies of exclusion and marginalization.

However, for most existing mainstream theaters, the obstacle opens up an opportunity. An audience dominated by educated, affluent white people—people with privilege and a degree of cultural power—elects to attend theatrical events at which we can grapple with racism. For ninety minutes to three hours (depending on the duration of the particular event), we turn off our cell phones and focus our attention on pervasive problems caused by white supremacy, including police brutality, cultural appropriation, segregation, and educational inequality. We take emotional journeys and make the familiar strange. After many events, facilitated discussions help us process feelings, work through the language to discuss new understandings, and learn about concrete actions to take in the real world. At their best, these theatrical events operate as pedagogical spaces in which educated white audience members work on learning how to use our structural privileges to help dismantle white supremacy.

In the wake of the election of Donald Trump to the presidency of the United States in 2016, audience members are hungry for these spaces. Many educated, urban, politically progressive white people were taken by surprise that an overtly racist, xenophobic, sexist reality television star could rise to power not in spite of those traits but because of them. We understood that we had, in comfort and complacency, been blind to the persistence of such problems. We came to the theater to figure out what had happened and what we could do to fix it.

## White Habitus

The social and cultural scripts identified with "whiteness" in the contemporary United States are rooted in the habitus of a college-educated, professional/managerial/intellectual upper middle class. Bourdieu developed the concept of *habitus* as embodied systems of cultural power, the bone-deep manifestation of the tastes, habits, attitudes, skills, and dispositions developed over a lifetime of culturally specific experiences.[15] Harvey Young emphasizes the ways habitus are not fixed; people organically develop multiple habitus through a lifetime of varied experiences, acquiring new tastes and growing into new roles.[16]

The tastes, habits, and dispositions common to a college-educated upper middle class are not the exclusive provenance of white people, nor are they common to all people with fair skin. This habitus performs and signifies a position of relative status within the social hierarchy of the contemporary United States. Skills like speaking and writing fluent Standard English with the complex syntax and vocabulary of the college educated are coded "white"; this "racing" of class is part of the fabric of white supremacy.[17] Cultural markers of class and status are misrecognized as racialized performances as a myriad of social skills required for smooth participation in spaces of power are coded "white."

This masking enables actual racialized performances of whiteness to go unmarked. Eduardo Bonilla-Silva defines *white habitus* as a "racialized, uninterrupted socialization process that conditions and creates whites' racial tastes, perceptions, feelings, and emotions and their views on racial matters."[18] White habitus manifests in many ways—for example, the way segregated white neighborhoods and schools appear normal and neutral to many white people.[19] The theatrical events I study throughout this book often attempt to use the live, collective nature of the theatrical event to socialize white antiracist perceptions, feelings, and views on racial matters. As the opening anecdote to this introduction suggests, audience members perform their existing white habitus in response, sometimes revealing uncomfortable truths. However, many of them perform sincere efforts to develop their capacity to tolerate racial discomfort and enfold ongoing self-awareness into their routine interactions. For some audience members, this process is well under way, while others display evidence that they are at the start of their journey. At times I am able to catch glimpses of moments in which new feelings and perceptions have been seeded, have not yet taken full root, but are perhaps beginning to grow.

Bourdieu theorizes that reflexivity allows people to consciously change our habitus and that "reflexive labor might be undertaken most effectively not by the solitary or heroic intellectual but by a community of inquirers bound together by a logic of peer competition and 'regulated struggle.'"[20] I watch audience members come to the theater to consciously work to change their white habitus. Theater cannot do this on its own; it works in concert with a wider array of cultural forces, and those cultural forces drive this audience to attend these theatrical events and reinforce their messages when the performance is through. In chapter 4 I will discuss how much public pedagogy around racial discourse takes place through digital performances on social media, disconnected from the embodied experience of watching others react to moments of performance nonverbally and in real time. In the theatrical event, audience members watch other people respond to moments of performance—both the matrixed performances of actors onstage and the nonmatrixed performances of other audience members in moments in which actors request audience participation and in post-performance discussions. From these responses—some overt (such as applause), some verbal (such as direct responses in discussion), some subtle and nonverbal (such as averting the eyes or physically closing off the body)—they take social cues surrounding decorum and the boundaries of community.

But I do not want to paint too upbeat a picture. In this study, I also examine unsettling evidence of how at worst, antiracist theatrical events *support* oppressive systems of power by operating as a mechanism for white upper-middle-class social reproduction, exacerbating class inequality and reinforcing the dominance of affluent, educated whites. The subtly exclusionary responses privileged audience members have within theatrical events *designed to include* work against artistic and institutional efforts toward inclusion and equity. Some of the same actions that help white audience members start to develop racial self-awareness reinforce the dominant whiteness of the theatrical space. Many of these actions reinforce the moral superiority of the white people choosing to attend the antiracist theatrical event. Even when facilitators attempt to intervene in such discourses, audience members often persist in blaming *other, bad white people* for the continuing problem of white supremacy. At worst, such events assuage the impulses bringing audience members to the theater, sending them back into the world feeling they have done something to dismantle racism by attending a theatrical event and have as such fulfilled their responsibility to help create a more equitable world.

Changing one's habitus is hard, and I watch white audience members work at it. The display of this reflexive labor comes with its own double bind. In my classroom, white students express anxiety that their allyship will be read as performative—that is, that their visible labor to develop racial self-awareness and work on dismantling white supremacy will be interpreted as insincere. This anxiety paralyzes. I watch well-meaning white people who want to fight racism fear they will be socially ostracized for visibly laboring to do so not because it is *bad* to fight racism but because doing so in a white body might be read as performing moral goodness for the purpose of increasing individual cultural capital. Judith Butler's foundational concept of performativity has been co-opted by popular discourses of "performative allyship" and stripped of its complexity. Butler's theory of gender performativity shows "that what we take to be an 'internal' feature of ourselves is one that we anticipate and produce through certain bodily acts, at an extreme, an hallucinatory effect of naturalized gestures."[21] Performativity highlights the ways in which humans construct identities through repetition of a readily available repertoire of speech acts and nonverbal gestures; such repetition helps make us who we are. The repertoire of readily available actions is produced by larger power structures; through embodied repetition they come to feel natural and we cease to analyze their systemic roots.

The popular definition of *performative allyship* takes on a decidedly antitheatrical bent, painting "the performative" with what Erving Goffman might call a "cynical" brush. To Goffman, performances can be cynical or contrived (that is, intentionally deployed for personal gain or one's sense of the good of a group), or they can be sincere (that is, a reflection of genuine beliefs). Most social performances fall somewhere in between. When an individual presents a front adhering to the values of the group, she knows she is doing it—that is, she knows she is fitting in. That consciousness does not mean that she does not agree with or believe in any of the group's values. Goffman recognizes that when an individual begins to learn a social performance, the effort of learning makes for a contrived performance. With repetition, the social performance grows more organic and more ingrained.[22] I believe the majority of antiracist white performatives I describe throughout this book reflect genuine desires and beliefs, though many are marked by the effort required to learn.

Shannon Sullivan highlights how the categories through which the white body can be seen in relation to matters of race fit a narrow binary: good/not-racist or bad/racist. *Good white people* know and act in adherence to the rules of appropriate antiracist behavior, distinguishing themselves from *bad, racist white people*.[23] This ontological split creates a false, hierarchical division between the morally good not-racist white people (the allies) and the morally bad racist white people (the *other* white people). These are treated as essentialist categories; a bright line divides this binary. The anticipation of racism, to borrow from Butler, "conjures its object," and so all actions taken by white people in relation to matters of race support this binary.[24] The unmarked nature of whiteness insists that actions taken in white-segregated contexts that do not acknowledge them as such are not racial performatives.

White people can avoid being categorized in relation to this binary by maintaining segregation and avoiding direct discussion of race. Many do.

Antiracist cultural capital is valued within what Sullivan calls "middle class" contexts, consciously using this term as "less a precise economic category than a broad rhetorical designation for the vast majority of Americans who see themselves as the moral norm: hard workers who deserve their success and who have endless possibilities for improving their lives further."[25] The United States is plagued by conspicuous silences on the topic of class, and widespread use of the term *middle class* to include much of the middle, upper middle, and upper classes obscures inequality and class stagnation. Richard Reeves describes a contemporary United States in which households in the top fifth of income distribution in the United States operate within an increasingly separate cultural landscape. He argues that a distinct class gap can be seen between the richest 20 percent of households and the rest of the country in terms of education and occupation, family structure, security, health outcomes, and civic participation.[26] The upper middle class is not monolithically white, but 75 percent of households in this class are headed by individuals self-identifying as white.[27] This class division is reflected economically, socially, and culturally, manifesting in segregated schools and neighborhoods that reinforce and reproduce social capital.

Sullivan argues that the binary of good antiracists and bad racists serves to support the continuing class dominance of an affluent, white minority through the abjection of working-class and poor whites—constructing those who do not have the capital of what she calls "race-class etiquette" as morally bad racists who therefore deserve to be disenfranchised.[28] The class most likely to have and benefit from the cultural capital of such etiquette is what Barbara Ehrenreich and John Ehrenreich label the "professional-managerial class" of college-educated professionals.[29] To return to an earlier point, theater attendance in the contemporary United States can operate as a method to build and perform cultural capital valued within this same class context. It is for this reason that artists and leaders creating theatrical events with goals of intervening in white supremacy must pay attention to the impact of these events on real audience members. Audience members at antiracist theatrical events can displace racism as elsewhere, positioning themselves as enlightened *good white people* in contrast to the imagined other *bad, racist white people* who did not attend the performance, who live in a geographic region they consider less enlightened, or whose work to change their white habitus presents itself in an awkward or messy way.

Scholars of theater and social change have, for decades, taken heart in the counterhegemonic possibilities of resistant readership and spectatorship. Antonio Gramsci and Michel Foucault each articulate the mechanisms by which dominant power structures produce compliance in mainstream populations, and Michael de Certeau writes about ways in which individuals can resist these mechanisms.[30] Jill Dolan highlights the ways in which marginalized subject positioning informs resistant reading.[31] At the heart of these foundational theories of resistant readership is a hard truth openly acknowledged by its authors: *most* readers and spectators *do not* default to make counterhegemonic meaning of the work they read and see. Many people who will make counterhegemonic meaning are individuals whose lived experience runs against the grain of the dominant narrative; those who benefit from the status quo, as Dolan puts it, "applaud at the curtain call" and tend not to think too much about how imbalances of power are reflected in and naturalized by cultural products.[32]

The act of watching is interpretive and active, and spectators make their own sense of performances in relation to their preexisting understandings of the world. Susan Bennett's foundational study of theater audiences recognizes spectators as "productive and emancipated" makers of meaning.[33] Readers make active, resistant meaning, according to Roland Barthes, through a redistribution of language:

> Now *such redistribution is always achieved by cutting*. Two edges are created: an obedient, conformist, plagiarizing edge (the language is to be copied in its canonical state, as it has been established by schooling, good usage, literature, culture), and *another edge*, mobile, blank (ready to assume any contours), which is never anything but the site of its effect: the place where the death of language is glimpsed. The two edges, *the compromise they bring about*, are necessary.[34]

A dialectic forms between an "obedient" reading of the text as set down by the author and "another" uncontrollable and unpredictable reading determined by the reader, which combine to create the meaning the reader makes of a work. Dialectics rely on opposition—two opposites are drawn together to explode into something new. Barthes's language of obedience, conformity, and plagiarism telegraphs to the reader a preference for the unpredictable edge of this dialectic as he situates the more predictable edge as the product of institutional systems of cultural power.

The mainstream notion of a politically resistant reading relies on the "obedient" reading of the text to be in keeping with hegemonic values, so the unpredictable reading can run against the grain of dominant discourses. In this way, it presupposes that the now-dead author is fundamentally conservative, supporting an oppressive status quo. Within a Frankfurt school worldview, this will always be true—as Louis Althusser argues, there is no "outside" ideology, and all of us (regardless of political leanings) are embedded in the status quo.[35]

Emancipated spectators filter signs and symbols and actions and stories through our own individual experiences and culturally mitigated understandings. All acts of communication are acts of translation, as we spend our entire lives trying to bridge gaps across each other's understandings. "Distance is not an evil to be abolished, but the normal condition of any communication," Jacques Rancière argues.[36] This distance is the gap between the "edges" Barthes invokes. Rancière describes how the spectator "observes, selects, compares, interprets. She links what she sees to a host of other things that she has seen on other stages, in other kinds of places."[37] The "edge" Barthes earlier describes as "blank (ready to assume any contours)," Rancière understands to be defined by a lifetime of already-consumed stories and already-lived experiences. Emancipated spectators "develop their own translation in order to appropriate the 'story' and make it their own story."[38] In so appropriating, they create a dialectic between Barthes's "obedient" edge and an edge created by their own preexisting understandings of the world.

Those understandings are not fixed. The subfield of "theater and social change" is based on the premise that the dialectic process I have described can shift spectators' preexisting understandings of the world in the direction of social justice. However, sometimes the "obedient" edge reflects progressive ideologies popular with many artists and intellectuals, and the edge created by spectators *does not* collide to facilitate spectators' understandings in the ways artists hope. Many people do not want their actions challenged and beliefs changed. As I illustrate throughout this book, many white audience members interpret antiracist performances in ways that maintain their own sense of themselves as *good white people*, undermining and subverting the performance event's intent to intervene in white supremacy. Active spectatorship can operate as readily in conservative directions as in progressive ones.

That does not stop many artists from wanting to use theater as a counterhegemonic technology, unsettling the status quo for the purpose of making progressive social change. Many are inspired by the work and legacy of Bertolt Brecht, who advocated for theater to foster critical thinking by distancing spectators from theatrical action, leading them not to laugh and weep along with the characters in the drama but to "laugh when they weep [and] weep when they laugh."[39] Brecht and then later Augusto Boal both characterized theater emphasizing emotional identification with a hero's journey as supportive of the status quo, promoting rugged individual effort (rather than collective action) as the default means to overcome adversity.[40] Following in their footsteps, generations of artists committed to using theater to make social change have employed artistic strategies to distance audience members from dramatic action. Many of the performance events I describe throughout this book use theatrical devices such as fragmented narrative, direct address, actors playing multiple roles, and attention drawn to the mechanics of theatrical event creation. Many also include overtly Brechtian elements such as signs or titles signaling points of dramatic action before they occur or juxtaposition of contradictory elements (such as projections and staged action intentionally telling opposing stories). These aesthetic elements are designed to interrupt the process by which spectators read themselves into a natural-seeming story.

This attempt does not always work as intended. I found that, regardless of a theatrical event's aesthetic setup, white audience members tend to interpret what they see in a way consistent with their own sense of themselves as morally good. When sympathetic white characters are present in a multiracial landscape, white audience members often seem to identify with them regardless of the aesthetic mode in which the production operates. They speak in post-performance discussions and informal interviews in ways constructing the moral goodness of those characters—even when the plays clearly implicate those characters in the problems in which the plays look to intervene. When overtly racist white characters are present, audience members identify them as *other, bad, racist whites*, differentiating them from the *good, antiracist whites* who choose to come watch an antiracist play. In theatrical events in which either no white bodies are present onstage or the only white characters are *bad racists*, white audience members construct themselves as allies to sympathetic people of color, negating the conspicuous absence of such allies in the narratives. These patterns track across theatrical events with many distinct aesthetics. As I will discuss in greater detail in chapter 5, I did not see performance events achieve much success in getting white audience members to recognize the ways in which the choices we, ourselves make (for example, living in segregated neighborhoods and sending our children to segregated schools) perpetuate and exacerbate white supremacy.

Theatrical events seemed more successful in creating opportunities for white audience members to start to understand and empathize with people they do not often encounter in their day-to-day lives (and may not be able to *hear* when their paths do cross). For example, many white people may recognize excessive police force to be a problem in the abstract but do not understand how it leads law-abiding people of color to live in fear of the police. A vicarious emotional journey can help them understand the urgency of a distant problem like this one. Critical distance can be just as helpful in understanding the underlying reasons for this problem's pervasive existence. White audience members struggle to understand what they, personally, can do to help solve this problem. Their previous ignorance and lack of fear of police open up spaces to understand their own privilege, which is a necessary first step in dismantling it.

These findings open up a double bind. White audience members need critical distance to be able to access the problem of white supremacy. However, the events that seem most successful in getting us to grapple with it focus on problems the audience members are too far away from to know how to solve. The theatrical events tackling the quotidian ways in which white audience members actively support white supremacy are, in some ways, the least politically successful ones I encounter. Many theatrical events seem to get people to think and care; many help white audience members build vocabulary and capacity to discuss racism and privilege. I did not observe any theatrical events appear to get white audience members to make material changes within the domains over which we have the most power.

## Whiteness: Some Key Concepts

A number of key concepts drawn from critical whiteness studies circulate through this book. I present brief descriptions of them in this section.

*White supremacy* is the hierarchical sociopolitical system of racialized power in which whiteness comprises the dominant category. This system spans far beyond the conscious, overt racism of hate groups—who do not appear in this study—encompassing, as David Gillborn puts it, the "comprehensive condition whereby the interests and perceptions of white subjects are continually placed centre stage and assumed as 'normal.'"[41] White people who consciously oppose racism still unconsciously carry widespread, hegemonic ideas about white superiority and entitlement around in our heads. As white people in the United States overwhelmingly control cultural, economic, and political power, these ideas manifest in the routine practices of institutions, maintaining a status quo of continuing white domination. Frequently, a discourse of what Joyce Bell and Douglas Hartmann call "happy talk" around the benefits of diversity and multiculturalism masks material practices upholding white supremacy.[42]

This book contains few individual, conscious acts motivated by racialized hate. It includes many moments in which well-intentioned white people unreflexively and unintentionally act in ways perpetuating racist structures. Actions taken in ignorance can cause real pain, and it is important to differentiate between intentions and impacts. When our well-intentioned actions unintentionally cause pain, it is our responsibility to help alleviate that pain and learn how to avoid causing such pain in the future. Robin DiAngelo writes that "naming white supremacy changes the conversation in two key ways: It makes the system visible and shifts the locus of change onto white people, where it belongs. It also points us in the direction of the lifelong work that is uniquely ours, challenging our complicity with and investment in racism."[43]

The theater productions I study largely look to draw the attention of white audience members to the problem that when we passively benefit from oppressive systems of power, we tacitly support them. The comfortable path of least resistance upholds white supremacy because maintaining that comfort oppresses people of color. Once a white person understands this—and this is the lesson many of these performances look to teach—the choice to ignore it when convenient becomes a conscious act.

*White privilege* is the term used to describe the unearned advantages enjoyed by people whose skin marks us as belonging to the dominant racial group. It manifests in myriad ways, quietly smoothing rough edges and cracks to make the path trod by the dominant a little less fraught with friction. Peggy McIntosh owns, "Some privileges make me feel at home in the world. Others allow me to escape penalties or dangers which others suffer. Through some, I escape fear, anxiety, or a sense of not being welcome or not being real."[44]

Recognizing white privilege is a step in dismantling white supremacy—that is, identifying the unearned advantages whiteness brings enables us to start to build a more equitable world. *Privilege*, however, is baggage-laden word. While the term is ubiquitous within academic and social justice activist contexts, it is not universally recognized by audience members as a structural designation. Phoebe Maltz Bovy highlights how *privilege* colloquially operates as "a synonym for 'entitled and willfully obvious' " implying "horrible person-ness."[45] When used or interpreted in this way, the term personalizes and individualizes; it can be used or misinterpreted as an insult. Bovy points out that until recently, the popular use of the term outside of scholarly circles implied inherited financial wealth, or "old money."[46] "The conflation of all forms of relative advantage with the *financial* form," Bovy argues, alienates poor and working-class people from the term.[47] This conflation makes it difficult for working-class and poor people who benefit from being born white (or for that matter, able-bodied or straight or male) to recognize these unmarked subject positions as "privilege." After all, it is possible to enjoy privileges by virtue of belonging to a dominant social group without *feeling* privileged, in particular if one compares oneself with other individuals within that social group.[48]

As Michael Kimmel points out, even people who "are willing to engage with these questions [of inequality] tend to personalize and individualize them," acknowledging the systemic nature of inequality while simultaneously treating racism (also sexism, homophobia, ableism, etc.) as "bad attitudes held by bad people."[49] Such slippage from the structural to the individual makes the term itself a nodal point for conflict, obscuring our capacity to openly discuss systemic inequality.

*Whiteness as an unmarked racial identity* means that, in the United States, white people are configured as "people" and white stories as "universal." The conspicuous invisibility of whiteness posits white experience as the default human experience. Richard Dyer points out, "This assumption that white people are just people . . . is not far off saying that whites are people whereas other colours are something else."[50] Marking white racial identity disrupts such a dehumanizing assumption, constituting all people as racialized subjects operating within the social order. Robin DiAngelo analyzes how the unmarked nature of whiteness makes it particularly difficult for white people to view *white people* as a social category—that is, a group sharing generalizable features.[51] White people are socialized to consider ourselves unique, exempted from the group by virtue of the particulars of our lived experience. We push back against our inclusion in the generalized category of *white people*—a category of people whose actions and unconscious biases maintain our dominant status within an oppressive, hierarchical status quo. When we see the impacts of such actions and biases represented onstage in mainstream theatrical events, we find ways to excuse ourselves from the social group represented as the oppressors.

*The white gaze* is a concept whereby white people resist inclusion in a racialized category yet render people of color as representatives of racialized groups. These generalized categories are overdetermined, weighted with stereotype. George Yancy warns of how the white gaze "distorts, caricatures, oppresses, and dehumanizes" the black body.[52] This distorted gaze flattens the *racialized other* into a generalized figure that is somehow less human and less individualized than representations of white people. At its most dangerous, the white gaze can lead a white spectator to misrecognize a black body as an object of fear. As Joe Feagin argues, such stereotypes emerge through "automatic mental processing," having been conditioned in through a lifetime of biased cultural messaging.[53] Individuals have agency as to the degree to which we act on or ignore the stereotypes, and many white people work to ignore them. As such we would like to exempt ourselves from the group instinctively gazing with their overdetermined weight. To begin the process of decolonizing the white gaze, white spectators must recognize the existence of and reasons for the unconscious biases coloring our fields of vision.

*White fragility* is defined by DiAngelo as "a state in which even a minimum amount of racial stress in the habitus becomes intolerable, triggering a range of defensive moves. These moves include the outward display of emotions such as anger, fear, and guilt and behaviors such as argumentation, silence, and leaving the stress-inducing situation."[54] White people are frequently insulated from racial stress. The unmarked nature of whiteness means that most white people do not think of ourselves as racialized beings and often do not recognize how our race shapes our perception of the world. Whiteness's dominance means that we feel racial comfort in spaces of status and prestige; we are surrounded by narratives quietly affirming our racial superiority. This racial comfort is punctured when we are challenged racially. An example of a racial challenge is when a white person is asked to look critically at his or her complicity in supporting racist structures. White people frequently respond defensively to racial challenges out of definitions of racism as conscious individual acts of cruelty motivated by racialized hate and investment in a racist system from which they benefit and which they misrecognize as meritocratic. White taboos against direct discussion of race frequently leave white people racially ignorant; white fragility is an obstacle preventing us from developing a clearer view of how racism works.

*Whiteness as a social construct of dominance* places the meaning of skin tone in relation to systems of social hierarchy in a way that is culturally constructed. Matthew Frye Jacobson highlights how race is a conceptual category as much as a perceptual category, pointing out how "the American eye sees a certain person as black, for instance, whom Haitian or Brazilian eyes might see as white."[55] Races are invented categories, sifting people into groups marking lines of difference. Racial boundaries change over time and are marked differently in different places. Jacobson describes the slippery ways in which whiteness has been defined and redefined through US history, operating as a signifier for "who belongs and who does not, of who deserves what and who is capable of what."[56] In the nineteenth century, immigrants from southern and eastern Europe were considered racially distinct from—and lesser than—the descendants of western European immigrants who had already settled in the United States. Starting in the 1920s, the racial distinctions between categories such as Jewish, Italian, Irish, and so on consolidated into the unified *Caucasian* in current use. This shift in racial logic was due, in no small part, to the migration of African Americans to the north and west; the social inclusion of some groups relied on the social exclusion of others.[57]

*White racialized performativity* is a concept that recognizes that performances of whiteness are complex and varied. Bryant Keith Alexander defines *racialized performatives* in the following way:

> The expressed or scripted performance of raced individuals, are possibilities that emerge from the depths of sedimented histories, which do not operate outside the realm of the real but in the processes of their embodied reenactment—both policing and resisting the scope of expressions affixed to the racial performances under scrutiny, in the company of members of that particular and practiced racial community.[58]

White people have ready access to a repertoire of context-specific actions (speech acts, gestures, etc.) to perform our white identities. Because whiteness often goes unmarked, we do not typically recognize our racialized performances as such. As George Yancy, Claudia Rankine, and many other scholars and artists of color have noted, white racialized performances unintentionally reveal ugly truths about the pervasive and insidious nature of racism.[59] As Faedra Chatard Carpenter reminds me, artists of color have a rich history of performing whiteness, and white people have much to learn from the specificity with which they recognize our racialized performances.[60]

At the historic moment at which I conduct this study, the repertoire of readily available antiracist white performatives is narrow and specific. I describe elements of these performance codes throughout the book, as well as white performances policing the scope of such expressions. These performances of whiteness reveal much about the ways even well-meaning white people are more comfortable disavowing racism than confronting the ways in which we continue to tacitly, materially support it.

## Audience Research

Many activist, applied, and educational performance projects are created with the goal of shifting the perspectives of participants, audience members, or both on a particular issue. Yet scholars and practitioners of theater and performance tend to be skeptical of rigorous evaluation of the impact of such artistic work, fearing that what James Thompson identifies as "beautiful, radiant things" such as beauty or joy will wither and fade performance from art to instrument.[61] Theatre Communications Group's recent study of audience engagement makes it clear that this is a continuing challenge within the theater industry, as artists express anxiety around "being boxed into traditional outcome-based measures that are inherently transactional." The study found that "knowing how to evaluate, determine and communicate success was a struggle" even as artists recognize a need for "constant vigilance around impact—often without having obvious measures to determine success."[62] The study works to address this methodological gap by using qualitative research methods to capture and analyze rich, complex, messy evidence of how performance events are affecting their audiences intellectually, emotionally, and socially.

Much of the most readily available research on theater audiences is generated by theaters or arts agencies for marketing purposes and tends to focus on demographic details related to marketing categories. Kirsty Sedgman questions the epistemological ramifications of overreliance on quantitative research collected for the purposes of marketing and advocacy.[63] Such research rarely attempts to capture the complexity of audience experience of theatrical events. Sedgman argues for qualitative audience-centered research as a method to help break down false divisions between "impact" and "affect," helping theater scholars and practitioners "re-envision value as a process rather than an outcome."[64] She views "value not as an *end point*—'benefit,' 'impact,' 'outcome,'—but as a *process*: something that is constantly negotiated and always in flux"; qualitative study of audience members' responses to theatrical events enables us to "get a sense of this process in action."[65]

Theatrical events are comprised of "artistic" conventions of communication, "organizational" structures governing the setup of the encounter itself, and the "structural" social and material conditions of production and reception.[66] Studies of theatrical events, like this one, analyze the interplay of artistic, organizational, and structural elements. I pay particular attention to the ways in which organizational and structural conditions can amplify or hinder the social impact of carefully considered artistic choices.

To study such impact, I draw direct evidence from audience members' behavior at theatrical events. Methodologically, I borrow from Caroline Heim, who explores how "the embodied actions of audience members constitute a performance."[67] She uses Goffman's "repertoire of actions" as a framework through which to analyze audience behavior at mainstream theatrical events. Heim observes, "Contemporary audience members in mainstream theatre playing the role of audience have a limited repertoire of actions to perform: laughing when appropriate, occasional crying, applauding at the right time," as well as "the shuffle and the fidget" and the rare but powerful "walk out."[68] To this list I add a repertoire of quiet low-focus gestures, such as physically closing off the body by contracting the torso back into the farthest reaches of the seat and crossing both arms and legs. Such embodied actions can have multiple meanings—for example, an audience member might perform this action because she is physically cold in the theater, emotionally repulsed by onstage content, or angry at a companion for reasons unrelated to the play. It is impossible to know the motivation behind a single performance of such an action without asking about it and, in so doing, drawing attention to that it is being watched. However, when a similar action is repeated by many audience members during the same moment at many performances during a theatrical run, the pattern can be interpreted. Actors and stage managers routinely pick up on and use these patterns during performance runs, timing entrances, lines, and cues in anticipation of expected moments of laughter or tension. This study examines the cultural meanings we can make from such patterns.

I describe specific examples of audience members' performances throughout this book, using thick description to invoke particular moments of behavior. These moments are usually representative of larger patterns of audience response and have been selected because they illustrate the pattern. I do describe singular moments of audience response—such as a walkout in chapter 3—when they take so much focus that they visibly become part of the performance event for the rest of the audience. These singular moments are clearly marked within the text as distinct and are often contextualized with additional information about the action gathered from that audience member's comments during a post-performance event, an artist's account of a conversation they had with the audience member, or an informal interview I conducted with the audience member.

Most of the qualitative data I collected for this study focuses on the public performances of strangers; this data was collected through anonymous participant-observation. There are some case studies in this book in which I worked with a team of research assistants who operated as participant-observers to collect data on audience responses to every performance of a show's run. For other case studies I worked alone, collecting data at a representative sample of performance events and including artists' descriptions of distinct audience behavior at performance events I did not attend. One set of case study data is drawn from archival sources, focusing on critical and social media discourse. Specific methodological details are included in the description of each case study. Heim identifies how "actors are the audience's audience," and in several case studies I include data I collected from interviews with actors, contextualizing what I can see from my seat with what they can see and feel from the stage.[69] Doing so is particularly important in performances in intimate spaces eschewing the convention of the fourth wall, in which audience members functionally operate as an actor's scene partner. I include the voices of diverse artists and research assistants throughout the book triangulating and contextualizing what I can see from where I sit—literally in my single seat on any given night, but also within my white skin.

As the project developed and I grew more accustomed to studying audiences, I became less shy about striking up conversations with the audience members around me. My embodied presence as an educated white woman of about forty appears unremarkable in mainstream theater audiences—my race, gender, age, and apparent class positioning all unmarked for their dominance in such spaces. Some post-performance events included breakout discussions with small groups of other audience members, and my research assistants and I participated fully in these discussions. In all conversations with fellow audience members, I was transparent about my project, most frequently telling people I was writing a book on theatrical interventions in white supremacy and studying the impact of the play on the audience. Some theatrical events created environments in which it felt organic to conduct informal interviews at intermission or after the show. I re-created all informal conversations to the best of my ability from memory when drafting my field notes after each event, and when they are present in the text, I appear as a character in the narrative, contextualizing other audience members' responses within the full conversation. I did not collect identifying information from any audience members.

During some high-focus post-performance events—that is, some panels and full-room discussions hosted by a central facilitator in which all comments and questions are performed for a full room of strangers—archival audio recordings were created. I was able to refer to transcripts of these archival recordings when re-creating the details of pivotal moments of discourse or action in these post-performance events; these are cited as such throughout the book.

Participant observation relies upon visible markers of racial identification, which do not always track neatly with racial identity. This method foregrounds the significance of racialized perceptions in social interactions, as people (including me) interpret and respond to actions in relation to visible markers of race. As I discuss in chapter 6, when such interpretations prove incorrect, audience members' responses reveal the ways in which perceptions of racial identity color social performances. My research teams and I were often able to verify audience members' racial identities via informal interviews and interactions, and comments within the scope of post-performance events almost always referenced the racial identity of the speaker in implicit or explicit ways. However, a limitation of this study is we were not able to we speak with every audience member we observed, and so is possible that we have misidentified the racial identities of some audience members. Broad patterns of observed nonverbal behavior described in the text are based on visible markers of racial identification. Detailed examples within the text focus on audience members with whom we had enough interaction or context to verify their racial identities.

Alexander critiques the field of critical whiteness studies as ostensibly engaging with "the abolitionist project of deconstructing and moving away from Whiteness as a dominant paradigm [that] actually, in content and method, becomes centripetal by centering Whiteness in discussions of race and multiculturalism," stealing center stage from people of color in one of the only pockets of the academy they have carved out as their own.[70] An inherent tension lies at the core of critical whiteness studies—its project is to make whiteness visible, exposing its specificity for the purpose of moving it away from a position of dominance. To do that, it centers a discussion of race and diversity on whiteness, giving yet more attention to white institutions and white voices. I am sensitive to this critique. As a white person writing about white behavior in white institutions, I recognize that I risk centering the overrepresented white voice. This makes for a dilemma I cannot fully resolve as I work to better understand how to disrupt white supremacy by using my insider positioning to study the slippery ways it works on and through the bodies of well-intentioned white people.

This book is written for an audience including scholars and students of contemporary activist performance and theater practitioners interested in equity and inclusion. A majority of theater scholars, artists, and students are white, and as such I expect that many—though by no means all—of the people who read this book will be white people. I am embarrassed to admit that when I began this study, I was surprised and shocked by many white racialized performances in theater audiences, and I was horrified that I had not noticed them earlier. It is my hope to help other white artists, artistic leaders, and audience members see a little more clearly the impact of our whiteness on theatrical events, using this facet of my white privilege to help combat institutionalized racism in the theater. Dismantling the haunting whiteness of theater spaces is work white people must do.

I recognize that readers of color do not have the luxury of ignorance of how white people perform our privileges in public, and as such they are likely to recognize behavior patterns I describe in this book. I hope my documentation of these patterns affirms the experiences of such readers. Artists and scholars of color have developed a rich body of work critiquing whiteness, and I am indebted to their insights. This work informs much of my analysis, and I encourage readers to read deeply of this canon.

My focus on white audience members is not intended to erase or ignore the presence, responses, and experiences of audience members of color, who are present at many of the theatrical events I study. I include their responses throughout the study, attending both to moments in which people of color respond differently than white people do and moments in which white people perform differently in the presence of people of color. The haunting, pervasive whiteness of mainstream theater spaces requires that attention be paid to white racialized performances as such; I place whiteness at the center of this study in an effort to make it visible and highlight its strangeness.

This book focuses on the specifics of theater audiences in the United States, engaging with the nuance of its particular cultural context. However, upper-middle-class white audiences dominate mainstream theater events in the United Kingdom, Canada, and Australia, and the racial dynamics I describe in this book resonate across national borders.[71] I contextualize US-based case studies with theory written by international scholars, situating them within a global conversation on the capacity of theater and performance to make progressive social change. The case studies I analyze in this book represent a range of mainstream theatrical events—they were produced by large institutional theaters and small ensemble theaters, employ a wide variety of aesthetic and storytelling structures, and tackle a range of issues stemming from white supremacy. They include plays by black, Latinx, and Asian American artists produced by theaters led by predominantly white artistic leadership teams. This choice is not intended to negate or ignore the important work done by culturally specific theater companies but rather to highlight the nonneutrality of white institutional spaces, making strange the pervasive whiteness of a theater industry whose discourse lauds diversity, inclusion, and equity. Many of the case studies in this book deal with the ways white supremacy manifests as antiblackness; four chapters focus on theater inspired by the Black Lives Matter movement and its reception by white audiences. This emphasis reflects the programming patterns of mainstream theaters during the years in which I was collecting data, a larger, related trend in the United States for discourses of race to default to a black/white binary, and the specificity and severity of antiblack racism and state-sanctioned violence against black people.

Part 1, "Come Closer," engages with two case studies of productions attempting to use the liveness of the theatrical event to dismantle white supremacy through empathy and interpersonal relationships. The chapters focus on contrasting productions from American Repertory Theater's 2017–18 season, navigating relationships between artistic work and formal post-performance programming within the context of a large institutional regional theater. Chapter 1, "Making Whiteness Visible," analyzes how exclusionary responses white audience members perform within theatrical events work against artistic and institutional efforts toward inclusion and equity, focusing on the ways the facilitation staff for A.R.T./ArtsEmerson's large, high-profile production of Claudia Rankine's *The White Card* worked to address this problem. Chapter 2, "Critical Catharsis," examines the ways in which post-performance events can amplify or interrupt a performance's potential to get audience members to take responsibility for helping to solve the problem in the real world, focusing on Keith Wallace's intimate solo performance *The Bitter Game* at A.R.T. Oberon.

Provocation and outrage as tactics for dismantling white supremacy are the focus of part 2, "Rage against the Machine." Chapter 3, "Peeling Back the Veneer of Decorum," examines the impacts of contemporary blackface minstrel performance, taking Sleeping Weazel's 2017 production of James Scruggs's *3/Fifths Trapped in a Traveling Minstrel Show* as a case study.

Chapter 4, "Outrage and the Boundaries of Community," examines digital performances of outrage in response to controversial incidents in the theater community, examining how artistic communities perform and enforce their social norms. It takes as case studies the controversies surrounding Steppenwolf's *This Is Modern Art* in 2015 and *Pass Over* in 2017.

Part 3, "Decolonizing Gazes and Spaces," focuses on ways to do just that. Chapter 5, "Maintaining White Racial Comfort," examines obstacles to decolonizing the white gaze, studying the ways audience members avoid looking at how the choices we ourselves make (for example, living in segregated neighborhoods and sending our children to segregated schools) perpetuate and exacerbate white supremacy. It draws evidence from three theatrical events I participated in between 2013 and 2015 in Chicago and its close-in suburbs: Steven Simonic's *Broken Fences* at 16th Street Theater, Collaboraction's *Forgotten Future: The Education Project*, and Kirsten Greenidge's *Luck of the Irish* at Next Theatre. Chapter 6, "Building Diverse Community," highlights the way many small and fringe theaters perform to audience bases comprised mostly of the friends and family of artists. I examine this phenomenon as a *feature* rather than a *bug* of small theater production, examining how this feature can help bridge social divides and create theatrical events that are *not* hauntingly white. It examines Halcyon Theatre's 2017–18 productions of Lloyd Suh's *American Hwangap*, Marisela Treviño Orta's *The River Bride*, and Caridad Svich's *De Troya*. A brief, action-oriented "Conclusion: More Work to Be Done," synthesizes some of the specific tactics that seem to make the greatest impact in dismantling white supremacy, offering recommendations for artistic leaders, dramaturgs, facilitators of community engagement programs, and audience members to consider when tackling and watching antiracist theatrical events.

# Part 1

✦

*Come Closer*

## Chapter 1

✦

# Making Whiteness Visible

Climbing the steps to the Paramount Theatre's performance space, the doorway glows blindingly white for the world premiere of Claudia Rankine's *The White Card*. Produced by American Repertory Theater (A.R.T.), presented by ArtsEmerson, directed by Diane Paulus, and dramaturged by P. Carl, this high-profile production would perform to sold-out houses throughout its run in February and March 2018 at ArtsEmerson's Paramount Center Robert J. Orchard Stage in downtown Boston.[1] Riccardo Hernandez's set is completely white: white walls, white stairs, white furniture, white coffee table. The audience of about three hundred people sits in an alley stage configuration, on display within the white box.[2] On one wall hangs a photo of police officers shrouded in smoke; on the opposite wall, a photo of a crowd of black people raising their hands. The two portraits face each other on opposite sides of the room. On the couch rests a copy of Ta-Nehisi Coates's *Between the World and Me*.

*The White Card* depicts a small dinner party thrown by Charles, a progressive white art collector, for Charlotte, an acclaimed black photographic artist whose work he wants to acquire. The white characters perform a series of unrecognized biases the audience is intended to recognize as such, while Charlotte demonstrates the grace with which a successful black professional must push them aside. The play illustrates how white people often fail to understand our power within racialized social contexts, showing the ways in which this ignorance manifests in problematic performances of whiteness.

A facilitated discussion with a stated goal of getting audience members "to stay in the room together and have a conversation about race" is framed as the second act of *The White Card*.[3] Interracial teams of two trained facilitators run each event using a common structure. They introduce themselves and the event, break the audience into low-focus "buzz" groups to discuss where they saw themselves in the play and what challenged them, and the audience returns for a high-focus discussion reporting back on their buzz groups. At the end, audience members are given white index cards and asked to write down one thing they can concretely do moving forward to address racial inequalities identified in group discussions. Rankine and Carl articulate the reason for incorporating this interactive discussion into the performance event and their goals for this project:

> The play exists to consider a way forward. It looks at what feels like a fault line so wide that we will never be able to find each other on the other side. And yet, we are in each other's way every day without knowing what to say. As we sit in the theater in such close proximity to one another, as we embrace the discomfort of the words and histories we fear to speak, we hope the play sparks the kind of risky, vulnerable, and nuanced conversation that the urgency of our situation demands.[4]

For this case study, I assembled an interracial team of research assistants to help me study the audience's response to the production: Pablo Hernandez Basulto (who is a light-skinned Latinx man from Mexico), Liam Hofmeister (who is a white man from the northeastern United States), and Amos Nasongo (who is a Kenyan immigrant raised in the southern United States).[5] We operated as participant observers throughout the run of the play, keeping field logs and analytic memos on audience responses to moments of performance of the play proper and the participatory act 2 program. We collected this qualitative data anonymously. We did not know the identities of most of the audience members we encountered, and I redacted from our data set any information I thought could potentially be used to identify audience members. The initial plan was for a team member to watch the audience through every performance, but the run sold out quickly and we adjusted our plan to collect data at select performances of the play and at every performance's participatory act 2 discussion.[6] My research team stayed in dialogue with the act 2 facilitation team throughout the run, communicating what we saw and keeping track of adjustments the team made in response. After the completion of the run, I held focus groups and interviews with some of the act 2 facilitators, triangulating what my team saw with their experiences facilitating the events.

The theatrical event operates as a pedagogical intervention for white people, encouraging white people to "make yourself your own project" and make white privilege visible.[7] The program gets its target audience of older, affluent white theater patrons to think critically about how, in the words of the play, "we were all raised wrong," stay and talk about their discomfort seeing themselves in unflattering characters, and start to think about their complicity in the structural systems of power from which they benefit.[8] However, the audience for this production is not exclusively white, and the targeted intervention of the act 2 community engagement program at times appeared to alienate audience members of color and reinforce the haunting whiteness of the institutional theater space. As audience member Divya Amladi tweeted, "The whole discussion/homework thing made it seem like the play was only for white audiences who need to #StayWoke."[9] The facilitation team recognized this problem early on and made adjustments to try to accommodate it, but the team members found themselves locked into a structure that did not allow them to fully resolve this substantial issue.

Michael Finneran and Kelly Freebody "provide a vital counter-narrative to the received idea that simply by intending to do 'good,' drama work will therefore automatically, always do 'good.' Besides, with the complexities that exist between practice, context and intention—maybe good isn't good enough anymore."[10] *The White Card* looks to intervene in the problem that, as facilitator Maureen White puts it, "white folks in this country [the United States] are abysmally unpracticed at discussing race."[11] It is impossible to decode a lifetime of ignorance and develop this nuanced skill set in ninety minutes by watching a play. White people who do not know how to talk about race and who are just beginning to realize that they unintentionally hurt, insult, and exclude people of color *sometimes talk about race in ways that hurt, insult, and exclude the people of color in the audience.* As act 2 facilitator Ashley Herring describes:

> What surprised me, and it shouldn't have, were the white people who watched a play about whiteness, about white supremacy, about all things white and they were still their worst white selves when commenting. Not only were some white audience members full of their white selves in the share out but other white [*sic*] said nothing or didn't stand up to terrible shit being said. It was all a larger extension of the play.[12]

The subtle (and sometimes not-so-subtle) exclusionary responses privileged audience members have within theatrical events *designed to include* work against artistic and institutional efforts toward inclusion and equity. Some of the same actions that help white audience members start to understand their own white privilege reinforce the dominant whiteness of the theatrical space. This chapter examines what happens when an applied theater project creates contradicting and conflicting feelings and impacts—the very elements of a program that make the greatest change for one group of audience members wreak the most havoc on another.

The theatrical event was explicitly designed as an intervention in white supremacy targeting the older, affluent white people dominating audiences and subscriber bases at large institutional theaters. Judith Malina asks activist artists to think critically about the question "what do you want to say to which people?"[13] This intervention does just that, working to create the conditions in which affluent white people might be able to see, hear, and begin to understand the experience of middle-class black people circulating in the corridors of (white) power. Brenna Nicely, A.R.T.'s education and community engagement director, articulates how the event provided some productive "vocabulary and some space to unpack it" for white audience members "who are not confronted with race on a daily basis or are not aware of race on a daily basis."[14] For this portion of the audience, this event often does what it seems to have been designed to do—operate as a public pedagogy to get affluent white theater patrons to recognize whiteness as racial specificity, identify microaggressions as problematic, give them some language to name oppressions they recognize, and plant the seeds of continuing growth in the work to make whiteness visible.

In buzz groups, we frequently encountered white people who were visibly shaken by the play who had trouble putting their feelings and responses into words. Many audience members do not have a sophisticated vocabulary with which to discuss racism. They articulated that the play made them uncomfortable and that it made them think. They echoed phrases from the play, "we were raised wrong," internalizing the play's argument that they "need to look inwards" because they "might not be helping even though we think we're helping." They described discomfort at seeing themselves reflected in unflattering ways, recognizing their complicity in the problems the play represents. They expressed the sentiment, "I learned more than I expected to. Things I shouldn't have had to learn. Things I should have known already." Audience members who chose to fill out a post-performance survey emailed to them by A.R.T. overwhelmingly responded positively to the event, appreciating the thought-provoking play and the post-performance space in which to unpack it.

Many white people who appeared to be in their sixties and seventies commented that white privilege is a new idea to them, and in high-focus facilitated discussion, they often referenced how other people in their buzz group helped them understand this new concept. This informal feedback provides evidence of how the social, interactive nature of act 2 provided productive pedagogical space. However, these moments also reveal the ways in which these audience members can unthinkingly demand that the event center on *their* learning process and interests in ways that are detrimental to others.

To offer a representative example, at one performance, an older white man who does not have the microphone—that is, whom the facilitator has not called on to speak—says that a woman in his group had a great comment that he thinks she should share. He indicates a young woman of color, who grabs her face and shares an embarrassed laugh with the young white woman sitting next to her, whom she appears to know.

The facilitator asks if she's "being voluntold or volunteered?"

The older man says—as he holds a microphone toward the young woman—that ultimately it is her choice if she wants to speak. He hands over the microphone and asks her if she's comfortable in saying "the thing about Charlotte's subtext."

The other facilitator loudly says, "Yes, she can speak for herself."

The young woman of color, now holding the microphone, agrees to speak and says that she was moved by how Charlotte always had a subtext that she was being forced to speak for her race and how as a young woman of color she often feels that expectation that she needs to explain to other people the position of people of color.

The white man appears to miss the irony that he has created a situation coercing the young woman of color to do precisely the thing her comment critiques. Moments like this—and there are many such moments—reinforce the whiteness of the theatrical event. They tell the very people of color whose lived experience and perspective the play represents that the event is not for them—it is for the consumption and benefit of the white audience. Such moments communicate that their bodies and voices are present in the space to help educate white people—in the words of the play, to "spread out the work" of such pedagogy and amplify the veracity of the experiences represented in the play.[15]

Sara Ahmed describes how people of color "embody diversity by providing an institution of whiteness with color," thus masking the problem of an institution's haunting whiteness.[16] We watched white audience members treat the visible presence of people of color in the act 2 discussion as a kind of service they expected the institution to provide them, critiquing the dominant whiteness of the event as a way of distancing themselves from their own culpability in the problems the play presents. We saw more of these critiques in high-focus moments of act 2 than in buzz groups.

For example, one evening a white woman in her thirties comments that, "what made [me] uncomfortable is that the majority of the audience is white" and that "[other white audience members] were speaking from their comfortable seats, enjoying the play just as the characters in it are enjoying the black art." She focuses on the facilitators, asking what efforts A.R.T. and ArtsEmerson have "put out to get people in the room from different backgrounds or take the play to other more diverse places."

One of the facilitators tries to refocus the conversation on "personal reflections" and says that "she is happy to talk about their outreach efforts after the play."

Now without the microphone, the woman responds, "It is personal." The usher gives her the microphone back and she repeats, "It is personal." She says that she does not feel that she can have this conversation when "everyone here is white."

The facilitators deflect this comment and move on to "continue to give other people a chance to speak," but this woman continues to shake her head as the conversation moves on and ultimately walks out before the end of act 2.

This high-focus moment of open conflict is a touch more dramatic than was typical, but a number of white audience members did make comments indicating that they would prefer a more racially diverse audience, that the whiteness of the audience made them feel "uncomfortable," and several asked my research assistant Amos, who is black, why there are not more black people at the play.

Ahmed points out how "what 'comes up' as a problem is already dependent on interests that cannot and will not be declared. In other words, it is a critique of *how things surface*, which is to say, a critique of what recedes. So, for example, whiteness recedes when diversity becomes a solution to the problem of whiteness."[17] The woman who does not feel she can discuss the play in a room in which most of the people are white avoids engaging with her own whiteness, focusing instead on how the institutions producing the event failed to provide her with people of color with whom to discuss the play. In so doing, she reduces audience members of color to racialized representatives, framing their presence as a *service* an institution should provide for her edification.

Many audience members arrive at large institutional theaters with a horizon of expectations that they will receive services designed for their comfort. These theaters work hard to help make patrons comfortable, partnering with upscale dining venues and nearby parking garages, emailing instructions to help smooth audience members' paths to their comfortable seats. Frequent patrons come to expect that their experience at the theater will center their comfort, and audience members paying eighty-five dollars for a theater ticket frequently expect to be made comfortable by others in the same ways that audience members paying twenty dollars for a ticket frequently expect to take responsibility for their own comfort. That horizon of expectations can pose a problem when the artistic goals of a production are to make audience members feel *discomfort*.

As the aforementioned examples demonstrate, we routinely watched white audience members in act 2 attempt to transform an event designed to make them experience racial discomfort into one in which they can feel comfortable that they have some control. I do not want to insinuate that *all* white audience members at *The White Card* behaved in these ways—most did not—but this vocal minority's performances disrupted the event for the entire audience and reinforced the haunting whiteness of the space.

## Believable

Charlotte, as a working artist, needs the admiration and patronage of the white philanthropic class; the play depicts her journey to recognize that their gaze and their money undermine and contradict everything she stands for. The very things that she works for cause her pain. Lauren Berlant theorizes, "A relation of cruel optimism exists when something you desire is actually an obstacle to your flourishing."[18] Charlotte finds herself caught in a situation that ultimately forces her to cut off the relationship and chart a new direction with her artwork.

Rankine represents this journey through a realistic, narrative aesthetic with a classic Aristotelian dramatic structure. Charlotte is the protagonist;

Charles is the antagonist. The inciting incident: the black artist Charlotte comes to dinner at the home of Charles, a white art collector who wants to collect her work. The rising action: Charlotte endures a series of microaggressions. The climax: Charlotte rejects Charles's patronage in an explosive visual metaphor I will describe later in this chapter. The denouement: Charles visits Charlotte in her studio a year later and they have a conversation in which he is ultimately able to listen to what she has to say and start to take in her critique of his actions. The resolution: they chart a new artistic path together, making whiteness visible and openly acknowledging the relationships between their historic selves.

This dramaturgical structure positions the audience to take an empathetic emotional journey with Charlotte. Many audience members of color report identifying with Charlotte and recognizing their own lived experiences in the play. Several make comments about how "to survive or succeed, [they] need to exercise an understanding of whiteness and present themselves in a way that appeals to white people to survive." They comment on how "exhausting" it is to "be the only black person in the room and have to act as a spokesperson." Artists of color identify moments of tension in which they recognized themselves creating art "with an internalized gaze that wasn't my own."

White audience members generally respond in ways indicating they are sympathetic to Charlotte's plight, trapped in a dinner party with people she must impress who are unintentionally insulting her at every turn. They laugh at the clueless white characters' bad behavior. But to many white audience members, these characters appear "unrealistic" and "cartoonish"—exaggerated versions of racist white people insincerely and poorly performing allyship. Some report feeling further alienated from the characters because they are extremely wealthy; they find them "unrelatable." They are "caricatures" to laugh at with scorn. For these audience members, the play is not so dramatically or politically successful as they frame themselves as good white people distancing themselves from characters who perform unconscious biases in unsubtle ways.

When such comments began to emerge frequently during act 2 in previews, the facilitation team adds a line to their introduction asking audience members not to "be theater critics" and to instead focus on "where they saw themselves" in the play and "what challenged them." This adjustment curbs the frequency of such comments in the high-focus portions of act 2. However, they continue to surface in the low-focus buzz groups, often prefaced with, "I know we're not supposed to be theater critics, but . . ."

In public conversation with Rankine, P. Carl poses a rhetorical question, "What are real people then if these are not real people, and why can't white people believe how white people behave?"[19] Rankine responds with a story of a real dinner party she attended recently, rife with moments similar to those depicted in the play, summing up the veracity of the dramatic scenario, "so, you know, so when people say to me, this is not believable, I think that what they're really saying is, I am not in the room with black people ever."[20] Rankine and Carl go out of their way to highlight that every moment of the play is rooted in a real experience Rankine has had circulating in the corridors of power—white power, the only kind in the contemporary United States. If white audience members don't recognize ourselves, it's because we aren't paying attention. As Charlotte articulates, "it's as if there's a fault line that runs the entirety of our lives between us. On your terms there's no way for me to get to you on the other side."[21] The stark difference between the ways in which white audience members deny the believability of the very scenario audience members of color recognize as common highlights the central problem in which the play seeks to intervene. It highlights the fault line.

Rankine and Carl's intervention in the spectator's experience asks white audience members to ask ourselves why we are distancing, to lean into the act of being distanced, and to reflect on why we are responding in this way. Some audience members do just this and articulate feeling uncomfortable that they are distancing themselves from culpability. They make the act of distancing the site of reflection.

However, many white audience members simply report frustration that they have difficulty taking an emotional journey with these fictional characters. The realistic, narrative aesthetic in which the play is written sets up this expectation for many audience members. The play works better if it is read as theater of the absurd, with the absurdity being white privilege, power, and supremacy. Rankine and Carl's intervention does what the realistic, narrative aesthetic does not do, which is signal that the play should be read from a critical, distanced position.

## Reinscribing the Whiteness of the Event

At a pivotal moment of the play, Charles places a large, flat rectangular object on the floor. This object has been covered by a shroud, leaning against the wall throughout the play. It is a sculpture entitled *An Anatomy of a Death*, he tells Charlotte. The cloth covering the large slab is removed to reveal a life-sized black-line representation of Michael Brown's autopsy report. Michael Brown was an unarmed eighteen-year-old African American who was shot and killed by police officer Darren Wilson in an altercation in Ferguson, Missouri, on August 9, 2014; Brown's body lay in the street for four hours following his death, and Wilson was exonerated of all charges. Michael Brown's death galvanized the Black Lives Matter movement in the United States. On the piece now lying on the floor, black lines on a white field indicate the outline of a body; black marks indicate the six bullet holes in Brown's body.

Charlotte and Alex, Charles's white nineteen-year-old son, stare at the artwork in silence and horror. Alex grabs his hair and bites his hands in disbelief. Charles defends the piece as "a representation of violence against

Fig. 1.1. Colton Ryan, Patricia Kalember, Karen Pittman, Jim Poulos, and Daniel Gerroll in *The White Card*. Photograph by Gretjen Helene, www.gretjenhelene.com.

Brown" documenting "the violence inflicted on a black man," arguing that it "gestures toward structural racism" and "if it's a portrait of anyone it's a portrait of [Officer Wilson]."[22] Charles analyzes the piece from a cool, intellectual distance.

Charlotte recoils in horror, viscerally affected by the object lying on the floor in front of her. For the first time in the play, her calm, cool demeanor crumbles and she displays the fullness of her emotional response, saying, "Feeling bad by looking at black lines enclosing a white space doesn't come close to experiencing the dread of knowing you could be killed for simply being black."[23] She tries to get the white characters to understand how the piece erases Brown by replacing him with the generic public record of his death. Charles and art agent Eric, who is also white, respond by refuting Charlotte's analysis of and response to the piece, arguing that "this representation is no different from [her] work."[24] "If you think what I'm doing is no different than this then I fail," she responds in shock.[25]

The conversation devolves into a screaming match between the white characters, as Alex attacks his father for "perform[ing] white supremacy" and "upper class terrorism."[26] The white characters get caught up in their own drama, which moves them to one side of the room, leaving Charlotte alone with the canvas. Charlotte lays her body over the autopsy portrait, fitting her body to the frame of black lines (fig. 1). When Charlotte replaces the generic outline of a black body with the specific contours of her own, she transforms the visual representation of overgeneralized black death into a portrait of her own death. The white characters continue to fight for a few moments before they notice Charlotte.

The theater falls into a deep silence. Hands rise to cover mouths in shock. A young black man with long dreadlocks hides his face in his hands when the image is revealed; his white boyfriend reaches over to hold his hand and intertwines their arms, resting his head on his shoulder.

*Anatomy of a Death* erases Michael Brown's body, commodifying it and making it fungible, reducing specific black life and experience to interchangeable black victimhood. It serves as a disturbing reminder that any black body can be misrecognized as dangerous, murdered, and reduced to a sterile autopsy report. The argument appears obvious to people who share Charlotte's lived experience of navigating US society in a black body. Throughout the run of the play, when audience members who visually present as black referenced this moment in act 2 discussion, they often echoed Charlotte's emotional and intellectual response to *An Anatomy of a Death*. Some described how the piece created for them an "experience [of] dread," and many brought up the problem with treating a portrait of black suffering as a metonym for all of black human experience.

The theatrical moment in which *An Anatomy of a Death* is revealed stages a failure of communication—Charlotte cannot put words together that can enable the white characters to understand her experience of the piece of art. The white characters cannot listen to what she is trying to tell them. The moment represents how, as Jared Sexton puts it:

> Our grand involvement across the color line is structured like the figure of an envelope, folds folded within folds: a black letter law whose message is obscured, enveloped, turned bout, reversed. Here a structure of violence is inscribed problematically in narrative, an inscription that can only struggle and fail to be something other than a writing-off, or a writing-over.[27]

Language fails Charlotte; she uses embodied visual spectacle to communicate. Within the world of the play, this gets the white characters' attention, but it, too, fails to make clear and specific enough meaning to the white characters. When Charles later comes to see Charlotte, he may be embarrassed that his dinner party devolved into a shouting match, but he demonstrates no remorse for fetishizing black death.

We saw uncritical echoes of this staged problem in act 2, as many audience members failed to make clear and specific meaning of the theatrical moment. When audience members who visually present as white, East Asian, and South Asian referenced this moment, they recognized it as "powerful" and it made them "uncomfortable," but these audience members did not engage with Charlotte's interpretation and reaction to it.[28] The significant difference in the reception of this moment between people who do and do not share the lived experience of moving through US society in a black body highlights the specificity of antiblack racism in the United States.

To take as an example a moment from our study captured in his field notes, Amos is in a buzz group with three white men—one in his fifties or sixties and two in their late twenties or early thirties. The men bring up *An Anatomy of a Death*. The older white man says that if he saw *An Anatomy of a Death* in a gallery, he would remember it. One of the younger white men tells the group that he didn't understand why Charlotte disapproved of it so much, and the three white men agree that they like the piece, finding it memorable and emotionally impactful. Amos, the lone person of color in the group, speaks up and says he doesn't like the piece, explaining to the white men how, to him, the piece turns Michael Brown from a person with a life into an object to provoke an emotional reaction.[29] Tension ripples from Amos's field log; Amos makes it clear that the conversation makes him uncomfortable and upsets him.

In their discussion, the white men operate as emancipated spectators, "develop[ing] their own translation in order to appropriate the 'story' and make it their own story."[30] To do so, they "observe, select, compare, interpret"—observing the artwork and the scene, comparing the interpretations and responses of the white art collector and the black artist, selecting the side of the white art collector and discarding the details the play provides that contextualize his actions and interpretations as hurtful and misguided. They write themselves into the story, placing themselves in Charles's shoes.

In this moment of act 2, the three white men not only do not appear to understand Charlotte's argument (a central argument of the play, referenced again in critical moments later in the performance), but their speech acts negate it, subsuming her critique to their own aesthetic pleasure. Amos repeats Charlotte's argument, essentially reperforming this scene of the play in his act 2 buzz group. The white men do not seem to recognize how they have written themselves into the play in a way that contradicts its central message. They do not seem to recognize how and why their conversation about *An Anatomy of a Death* upsets Amos—they simply do not seem to have frameworks in place to see the relationship between the artwork and Amos's own body to understand why he, like Charlotte, responds to the work in so personal a manner. In this moment, they provide evidence that they did not learn the lesson that this moment of the play is trying to teach. The play as a whole hammers home a message that a diverse, inclusive, and equitable society requires that white people listen to and build reciprocal relationships with people of color. The white men in Amos's buzz group fail to do this.

On another night, Liam is in a buzz group with a white man in his sixties and a young black woman who is a student at an elite university. The older white man peppers the young black woman with questions about her experiences with racism at the institution, and she attempts to redirect him away from her personal stories back to the play and the structural systems of power it represents. He tells her he "doesn't see color"; Liam watches her clench her jaw at the color-blind discourse as the facilitators call the audience back to the high-focus portion of act 2.

At the end of the event, the young black woman reengages the older white man. She tells the man that it's important for everyone to look at their language closely when they speak. She asks, "What are you suggesting when you say you don't see me as black? I'm proud to identify as a black woman." She tells him she felt like his questions probed into her experience without requiring him to look at himself and his own experiences, and she wants him to think about that.

He responds that he is thankful she said this and that he's not sure how to have conversations like these. He says he was just trying to be honest. She says she appreciates that, but it's important that she let him know how it made her feel.

These examples are representative of larger patterns we saw in interracial buzz groups throughout the run, and we got glimpses of this dynamic in high-focus moments of facilitated discussion following the buzz groups at some act 2 events. Both of the examples I offer from buzz groups ended differently—the first does not seem to alter the understandings of the white audience members, while the second appears to operate as a productive intervention—but they share a common feature. Both put young people of color in uncomfortable positions and required them to educate older white audience members in order to reinforce lessons the play itself attempts to teach. The play itself is about Charlotte's experience of discomfort as an isolated black person called on to perform the pedagogical labor of teaching white people about racism; even when this dynamic was explicitly and repeatedly named as a problem, we watched it persist in interracial act 2 buzz groups.

Multiple audience members of color commented to facilitators following act 2 events that they wish they had not stayed. White audience members reproduced the problematic dynamics the play depicts, at times transforming a theatrical event with goals of inclusivity into one reinforcing hegemonic white supremacy. Michael Finneran and Kelly Freebody remind us, "We have to acknowledge that whilst we control something of the aesthetic transmission, that the beauty, wonder, awe, admiration, understanding, empathy, anger and impact that our audience and participants feel is beyond our control, but deeply valid nonetheless."[31] Active spectators usually make meaning reinforcing their preexisting sense of how the world works, informed by and rooted in their own lived experiences. Therefore, most of the audience members viewing *The White Card* put their lived experiences of whiteness in the center of their understanding. A central message of the play is for white people to decenter this white experience—but any form of reflection is by definition about looking into your own experiences, feelings, and thoughts.

As a result, when white audience members reflect out loud, we reassert our white understandings into the white box when white audiences dominate the event. In this way, to follow Sara Ahmed, power is "*redone* at the moment it is imagined as *undone*."[32]

The act 2 facilitation team recognized this dynamic when it emerges and went out of its way to highlight the perspectives of audience members of color during the high-focus portion of the event. The facilitators chose people of color to speak as often as they could, and a little over one-third of the total act 2 comments we documented were made by people of color.[33] But, as Brenna Nicely articulates:

> When we had the breakout groups, there was no way for us to be monitoring or responding as facilitators to what was happening in every group. Even with the best intentions, folks who were inexperienced with conversation in cross-racial or intergenerational groups said or did plenty that replicated what was going on in the play. These problematic interactions might not seem like a lot on the surface, especially from the person causing the problem, but could have been received in a damaging way—particularly, I think, by younger folks and folks of color.[34]

The facilitation team made minor adjustments to their script to try to counter this problem throughout the run. For example, in the closing moments of act 2, audience members are given white index cards and asked to write a concrete thing they commit to do after they leave the theater. Early on, this action was framed with the question, "How can you make yourself your own project?" echoing a suggestion Charlotte makes to Charles in the final scene of the play. This question, we discovered, reinforced the hegemonic whiteness of the event, implying an assumed white "you." The team adjusted the language to be more inclusive, framing the act of committing to a follow-up action with a comment on a card, "For some of you it might be what you can commit in changing in yourself. Maybe for some of you what you commit to is taking care of yourself." Each facilitator selected their own language, and so there was variation from night to night.

However, the facilitators found themselves locked into a format that is not flexible enough to ever fully solve the problems I have described. Act 2 was written, designed, and staged by the production's artistic team; it is artistically treated as part of the performance of the play. As such it was fixed in form by the end of previews along with the rest of the production. The facilitation team was not empowered to make major revisions to act 2's structure. They were, however, allowed to adjust the language they used within the fixed structure. A.R.T. editor and assistant dramaturg Robert Duffley explains that facilitators began to explicitly "name that this [is] not a space for people of color to educate or be called on to explain things to white people."[35] Some facilitators foregrounded the politics of the act 2 event by stating their commitment that black lives matter. But as Maureen White points out, "this work needs to take time," and the facilitation team recognized that twenty minutes in a room full of strangers is not the best format for equity, diversity, and inclusion work.[36]

I have been focused on white racialized performances of audience members for whom the ideas of the play appear to be new, but many white audience members arrived at the theater familiar with the vocabulary and concepts the play presents. Many people either directly referenced how the antiracist ideas the play presents are familiar to them or structured smooth discourse using sophisticated language to discuss complex social justice concepts. Such comments occurred at more than twice the rate as comments indicating that the play has introduced new ideas.[37] Some of these audience members reported that the play does not cover new ground for them and that its messages are "obvious." However, most of these audience members approached act 2 with a spirit of generosity and took the lead in helping fellow audience members develop vocabulary and frameworks through which to interpret the play. They introduced concepts such as *white fragility*, reflected on their own impulses to be *white saviors*, described the "four I's of oppression: ideological, interpersonal, institutional, and internalized," and suggested we not shy away from the language of *white supremacy*.

Moments of act 2 like the ones I invoke in this section expose the limits of *The White Card*'s capacity to lead white audience members to recognize specific behaviors as oppressive and immediately alter those behaviors. Monica Prendergast asks, "What opens up when an audience begins to doubt the efficacy and effectiveness of a given performance?"[38] When white audience members witnessed other white audience members making people of color uncomfortable or causing overt conflict, they appeared distressed and uncomfortable. A number of audience members in post-performance surveys included critical responses to other audience members' comments in act 2. Some analyzed how this discomfort highlights the pervasive nature of the problem, sharpening their understanding that attending an antiracist play does not by itself solve the problem of white privilege and white supremacy. However, as Ashley Herring pointed out in the opening section of this chapter, we rarely saw white audience members intervene in problematic moments in act 2.

Saidiya Hartman asks us to look critically at the fineness of the line between witness and spectator, proposing that the act of "witnessing" is "a kind of looking no less entangled with the wielding of power and the extraction of enjoyment."[39] Hartman demands that we consider "the pleasure of indignation yielded before the spectacle of sufferance," reflecting critically on just what this discomfort *does*.[40] As I will discuss in greater detail in chapter 4, when indignation and discomfort manifest in performances of disgust, these performances can operate as a mechanism for social reproduction of antiracist norms, using social pressure to teach white people how to recognize and avoid acting on their unconscious biases. However, it is important to attend to the pleasure of indignation, as it can also operate as a mechanism by which *good white people* avoid culpability in racism by distancing ourselves from the *bad white people* who didn't understand the play. Such indignation is nonperformative, blocking white people who have a framework in place to recognize problematic performances of whiteness from engaging in the ongoing processes of self-reflection required to work to dismantle our own unconscious biases.

The final moment of the play nods toward the promise that the "chasm" between black people and white people can be bridged when white people recognize the depth of our privilege, make it visible, and work to relinquish the power it gives us.

Charles recognizes, "Good lord, all this skin shields me. It protects me from . . . from being you. It's like the badge of the police." He removes his shirt and turns his back to Charlotte. "I'm ready," he says. "Charlotte, you can shoot me now."[41] His shoulders cave in, forming a tableau that appears defeated, exhausted, despairing.

Charlotte considers her angle, sets up her camera to focus on him. She reconsiders and resets it in a different place to capture the full room. Charlotte turns over a wooden box, ties a shirt around her waist to visually approximate a dress, and steps onto the box, binding her wrists to re-create a tableau of a slave on the auction block. The audience is very still and very tense. Charles turns around to see her standing in this tableau and a look of horror registers on his face (fig. 1.2). He turns back around to resume his pose for the photograph, understanding that the picture is of both of them, bound by the weight of history. The closing image of the play—the art she creates—is projected: A black slave woman on an auction block looking across a gaping white rectangular canvas at a shirtless white man, who stands with his back to her and his shoulders caved in defeat, despair, and exhaustion. The center of the canvas is marked by a faint line.

Saidiya Hartman argues that "the desire to don, occupy, or possess blackness or the black body as a sentimental resource and/or locus of enjoyment is both founded upon and enabled by the material relations of chattel slavery."[42] Rankine invokes this argument in Charlotte's closing image, subverting the object of chattel slavery as the gazing subject, removing Charles's power to possess blackness as a sentimental resource. This image makes explicit a dynamic that has been present throughout the play in Charles's desire to add Charlotte to his collection.

Berlant defines optimism as "the force that moves you out of yourself and into the world in order to bring closer the satisfying *something* that you cannot generate on your own but sense in the wake of a person, a way of life, an object, project, concept, or scene."[43] The optimism of this closing tableau does not *feel* optimistic; it is not a *happy* ending per se. Rather, it embodies "the *affective structure* of an optimistic attachment," which "involves a

Fig. 1.2. Daniel Gerroll and Karen Pittman in *The White Card*. Photograph by Gretjen Helene, www.gretjenhelene.com.

sustaining inclination to return to the scene of fantasy that enables you to expect that *this* time, nearness to *this* thing will help you or a world become different in just the right way."[44] The closing moment of *The White Card* visually manifests this affective structure, binding Charles and Charlotte together. The moment argues that whiteness must be made visible and decentered of its hegemonic power, and that the only way to begin to heal the gaping wound in the culture and collective psyche of the United States left by slavery and colonialism is to address it directly and deal with the ways in which white US culture refuses to do so.

White audience members largely did not seem to know what to do to with the explicit visual reference to chattel slavery. They brought it up in conversation—the moment makes for an arresting image—but many seemed reluctant to attempt to interpret it with groups of strangers. Some white men in their fifties and sixties pushed back against it, complaining that "the notion of slavery as relevant to modern issues is overemphasized," but such comments were relatively rare. Many white audience members for whom the ideas of the play appeared to be new seemed to take actionable suggestions from the closing moments of the play. Their comments at times were laced with unconscious biases and out-of-date vocabulary, but they appeared resolved to listen openly and work toward making whiteness visible. They may not know what to do with the visual reference to slavery, but these audience members seemed to understand that they have the power to do what

Charles is doing in the closing moments of the play—listening actively, making himself vulnerable, decentering his authority, and tolerating discomfort.

Other audience members interpreted the closing image pessimistically, viewing it as an inescapable condition of stasis from which neither the characters nor we can escape. They echoed Jared Sexton's sentiment that "the intimacy of power suggests the sheer difficulty of difference" and drew from the play the message that it is impossible to understand the lived experience of the Other.[45] They described the chasm between Charles and Charlotte as unbridgeable, the stasis in which they freeze unbreakable. They could not imagine Charles relinquishing his power beyond the isolated moment. Black audience members, in particular, made comments indicating pessimistic readings of the image—though this interpretation cannot be separated from the larger context of their experiences of act 2.

## Public Pedagogy and Citizen Read

Monica Prendergast argues that audience members have to be taught how to productively engage with live performance as critical, active interpreters and cocreators. She describes a three-part structure for moving audience from "passivity into creative interaction with performance": *preperformance, performance, and post-performance*.[46] Preperformance programming prepares audience members to encounter the production.

In conjunction with the production, A.R.T. and ArtsEmerson cosponsored Citizen Read, in which participants read Rankine's *Citizen: An American Lyric* and then participated in a two-hour facilitated discussion. *Citizen* is a volume of lyric poetry describing quotidian scenarios of white people's unconscious racial bias:[47] A moment in which a close friend "who early in your friendship, when distracted, would call you by the name of her black housekeeper."[48] A moment in the car in which "he tells you his dean is making him hire a person of color when there are so many great writers out there."[49] A lunch date who complains that she wanted her son to attend the elite college she and you both attended, "but because of affirmative action or minority something—she is not sure what they are calling it these days and weren't they supposed to get rid of it? Her son wasn't accepted."[50] These insults might, in isolation, appear minor. Rankine illustrates the experience of dissonance: the feeling of pain, the inner voice to just get over it. She highlights the labor required to maintain the decorum, the control, the sincere performance of full participation in a world subtly signaling it isn't built for you.

*Citizen* is written in the second person, framing the reader as the subject who experiences the microaggression. Rankine describes how the *you* says to the white reader, "We know that blacks are in pain. We know that they have been subjected to things no one, anywhere, should be subjected to. But what about your silent collusion with that. . . . Let's find you in here too. *Where are you?* I wouldn't be here if you weren't here as well."[51] Citizen Read extends this invitation, offering space for readers to navigate the work in a structured discussion.

Citizen Read is designed to operate as preperformance programming; the community engagement staff initially planned six book club events, all to be held at either Emerson College or A.R.T. However, overwhelming interest in the program led them to expand it to include many more events. Citizen Read facilitators joined existing community groups and book clubs at spaces including libraries, churches, schools, city hall, and private homes, facilitating sessions wherever those groups were already meeting. Brenna Nicely and Nicole Olusanya, her counterpart at ArtsEmerson, edited a facilitation guide for book clubs and existing groups to use on their own. In total, more than 1,200 people participated in Citizen Read book club events between January and March 2018. In addition, Claudia Rankine and P. Carl held a free, public dialogue at the Emerson Cutler Majestic Theatre, titling the program Citizen Speak. The Citizen Read and Citizen Speak events engaged people who do not necessarily go to the theater, pulling them in from book clubs and libraries and groups that do not have a financial barrier to entry. This programming operated as public pedagogy, leveraging theater spaces and institutional access to public intellectuals. For many participants, these events were not about *The White Card*, and the demographics for Citizen Read and Citizen Speak events skewed younger and more diverse than in the audience for the play.

The Citizen Read events are two hours long, include detailed ground rules for engaging in productive discussion, and consist of multiple scaffolded activities. They are overtly pedagogical spaces—people reported that they came to learn. This pedagogical slant is reinforced by the expectation that participants read to prepare for the events. Facilitation rules allow for honest responses that might hurt people's feelings, but at the events my team and I attended, we watched everyone tread pretty carefully. At these events, white people on the whole deferred to and actively focused on the things black people—mostly black women—had to say. This deference produced two effects—the white participants learned about the black women's experiences and perspectives (which largely echo and reinforce Rankine's text), and the black women reported that they felt heard. Because the events are longer and smaller, participants have more opportunity to build relationships with one another than they do in act 2. When moments of unconscious bias do arise, this little bit of additional social accountability helps aid participants and facilitators to navigate moments of conflict. In Citizen Read, we consistently watched white people bridge racial divisions in ways that respected and honored the dignity of the people of color in the room.

Reading *Citizen*, either independently or as part of the Citizen Read program, operates as a productive preperformance activity to prepare audience members to encounter *The White Card*. It offers audience members a specific frame through which to analyze and engage with the performance proper, critically examining the ways white characters inadvertently oppress Charlotte. When audience members in act 2 buzz groups had read *Citizen*, they often brought it up in conversation and found ways to relate moments of the play to moments of the book. Their post-performance encounter with the material was informed by the preperformance literary framing. That seems particularly helpful for *The White Card* because it can be difficult to catch the details of complex textual arguments in key moments of performance. Many of the points characters make in these moments are present in *Citizen* and emerged in the Citizen Read events. Audience members who were already familiar with these concepts and arguments from preperformance preparation recognized them when they heard them and had some vocabulary to discuss them in act 2. The success of the Citizen Read program demonstrates how artistic work can provide a rich pre-text for inclusive antiracist pedagogy. A two-hour event requiring prior preparation and including clear ground rules is likely to be a more constructive space for difficult dialogue than a twenty-minute postshow discussion.

However, for many participants, Citizen Read and Citizen Speak operated as separate from the production itself. Most of the people I talked with at the Citizen Speak event were either unwilling or unable to spend eighty-five dollars on a theater ticket or told me they had not learned about the production until the run was sold out. Three performances of *The White Card* were reserved for people who had participated in the Citizen Read program, but when audience members on those nights were asked to self-identify who had participated, less than a third of the audience had engaged with the preperformance programming. For all the success of the Citizen Read and Citizen Speak programs, they did not create a critical mass of audience members participating in the full sweep of *preperformance*, *performance*, and *postperformance* programming.

## Continuing Work toward Racial Equality

Participatory programs require, at an institutional level, the support and resources to make substantial adjustments in response to learnings. Such adjustments are frequently easier to accomplish within small organizations with relatively flat hierarchies than in large, hierarchical institutions. Community engagement programs are frequently marginalized within artistic organizations, positioned as secondary to the main event of artistic production. Act 2 is positioned as part of the performance itself, elevated to the status of an essential component of the play—this is a signal of respect and an effort to place community engagement at the center of the event. Its script, staging, and design were developed by the core artistic team. Facilitators were prominently billed by name on lobby signage.[52] Stage management's performance reports included a section on act 2. Within the context of an institutional theater, this treatment signals respect and status. However, as we discovered, freezing act 2 at the end of previews—as artists would freeze any element of a mainstream production—made for a substantial obstacle. Racial equity work requires flexibility, and facilitation differs from acting in a mainstream play. When the act 2 facilitation team recognized that the unfacilitated buzz groups were creating spaces that undermined the production's goals of equity and inclusion, they needed flexibility to make bigger adjustments than they were able to make. This barrier reflects the hierarchical nature of large arts organizations and the distance between artistic leadership and community engagement staff. As I will describe in chapter 3, when the leaders of the small professional theater company Sleeping Weazel found that their post-performance discussion format for *Trapped in a Traveling Minstrel Show* was not working for them, they were able to implement a new structure to address the problem they identified immediately. Their lean staff structure and flat hierarchy made this sort of adjustment straightforward. When large arts organizations undertake ambitious community-engaged projects, they need to be prepared to be similarly flexible.

The case study presented here in chapter 1 highlights some of the particular challenges posed by the high-status nature of this antiracist performance project, in which two elite institutional theaters collaborated to produce a play commissioned by a famous artist and public intellectual. The platform and resources supporting such work elevated its importance, and the attention it garnered highlighted the significance of the problems it raised, which in turn attracted an audience interested in attending high-status cultural events. These audience members may or may not have much prior exposure to antiracist activism. Projects like this one present an opportunity to focus the attention of white people with financial and social capital on their own racialized specificity for a few hours. Act 2 helps give this target audience some space to try out some language to discuss their new understandings about whiteness. But, as I have been discussing throughout the chapter, these audience members, in ignorance, frequently perform their whiteness in ways hurtful to audience members of color.

Racial equity work relies on ground rules and guidelines for conversation and time for unintentionally hurtful behaviors to be challenged, explained, and corrected. That is a difficult task to accomplish in most post-performance conversations, which are by design short public discussions among strangers. Interracial discussions following antiracist plays can be spaces of solidarity and coalition, but for them to be so requires participants to arrive at the theatrical event with frameworks and vocabularies for such coalition building already in place. Artists and artistic leaders cannot generally assume audience members have done this preliminary work, though sustained antiracist artistic programming will both help educate audience members and draw to the theater audiences who already engage with such activism. As Nicely puts it, "More work is always ahead of us."[53]

## Chapter 2

✦

# Critical Catharsis

A grieving mother, played by solo performance artist Keith A. Wallace, stands tall in front of a microphone stand. She takes a slow breath and begins to thank an array of government officials, reporters, and nonprofit advocates for their assistance in the fight for justice following the murder of her son, Jamel, at the hands of the police. Behind her, a makeshift memorial featuring evidence of Jamel's life displays a baseball cap and basketball, candles, a Vassar college pennant, teddy bears.

> In memory of my son.
> Jamel Smith.
> Jamel Smith.
> Please
> Say it with me.
> Jamel Smith.

The audience repeats Jamel Smith's name over and over. It's a fictionalized name, and the audience follows instructions obediently but quietly. Jamel's mother hands out white pillar candles, marked from previous use, and begins a call-and-response roll call of black victims of police violence. Sandra Bland. Trayvon Martin. Amadou Diallo. With each candle we repeat the name of a real victim, speaking each name with increasing volume and strength. We sit in the Oberon black box theater space at the American Repertory Theatre (A.R.T.) in Cambridge, Massachusetts, participating in Wallace's *The Bitter Game*, a theatrical event focused on a fictionalized act of police violence; as we enact the ritual dramaturgy of a vigil, we come together as a community mourning the real dead—victims of a structural, long-standing evil.

The roll call of names transitions into a soundscape of news coverage of these real shootings, repeating their names and layering them until they fade into white noise. In the moment of the vigil, the fictionalized Jamel—whom we care about and whose murder we witnessed a few moments ago—is at the center of our attention and part of a larger epidemic. Afterward, he fades. They all fade from consciousness as the world moves on. They become white noise.

*The Bitter Game* is a solo, interactive theatrical event created, written, and performed by Keith Wallace to battle the epidemics of excessive police force, racism, and trauma in communities of color. Wallace describes himself as an "actorvist," and his aesthetic and political goals for the piece are thoroughly entwined. The piece was originally commissioned by La Jolla Playhouse for its 2015 site-specific international Without Walls (WOW) festival and was directed and cocreated by Deborah Stein. It has since toured to high-profile institutional theaters including the Kennedy Center and the Public Theater's Under the Radar Festival in New York City, in addition to a range of community-based venues.

L. M. Bogad uses dramaturgical analysis to describe the impact of theatrical elements of protest actions. He identifies spectacles combining the "emotional power of Aristotelian identification with the agitating and radicalizing potency of Brechtian *Verfremdungseffekt* as *critical catharsis*; a catharsis that only finds release through political participation."[1] Events creating this critical catharsis combine "emotional investment in the fate of the victim" with Brechtian *Verfremdungseffekt* (distancing or alienating effect), "making the familiar strange and discomfiting, so that we see it anew and are unsettled and amazed."[2] Bogad exclusively deals with performances outside of the framework of formal theater. Much activist performance aims to achieve critical catharsis, and for a play to do so successfully, a precarious balance between aesthetic distance and real-world consequences must be struck. In the protest actions Bogad studies, this transference to real life is fairly obvious. Many theatrical events look to bridge the gap between the aesthetic distance of a play and real action in real life with a talkback, panel, or other post-performance program.

*The Bitter Game* is a rare theatrical event managing to balance aesthetic distance and reality to create critical catharsis, but this impact is fragile. I collected qualitative data as a participant observer at three performance events in September 2017—one performance followed by a formal panel on police violence, one performance standing on its own, and one performance followed by a facilitated discussion. In this chapter, I first analyze the aesthetic strategies Wallace uses in the piece to achieve both the identification and denaturalization required for critical catharsis and then look at the ways this impact is dispelled or activated in two post-performance programs. Oberon is an intimate venue, and *The Bitter Game* is a participatory event in which audience members can often see and hear each other's responses. I contextualized what I could observe with informal conversations with the subscribers, students, and activists who sat near me at each performance, took notes on what was said during post-performance events, and referenced transcripts from archival audio recordings of those events.

The material conditions of theater making in the United States structurally incentivize solo performances booked in short runs in high-status institutional venues. It is a common setup for a solo activist artist to tour institutional theaters, performing for a ticket-buying audience that is mostly affluent and mostly white. I examine the activist impact of *The Bitter Game* on this mostly (but not overwhelmingly) white, mostly middle- to upper-middle-class-looking audience who comes to see a play at A.R.T.'s Oberon performance space.[3] This chapter is about how it gets this audience to experience critical catharsis and start to understand and grapple with the steps it would take to dismantle the trauma and vicarious trauma experienced by communities of color as a result of police violence.

Critical catharsis relies on a degree of reality seeping into the theatrical event. If a theatrical event feels too fictional, we aren't motivated to take action in the real world. Moments in which the play dissolves the aesthetic distance of the theatrical event are vital. Oberon has about seventy-five seats set up on multiple levels on two sides of the space facing each other, leaving an alley between as a performance space. On a low platform to one side sit two coolers with soft drinks and water, adorned with cardboard signs: FREE. Before the show begins, Wallace circulates among the crowd out-of-character as they enter and settle in, bearing a cardboard sign proclaiming FREE SHIT! He greets audience members out of character, welcoming them in and offering them soft drinks. When he sees me, he gives me a hug and says hi. This initial introduction gives audience members a chance to see Wallace out of character, to recognize his tone and bearing as *real*.

When the play begins and Wallace is introduced as "Jamel Smith," Jamel welcomes the audience and delivers a brief preshow speech with the same tone and bearing with which Wallace welcomes us to the space in the preshow. Even though he has been introduced by another name, it is not initially clear whether Wallace performs this moment as himself or as a character. Harvey Young highlights how "the misrecognition of individuated bodies as 'the black body' creates similar experiences."[4] Wallace is a black man of about thirty from North Philly describing a childhood bock party from the perspective of a black man of about thirty from North Philly. He turns the problem Young identifies, that "an *idea* of the black body has been and continues to be projected across actual physical bodies," into an artistic strategy, collapsing the boundaries between his real body and the story he tells.[5] The fusion between actor and character is essential for the play's use of identification and empathy.

Participatory elements of the performance event plant the seed for a direct relationship between actor and audience. In the scene breaks, Wallace plays happily with any audience member who wants to play along. "Reach up an holler if you want candy!" he exclaims, throwing candy to enthusiastic participants who reach their arms in the air and make noise. The audience laughs with Wallace, building a convivial relationship. Wallace takes advantage of spontaneous moments of audience participation. A white woman in her sixties sitting in the front row shimmies her shoulders along to a moment of soul music; Wallace plays off her, shimmying in response. When audience members do not choose to interact with Wallace directly, they can still observe the interactions he has with others and the potential for interaction. He is charming, and it is hard not to like him. Over the course of the performance event, Wallace/Smith befriends the audience.

The core activist impact of *The Bitter Game* is that it gets audience members to care about a black man and see that he is in danger. This is a significant intervention for white audience members who unreflexively live in segregated white worlds, who do not have close relationships with the people whose lived experience the play reflects. Audience members of all races in post-performance panels and discussions do not refer to the fictional Jamel when describing or responding to moments of dramatic action; they refer to Keith by his real name. Jamel is killed, but Jamel has Keith's body. Jamel was killed for having Keith's body. Keith is in danger. The performance event takes the abstract evil of police brutality and makes it personal.

## Multiple, Overlapping Audiences

A white woman who looks like she's in her fifties sits down next to me and strikes up a conversation. She wears a casual black sundress, a statement wooden beaded necklace, and sneakers. I tell her I am new to Boston and she enthusiastically provides a number of recommendations of theater companies whose work she likes. She asks me what the play is about, volunteering that she is a subscriber and she just shows up and sees what she sees, trusting that "it will be interesting." From this exchange and others like it, I observe the presence of two overlapping audiences: a mixed-race, mixed-age audience of audience members who seem to come primarily to see a play about excessive police force, and an audience of white people in their late fifties, sixties, and seventies who primarily come to see a play at A.R.T.

Wallace tells me he designed *The Bitter Game* for two overlapping audiences: the mostly white, mostly affluent, mostly older subscribers of institutional regional theaters, and people of color whose lived experience resonates more directly with the events of the play.[6] These are not monolithic groups, and at A.R.T. Oberon I watched audience members enter into the space in mixed-race social groups, couples, and families more frequently than is typical at many institutional theater spaces. However, distinct and observable patterns of response do track across visible age and racial markers, in particular through groups of audience members who appear to have come to the theater with people of their own race and age.

Theater critics and artists alike can sometimes malign subscriber audiences as old rich people whose conservative artistic tastes skew institutional theater seasons away from adventurous aesthetics, contemporary plays by emerging authors, and diverse perspectives. But there's a reason subscribers subscribe: they love to see theater, and they see a lot of it. They come trusting artistic teams to take them on a journey, and they have not always spent time beforehand learning about what they are about to see. As a result, a visibly white, visibly older portion of the audience is taken by surprise by many moments of the play. At specific moments, they respond differently from the white audience members who self-identify as social justice activists, from audience members who arrive at the theater in mixed-race and mixed-age groups, and from audience members of color.[7]

Eight-year-old Jamel describes playing basketball with his older brother, trying to impress his sister's friend and goofing around like the kid he is. The moment is funny and light, and the audience laughs at his "eight-year-old moves." Until, "all of a sudden, in the distance, I just hear a *pop*."[8]

Half the audience responds. Bodies tense, a sharp intake of breath, a hand over an open mouth. These audience members lean in, still and silent; we cannot protect this child from the violence we know is about to happen. Stories of violence in urban black communities are familiar enough for this audience to recognize the setup. A hot summer day at the playground. *Pop pop pop* is not the sound of a firecracker. Meanwhile, the other half of the audience continues to groove with Jamel as he happily describes the day, celebrating, "It's like a holiday . . . one of them holidays where we set off whatchu call 'em . . ." and prompts the audience to supply the word *firecrackers*. These audience members are caught up in the energy of the block party; they don't realize what's happening until Jamel does. At that point, we all take the journey together with eight year-old Jamel Smith as he watches an older boy run by and another older boy run, stop, pull out a gun, and shoot. The two overlapping audiences unite into a collective, watching with bated breath as Jamel huddles on the ground with his basketball, transformed by a soothing "shh, shh, shh" into the sister he comforts and protects. We are all powerless to protect these children.

The production does not appear to be any less impactful on audience members who came to the theater because they wanted to come see a play at A.R.T. than those who came because they wanted to engage with an event about excessive police force. Many audience members came for both reasons. However, the moments of surprise, contextualized by some of the conversations I had with and overheard among subscribers, indicate that their somewhat accidental presence at a theatrical event about excessive police force opens up an opportunity for intervention that differs from the impact a production might have on people whose lived experience reflects the events of the play, or on white people who already spend a lot of time engaging the problems the play raises.

Bogad employs, with some self-aware irony, the metaphor of the air war versus the ground war in activist intervention. "Air War" actions "soften the cultural terrain, draw attention to a problem, change some minds or at least weaken opposition, and galvanize discouraged supporters."[9] Activist theater productions are typically "air war" actions. The "ground war" is "the hardcore, everyday organizing, in workplaces and communities face to face" to change policies and win elections.[10] This activity can only be done locally—on the ground, so to speak. The solo touring actorvist cannot by definition know how to fight the ground war at most stops on the tour. That requires a deep local knowledge and a network of relationships with local activist organizations already working on the problem a play addresses. Producing venues are local institutions, but their expertise and function is not typically long-form engagement with specific issue areas. It can be difficult for them to sustain partnerships with issue-specific activist partners when years might elapse between theatrical events engaging with the same issue. Well-funded institutions that can afford to pay artists a living wage typically have a deep local knowledge of philanthropy networks and funding relationships. When they produce plays as political interventions, their existing cultural capital contains the potential to get individuals with power and access to funding into the room. Large arts institutions like the A.R.T. (or the Kennedy Center or the Public Theater, just to name two other venues at which *The Bitter Game* has been performed) are not embedded in the activist "ground war," but they have cultural power. S. Jamil Ahmed highlights the impossibility of changing the world without engaging the powerful.[11] Activist performances at high-status, rich cultural institutions can open up a space in which the powerful can hear. This approach may not be satisfying to a radical sensibility wanting to dismantle the status quo, but it represents a pragmatic tactical use of available institutions and resources.

## Dramatic Irony: Making the Familiar Strange

Jamel's mother, Pam, lays down the rules. "No guns. I don't give a good goddamn if it was a BB gun, a water gun or a damn glue gun."[12] When police shot and killed twelve-year-old Tamir Rice for playing with a pellet gun in 2014, mainstream media drew white spectators' attention to the problem that black boys cannot safely play with toys that might be mistaken for guns by police officers wielding real guns. And so in 2017, many white audience members attending a play about excessive police force are aware that black children—and particularly black boys—in the United States get "The Talk."

Wallace subtly shifts the set of his shoulders, transforming his cisgender male body to evoke this female character. A brief moment of alienation occurs with this transition of gender performance, but the displacement is momentary. Pam feels real. And she is furious. Pam goes on to detail a litany of rules: do not run, no loud music, no headphones, no pockets, no backpacks; when you have car trouble, wait in a well-lit gas station with witnesses; when you find yourself in a dark space with a woman, give her space and "look her in the eyes, and soften your face, and drop your shoulders."[13] This instruction culminates in a participatory moment in which the audience is asked to repeat her text and gestures together, "so mommy knows you get it."[14] "One. Keep your head up. Two. Keep your eyes forward. Three. Keep your ego down."[15] Head up, eyes forward, ego down: the audience repeats three times. The first time a few people speak along and many gesture, and by the third repetition most of the audience speaks and gestures the rules. We have learned them.

The longer and more elaborate Pam's list of rules gets, the more it sinks in that her son cannot just *be a kid*; he needs to play by a very specific and somewhat arbitrary-feeling list of rules. I might *know* that this conversation really happens in many households, but framing me as the person who has to learn the rules makes me particularly aware that I made it to forty in my white body without needing to learn them. The dramatic irony of the moment crystalizes. It's not Jamel who needs to learn the rules. It's me.

"The Talk" sets up a piece of dramatic irony used later in the play, when the audience watches Jamel start to follow but ultimately deviate from some of Pam's rules during an altercation with the police. Regardless of an audience member's prior exposure to the problems the play represents, Pam has set up a framework within which audience members can know what Jamel "should" do in relation to police authority.

The audience watches Jamel exuberantly prepare for his mother's fiftieth birthday party. He is home from college, wears new clothes and new shoes, has purchased a nice gift, and is ready to take his mom to her surprise party. His pleasure is infectious, and the audience grins along with him. Until he describes renting a nice car. As Harvey Young points out, "While a luxury car could suggest that the driver is affluent and educated, a black body driving a luxury car may render the driver suspect to law enforcement."[16] Pam frames a rule in "The Talk": "Sometimes—you'll have to learn how to make yourself as small as possible."[17] Twenty-one-year-old Jamel does not seem to recognize that looking too nice and driving too nice a car violates this rule. A portion of the audience breaks from Jamel's exuberant energy as he prepares to pick up his mother in his rental car, responding to the dramatic irony of the moment with a sharp intake of breath or a subtle shake of the head. One white man in his sixties who identifies himself as a physician in post-performance discussion comments on "the predictability of what was going to happen," contrasting it with his "white privilege experience with the cops" in which he was pulled over for speeding in his luxury car and was sent home with a warning. He knows it's dangerous for a young black man to wear nice clothes and drive a nice car.[18]

Jamel realizes he is in danger in the moment a patrol car passes him:

> Everything in the car legit
> I got no reason to be nervous
> But I can never be too sure
> Check the rearview mirror.

Shit.

You already know.

They making a U-turn.[19]

Jamel takes deep breaths, reminds himself of the rules his mother has taught him, and tries to ignore the fear in the pit of his stomach. The police car turns onto another street and he pulls over to pull himself together. He tries to regain his confidence, refind the pleasure of wearing new shoes, let the crisp night air calm his fear, but it does not work. Jamel tries to pull himself back together with swagger, pulling his hoodie up over his head, playing his hip hop loud, singing along to the hook to Kendrick Lamar's "Alright," "We're gonna be alright. We're gonna be alright."[20] This coping mechanism expressly violates Pam's rules. No loud music. I watch the mouth of a white woman across from me drop open as she shakes her head, "no, no, no." We sit powerless in our seats as we watch Jamel try, unsuccessfully, to survive a traffic stop that in a better world would be as routine for him as it is for that white physician sitting in the audience.

Early in the show, Wallace remarks, "Now usually I do a whole bit about how I was worried for some of y'all being out here after dark. Blah blah blah. But let's keep it real. This is Cambridge."[21] In the moment, it seems like he's drawing attention to that we are in a predominantly white, affluent neighborhood where we (mostly white, middle- to upper-middle-class theater patrons) do not worry about walking at night in contrast to "some parts of this city."[22] The differences between these parts of the city are not named. It's an uncomfortable moment of dissonance for me as an audience member, highlighting the ways in which I feel safer in affluent urban neighborhoods that are predominantly white than in poor urban neighborhoods populated by people of color. This deeply embedded bias is part of the fabric of white supremacy, a stubborn reminder of my ongoing complicity in racist power structures. But the moment passes quickly, as the audience is welcomed into the block party and the discomfort is intentionally dispelled.

Later, I realize that the play is pointing out how black people need to worry about going out alone at night in a predominantly white, affluent neighborhood where they are more likely to be profiled as suspicious. There's a wry joke late in the play for affluent black audience members, "I know what some of y'all are thinking . . . if I move out to the burbs or start eating organic and shit that they gonna treat me differently."[23] This gets an "um-hum" of acknowledgment from an African American woman sitting next to me at one performance. Those parallel moments acknowledge that we are together in a space that is coded white—that is, a space haunted by legacies of exclusion in which it is potentially dangerous to have a black body.

Bogad highlights how "Different tactical performances involve "different stakes and dangers, and different matrices of risk considering the relative privilege of the protagonists."[24] Much is made of theater as a "safe space"; within the context of a larger conversation on police violence, *safe* takes on a physical urgency. To be *safe* is to be "free from hurt or damage," "preserved from some real or apprehended danger," and "affording protection or security."[25] The combination of visibility and status that theater can give to bodies of color can literally help keep activists safer than they might be in street protest settings. For, as *The Bitter Game* reminds me, safety is not a luxury every body can take for granted.

## Interrupting Critical Catharsis

Several months prior to the start of the run of *The Bitter Game* at A.R.T., Wallace asked the A.R.T. Education and Community Programs team to assemble participants for post-performance events based on the theater's local relationships. The staff recruited facilitators for the events who selected their formats and invited their panelists; these plans were approved by the Education and Community Programs staff and by Wallace.[26] I participated in two very different post-performance events during *The Bitter Game*'s brief Oberon run. The first event subverted the performance's potential to create critical catharsis; the second amplified it.

The first event was a panel discussion with Josh Dohan from the Massachusetts Public Defender's office, Sergeant Tommy Brooks from the Boston Police Department, and community organizer Mo Barbosa, moderated by facilitator Liz O'Connor. O'Connor initially recruited Dohan and Barbosa for the panel, adding Brooks the day before the panel to provide a diverse opinion.[27] The panelists and facilitator set up on one side of the performance space and the audience, who had been seated in an alley configuration, moved to sit in a more proscenium setup for the panel.

I sit high on a seating platform at the back of this new audience configuration and watch everyone stare at their phones while the loud post-performance music plays. We transition from a participatory, immersive, empathetic theatrical exchange to a proscenium panel in which we mostly sit quietly and listen to experts.

This panel focuses on the ways in which local police are working to build relationships with the black community, and on the importance of relationships and knowing each other in moments of conflict. Tommy Brooks and Mo Barbosa tell us about how they are building concrete programs to help combat this problem at a local level. That is comforting, and I learn many things about the ways the police and the local black community are working to solve the real-world problems the play addresses. What this panel *does* to the audience, however, is communicate that the problem is for the police and the black community to solve. That leaves people in the audience who are not black out of the solution; if the goal is to get us to go do something with the feelings we had during the performance, the panel tells us it's fine to go home knowing someone else is working on this problem and there's nothing we can do to help.

Audience members do try to find ways into the conversation. However, the "expert" setup leads them to do so by framing themselves as experts or offering specific expert resources. The first audience member to speak, a white woman who appears to be in her forties and wears funky eclectic clothes, introduces herself as having "been involved in the social justice movement for a long time in a bunch of different ways." She sets herself up as an expert, taking the cue from the panelists that the purpose of the panel is to offer additional information to audience members. She comments on a culture of fear:

> I walk through my neighborhood and I'm, like, growing up I was always out in the neighborhood, running around with my friends. When I talk to parents that I know, they don't let their kids run around. They're afraid something's going to happen to them. I'm, like, "Wow. We are really afraid of each other." That transcends our questions. I think it's between people of color and white people—there's a whole other dimension happening. And yet, in the larger sense, we really are living in a culture where there's a lot of fear of other people.[28]

In this comment, she transforms the parental fear in the play—a mother's fear that her black son will be killed by police—into a critique of parental overprotectiveness in her neighborhood. Given the content of this comment in relation to the content of the play, I can guess the kids she refers to are not black and the neighborhood through which they run is not regularly a site of gun violence. With this comment, she rejects the message of the play that Pam's fears for her son are well founded, rejecting the evidence the play gives of just how dangerous it is to be black in the United States. The audience member makes it, instead, about a nostalgia for an imagined past in which she as a white child could "run around with my friends"—a childhood that took place at roughly the same time but in a different neighborhood than the one in which Jamel and his sister cowered from gunshots. She flattens the real differences between Jamel's fear of the police and the police's fear of Jamel's black body. In attempting to "transcend our questions" and get to the "larger sense," she appropriates the story and makes it into a story with opposing meaning. This is a fundamental feature of emancipated spectatorship—to paraphrase Rancière, she's taking the story in and making it her story.[29] But this is a danger of empathy—she appropriates the story and, in trying to make it her own, she makes it comfortable for herself. She translates it in a way that sustains and supports her ongoing sense of the world as fundamentally safe, negating the message of the play that the world is *not* fundamentally safe.

The panel continues, and a black woman who self-identifies as having been raised by a single mother in the historically working-class Dorchester neighborhood of Boston highlights the veracity of "The Talk" and refocuses the panel on police accountability. She pointedly responds to the white woman commenting on the culture of fear, "I don't think this is generalized fear, unfortunately. Many of the friends that I have are familiar with the talk, fear of police, because of the color of our skin. Again, I don't think that has to do with what the community can do, but maybe it's a conversation of what the police would like to change for themselves?"[30] She prods both the white woman and Sargent Tommy Brooks to reengage with the problems raised by the play, attempting to recenter the focus of the predominantly white panel and audience on the experiences and perspectives of black people who have good reason to fear the police.

A few moments later, a white woman first jokes that "this is Cambridge so there may be some people who read books" and then suggests reading *New Jim Crow* and *Just Mercy*. She also makes the concrete suggestion, "I think people have to start doing whatever they do to change laws." This is the one suggestion emerging from the session to open up potential real-world actions white audience members could take to help solve the problems the play addresses. However, this suggestion does not go anywhere, possibly because policy and legislative advocacy are outside the areas of expertise represented on the panel.

A young man of color who appears to be about fourteen asks the panel a question, "Do you know what happened at Carnival? The shooting?"

Many of the people in the audience, including myself, cock our heads in confusion. This question references a real-world event with which I am unfamiliar. It stands in contrast with the rest of the audience responses during the panel—this is a real question about a specific local conflict, taking advantage of the expertise of the panelists in a productive way. This question maximizes the potential of the panel as a community forum on local relationships between the police and young people of color. The panelists are taken by surprise, and it takes them a moment to figure out how to answer the question without discussing the details of an active police investigation. Barbosa and Brooks fill in pieces of a response, telling us that there had been a shooting at a festival in Cambridge rooted in gang violence from across the river in Boston, and that two people had been shot. Barbosa explains to the uninformed members of the audience:

> Part of what we're struggling with is the response when that happens—is what the police should do, which is about securing the safety of everyone there. The experience of it, on the other hand, is I don't know what's going on. No one's telling me what's going on. And the police are telling me I have to go. That lack of communication creates some of the experience that folk are really pushing against.[31]

Barbosa highlights how he was at Carnival and describes how, when shots rang out and the police began to evacuate the event, he asked a police officer with whom he has a personal relationship for more information about what was going on. He tells us how the first thing that officer did was show Barbosa he was wearing a bulletproof vest. Barbosa tells us, "I've been walking around Cambridge for the last ten years, poking police officers in the chest, asking, 'Where's your vest?' " and telling them, 'I love you and I want you to be here,' and that when the bullets fly, you run in that direction."[32] Barbosa highlights the way he builds relationships with the police by acknowledging their fear of being killed in the line of duty. This story provides a model for the young man asking the initial question, demonstrating a method for building productive relationships with police officers that might yield useful information in moments of conflict or confusion. It also redirects an event ostensibly about, as O'Connor puts it, "police killing people," into a discussion about wanting to keep police safe in the line of fire.[33] This exchange highlights a rapport between Barbosa and Brooks, emphasizing that it is possible for black men to have positive relationships with police officers, but largely undermines the central point of the play that in the absence of such personal relationships, black men are in danger of police violence.

In the final audience comment of the evening, an Asian American woman dressed in expensive-looking clothing speaks with the resonant voice of an experienced public speaker, using the opportunity as a platform to draw attention to an unrelated organization:

> I want to share an organization that has been dedicated to promoting equality, diversity, and inclusion. We take the Albert Einstein approach to addressing this. Here is a very powerful quote that says, "You cannot solve a problem with the same consciousness that created it. You must stand on a higher ground." So, I want to share a message with all of you that speak to all of our consciousness. It says, "Are you greater than the sun that shines on everyone? Black, brown, yellow, red, and white, the sun does not discriminate." I want to share another quote with you by Mother Theresa. "I've come to realize over the years that being unwanted is the worst disease that any human being can experience." I hope when you go home tonight that you all take a moment to check out [our website] because we've been dedicated to sharing this message across America and around the world. This message has been turned into a song and we have a campaign right now . . .[34]

Audience members shift in their seats and roll their eyes as she gives her organization's web address. This digression attempts to hijack the panel with a set of "inspirational quotes" which, within the context of this comment, are saturated in *color-blind discourse*. Eduardo Bonilla-Silva describes how color-blind discourse negates the social reality of race, supporting white supremacy by cloaking racial inequalities in myths that racialized differences do not exist. Color-blind frameworks imagine that people of different races do not have different experiences of the world, rendering the mechanisms reproducing racial inequality invisible and implicitly rationalizing inequality as attributable to individual failings.[35] The production and the panel both focus on the ways in which black people—in particular, black men—experience relationships with representatives of state authority within an unjust, racialized social system. This audience member attempts to shift the conversation into a utopian color-blind framework, but the rest of the audience rejects the move. They seem to find both the color-blind framework and the blatant self-promotion distasteful, and they appear annoyed by the lengthy digression at the end of a long evening.

The panel ends and audience members are encouraged to stay and talk with one another and the panelists about real-world resources and actions they can take in the real world. Clusters of audience members form around each panelist and around Wallace, and some audience members remain to continue discussion. The woman encouraging us to check out her organization sits in her seat beaming hopefully; no one approaches her to talk about her campaign.

At the start of his residency at A.R.T., Wallace articulated that his goals for the post-performance events were for "audiences to leave the theater armed with 'language, information, and permission' to engage these issues (further)."[36] This post-performance event did give people language and information with which to engage with these issues—in particular, it shared specific information about local programs building relationships between police and local communities of color. The same post-performance panel, presented at a venue such as a national conference of police commissioners, could make a legitimate impact on the problem of excessive police force. But in this context, it took the onus off audience members to "engage these issues," relieving the audience of responsibility in answering the call to action charged by the performance. The performance leaves us with a challenge: nothing will change unless we—explicitly named—take action in the real world. The play demands, "Since people listen when you cry, cry for something real. Demand these cops be retrained . . . demand independent investigations of police murder . . . demand that they be prosecuted when they use excessive force . . . make examples of them, the way you make examples of us."[37] The panel absolves us white people, showing us that police and black community leaders are working to solve the problem. It shows us that police are individuals, humans, with fears and families. It asks us to all just get along—which is, of course, the utopian ideal. But it wishes away a real problem and offers a stable closure to the evening.

## Amplifying Critical Catharsis

Timothy McCarthy facilitated a post-performance discussion after the Saturday matinee. McCarthy is a faculty member of history, public policy, and education at Harvard and the host and director of the A.R.T. of Human Rights, an ongoing series of education/outreach events and dialogues programmed around A.R.T. performances.[38] For this event, audience members moved into the front two rows of chairs on either side of the playing space, maintaining the same fundamental spatial relationship in the post-performance event as in the performance itself while bringing participants physically closer to one another and to the playing space.

McCarthy initially asks participants to have a five-minute conversation with someone they do not know, discussing "something that struck you" about the performance and "what you were most challenged by" in the experience. After a few moments, McCarthy reconvenes the full group and solicits high-focus responses from participants. This *pair and share* facilitation strategy is widely used in many contexts; it warms up participants to talk and gets everyone talking, enables them to rehearse a comment they might then share with the full group, and offers space for people who might not feel comfortable saying something in front of a room full of people an alternate way to participate.

This facilitation strategy opens up a substantial space for reflection and discussion with this assembled audience. When McCarthy reconvenes the group for high-focus discussion, it is clear that audience members want to talk about what they have seen, and that many of them have a sophisticated vocabulary with which to discuss it. The discussion that emerges gets white audience members talking and hearing one another talk about their complicity in the structural systems of power underpinning the larger problem represented in the play. Audience members affirm the play's message that "white silence equals violence," and white audience members use the language *white privilege* to discuss the ways in which they do not feel as though they are in danger when pulled over by police for minor traffic violations. They identify that racism is too often treated as an individual rather than a structural problem and that "the stigma of the word itself" can be an obstacle to "fruitful conversations" about the larger problem.[39]

Their sophisticated vocabulary and comfort discussing racialized privilege lead me to believe that the people who choose to speak early in the high-focus part of the discussion have experience discussing these topics. These audience members arrive at the theater with frameworks in place enabling them to receive the critique of white privilege incorporated into the play along with the vocabulary to discuss it. When this prior exposure meets the substance of the theatrical event, audience members process the play by raising tough questions about their own complicity in white supremacy. The format of this event is similar to the format of *The White Card*'s act 2 discussions that were presented in chapter 1, but because this smaller event is more saturated with audience members who have experience having respectful and inclusive conversations about race, it does not suffer from the problems described in that chapter. This post-performance discussion operates as an intermediate-level seminar in white privilege, using the pre-text of the performance as a point of departure for a robust and frequently vulnerable conversation.

The white physician whose early acknowledgment of the "predictability" of the police pulling Jamel over that I cited earlier in this chapter grapples with the limits of fully understanding Jamel's experience and putting his thoughts into words. He demonstrates that he has received the play's message and is trying to internalize it. His previously smooth discourse gets choppy as he tries to find the right words, stating, "I can't see this through black eyes. The ability to get out of your own skin and see it in someone else's eyes when it's presented over and over and over again. I just can't explain that in conversation."[40] He mixes metaphors as he tries to articulate why the play is important—that it gave him a way to access a set of experiences he is aware of but does not fully understand. From his choppy language, I can see him trying to work through the limits of his embodied understanding. When his language breaks down and grows awkward, he provides evidence that he is in the process of grappling with a concept he has not fully mastered, and that he is willing to tolerate the discomfort of not understanding.

A few moments later, McCarthy tries to move the audience from discussing what struck them to what challenges them. One white man in his seventies initially does not seem to let him. This man tries to explain the impact the play has had on him, working hard to put into words the thing he learned about himself by watching the performance:

> As I've been—I have—I don't remember the last time I felt this much emotion, and so what struck me? One thing—the first thing that struck me is the incredible vitality of a block party in North Philly. I said, "We don't have anything like that." I don't have anything like that. I am not vital in that. So, then what struck me—I don't know. It's a thought about what drives—I mean, right now I'm talking about the police, but I'm ultimately talking about myself as a white person. What drives the police is fear. It's all fear-driven. I mean, I can understand why policemen would be afraid. They don't know what's—but the behavior, the whole way of being about life is fear-driven. That's my—in my opinion. And so what I'm noticing in myself is fear. That's what's present for me, and I suspect it's present in the room because usually if it's present here, it's in the room.
>
> So, I just want to say I am afraid, and I'm afraid of black people, and it's not like afraid of violence. It's something about the being of black people, that vitality. It's a threat to whatever little; teeny identity is that's over here. I never realized this before. I was left-wing as

> you can get in terms of what I think about myself, in terms of my beliefs, and—but for me—so, for me to actually get in touch with that fear has been an extraordinary experience.[41]

This audience member does not have a smooth, polite vocabulary with which to discuss racism. The bias in the comment is jarring—white people rarely openly admit to racialized bias in this way. The man identifies that he is full of feeling, and this overflow of emotion seems to power his need to speak as he works to reconcile his "left-wing" identity and his fear of black people. The performance event catalyzed his recognition of this tension. He visibly and publicly does the hard work of trying to understand his own fear. Wallace describes his reaction to this comment:

> And hearing those words, obviously, immediately the first reaction is . . . [a beat of silence]. But then, the more you think about it, I'm like, well, this is probably the greatest hope that I could ask for of the show, that it empowers somebody to take a look at themselves, kind of turn an eye internally and to ask themselves a different question or make an admission like that, especially publicly.[42]

Wallace does not name his initial reaction to the comment. His conspicuous silence seems to indicate a desire to avoid labeling the audience member *a bad person* for demonstrating the racialized bias he is attempting to dismantle, operating in tension with a gut-level negative emotional response to the racist sentiment. The audience member makes himself vulnerable in his comment and demonstrates self-awareness, and as a result, audience members and Wallace work to try to receive his comment in the spirit of critical generosity. It seems likely from his comment that this performance event marks the beginning of a longer journey that can continue outside the theater. That is, at least, the hope.

Most white audience members new to social justice frameworks and vocabulary choose not to talk in a high-focus way; they listen and watch as other white people take ownership of their white privilege. The audience members participating publicly in this post-performance discussion demonstrate a hunger for spaces in which they can have messy conversations about structural systems of power. This event gives it to them.

That said, conversation by itself can feel like *doing something* beyond watching a play and resolve critical catharsis without requiring anyone take any additional concrete actions. McCarthy shifts focus to Wallace, who charges us to continue these conversations in less comfortable contexts: "We know this is a space where people more or less understand where we're coming from and what perspective, but what about when you're in a hostile environment, at work, or at Christmas dinner with Auntie Doris, or whatever? Do you know what I mean?" McCarthy then hands out index cards and sends the audience back into the low-focus pairs from the beginning of the session, asking us to write down "the change you want to see in the world, and then what you're going to do to help change that." On the back of the card, he asks us to include our contact information, so the theater can collect the cards and follow up to hold us accountable.

My discussion partner and I stare at our index cards and look at each other.

"Hey."

"Hi."

"So, yeah."

This low-focus moment of discomfort is productive. My discussion partner, a white man whom I had never met before, is a political organizer, and he gives me a list of local organizations I can look into, including an organization organizing political campaigns for progressive candidates in local elections in the neighborhood I had moved into two weeks earlier and another organization doing antiracist work with white people. I, in return, give him a list of plays and performance events focused on racial conflict and social justice coming up in the next few months. Neither of us can, on the spot, come up with a satisfying and doable concrete action to write on our cards. We both identify things we had already planned to do as part of our professional lives but can think of no new actions as a result of this event. I am embarrassed and do not return my index card. But I keep thinking about it, an unresolved chord. And when I later sit down to write my field notes on the performance and take out the list of organizations I had scribbled on my program, I look them up and put one of their public meetings on my calendar.

Wallace describes his "ultimate hope," for these performance events to "check the empathy muscle . . . get that conversation going through that internal work . . . [and then] leave armed with information, knowledge, resources, language, and courage."[43] I admit, there's a degree of luck involved with my experience of this event, that the stranger sitting next to me happened to have a wealth of information on local progressive political resources two weeks after I had moved to a new city. But the thing that most gives me "courage" following the event was not the concrete information I had been given—the program also contains a list of local organizations, so my happenstance neighbor was not the only available source of resources—but the lingering discomfort that I had *not* been able to commit to an action on the spot. The lack of resolution—caused by the simple act of not handing in an index card—leads me to keep thinking about my ongoing responsibility to take action in the real world. It makes the familiar act of leaving the theater and *not* taking further action strange, amplifying the experience of critical catharsis and the power of the production to motivate action beyond the theatrical event.

# Part 2

✦

*Rage against the Machine*

## Chapter 3

✦

# Peeling Back the Veneer of Decorum

Actors Michael Bryan, who is white, and Wesley T. Jones, who is black, strut onstage in full blackface minstrel attire. Clad in vivid orange and green jackets, orange and green and purple paisley pants, striped shirts, bright ties, Afro wigs and blackface makeup designed by A. W. Nadine Grant, they join interlocutor Vienna Carroll, whose dreadlocks and dark skin contrast against dots of white makeup running down her forehead and nose. The ensemble greets the audience, singing a jaunty tune, "Woke up black again today / Jus' living my life gets in your way / My story, my struggle you'll never really know / Got me trapped in a Traveling Minstrel Show." The fifty seats in Nicholas Martin Hall at the Calderwood Pavilion in the Boston Center for the Arts (BCA) are packed this evening, November 3, 2017, for the opening night of the theater company Sleeping Weazel's production of *3/Fifths Trapped in a Traveling Minstrel Show* (fig. 3.1). The "you" in the lyric "you'll never really know" addresses and accuses the white people in the audience—and at most of the performances I would attend during the run of the play, most of the audience members would be white people—highlighting from the opening moment that we are part of this performance and the social problem in which it intervenes.

*Trapped in a Traveling Minstrel Show* uses the spectacle of blackface and the repetition of minstrel performance forms as vehicles to critique the continuing legacy of white supremacy in contemporary US society. The performance is overtly satirical as the performers' grins both embody and wink at the minstrel tradition in which black people are forced to perform for the pleasure of white people. Soyica Diggs Colbert highlights how "African American drama often introduces familiar racial performances that have historically been associated with the objectification of black people (i.e., lynching or minstrel-inspired style) and then challenges those performances by creating sites that interrupt that objectification."[1] This production, conceived and written by James Scruggs, who is black, and directed by Mark Rayment, who is white, fits into this tradition of African American drama. The use of blackface, to follow Colbert, metatheatrically separates the actors from their roles. She writes, "Blackface minstrelsy serves as one of the primary demarcations

Fig. 3.1. Wesley T. Jones, Vienna Carroll, and Michael Bryan in *Trapped in a Traveling Minstrel Show*. Photograph by David S. Marshall.

of the performative nature of blackness, which notably stands at a critical distance from black people."[2] The production manifests this distance through contrasts between historic form and contemporary content, overt use of irony in the deployment of minstrel tropes, and the literal removal of blackface makeup midway through the play. *Trapped in a Traveling Minstrel Show* "flips the epistemological script" to transform the hypervisibility overdetermining black people's physical bodies into a space to critique the damage such overdetermination wreaks.[3] The play confronts taboos head-on to try to get under the polite veneer of civility we maintain in order to minimize conflict in a diverse society. Doing so felt urgent and necessary in the autumn of 2017, a political moment in which the belief that a diverse society could be harmonious felt quaint and out of touch. From its short run November 3–11, the play went on to win a 2018 Elliot Norton award for Outstanding Production at a Fringe Theater.

The play is structured in three parts. The first part is a minstrel show featuring White Man (Bryan) and Black Man (Jones). The second part ruptures the minstrel convention as White Man stops the show and refuses to continue his blackface performance. The third part stages a trial of police officers exonerated of murders of unarmed black men. The production aesthetically links the dehumanizing properties of the white gaze with the epidemic of excessive police force, arguing that entertainments train the white eye to fear and objectify black bodies.

Playwright James Scruggs was inspired to create this play by the epidemic of excessive police violence against black men, fueled by a fear of black male bodies woven deeply into the fabric of US society. Scruggs looks to build a space in which white audience members could start to understand his lived experience as a tall, dark-skinned black man—the experience of living as an object of fear. "My skin being near you makes you nervous and makes you want to kill me," he remarks. "I think white people just don't understand that."[4] He hopes this play will get "white people to ask themselves where they are in this." This production attempts to intervene in white audience members' sense of comfort with the status quo. It does that, artistically, through head-on confrontation with taboo material, but also through humor, song and dance, documentary theater, and multimedia spectacle. It makes for a complex interweave, navigating the tensions between provoking the discomfort needed to shock complacent audience members into change and keeping them comfortable enough to be receptive to the play's message.

Entering the Calderwood Pavilion's glossy, shiny lobby through glass doors from the cobblestone curb of Tremont Street in Boston's upscale South End, audience members pass large framed posters of the productions playing in its multiple performance spaces. Between a poster for *The 39 Steps* and *The Velveteen Rabbit* is the arresting print image for *Trapped in a Traveling Minstrel Show* (fig. 3.2). The larger-than-life poster focuses on an archival image of Al Jolson in blackface, behind which stands an image of a bare-chested black man with his hands up in surrender and fear in his eyes. The image transgresses the polite decorum of the upscale theater lobby.

Blackface makeup is widely considered verboten—forbidden, taboo. Saidiya Hartman's foundational work frames the white body donning blackface as an obliteration of the black human it purports to signify.[5] As Jennifer Schuleter puts it, "black makeup on a white face is always an act of racial violence."[6] That said, as pointed out by David Krasner and by Yuval Tailor and Jake Austen, black artists historically donned blackface to perform in the minstrel tradition as a productive way to participate in a capitalist system allowing them few points of entry.[7] Black artists in the Black Arts Movement and through the post–civil rights era have deployed blackface and minstrel performance as tactics to critique the persistence of dominant white power structures, rallying the cultural volatility of the repertoire.[8] *Trapped in a Traveling Minstrel Show* fits into this tradition of radical critical black performance, and audience members mostly read its use of taboo makeup, language, and gesture as such. Even within an overtly critical frame, live blackface minstrel performance unsettles. Catherine Cole and Tracy Davis perhaps put it best when they articulate, "Artists have been repeatedly tempted to appropriate—and even to try to reassign—signifiers from this tradition, but blackface and its indelibly associated minstrel repertoire retain the power to reopen deep wounds."[9]

Fig. 3.2. Poster for *Trapped in a Traveling Minstrel Show* in lobby of the Boston Center for the Arts. Photograph by the author.

This is precisely the power *Trapped in a Traveling Minstrel Show* harnesses. The first part unapologetically features a white actor and a black actor performing minstrel repertoire together in blackface. The performance text's overtly antiracist content problematizes any easy revulsion to the performance convention. In using blackface on a black actor, the production highlights the continuing legacy of black debasement for the pleasure of white audiences and the economics of an entertainment system commodifying black bodies for white profit. Its use of blackface on a white actor performs racial violence in a clever, tricky way. Audiences tolerate the taboo convention because we interpret it as a radical tactic to critique white supremacy. Midway through the show, White Man breaks from the minstrel convention and, as I will describe more fully later in this chapter, reveals a racist hiding under the cover of antiracist performance. We realize that we have all along been watching—and taking pleasure from watching—a white supremacist perform in blackface. The racial violence inherent in the blackface performance is just that. In this moment the production exposes the contradictions present in its use of blackface to critique the very power structure it performs.

The first audience member to speak in the talkback on opening night articulates the fundamental tension inherent in watching blackface performance in 2017. A white male college student sitting in the front row of the audience comments on how "good the performances" are, and how he wanted to smile in response to the excellence of the performers while also not wanting to endorse the content of stories of oppression. "We want to show you we like . . . that you guys are all good actors, but at the same time we don't want to make it seem like we were all, like, 'Oh, wow, that was totally appropriate for those terrible things to be happening.' "

The first moment of blackface performance is shocking. As the actors sing and cakewalk, the audience sits politely. On opening night, they are very, very still. I sit in the back row, so I cannot see many people's facial expressions, but the faces I am able to see are blank. Audience members give nothing away as they adjust to the spectacle of the minstrel convention. Actor Michael Bryan told me in a later interview that in that first moment, as he greets the audience in blackface, they look at him "with disgust"; with no fourth wall, the actors get a clear sense of how the audience in the intimate performance space responds to them.[10]

"Good after-lunch," Carroll welcomes the audience with a malaprop-ridden 'stump speech,' insisting that the audience reply and setting up the convention that we will not be allowed to sit passively in our seats. Once Carroll gets the first laugh out of the audience, they start to relax into the convention and go with the flow of the performance. Audience members smile in response to the performers' satirical too-wide grins, laugh at their jokes, and nod their heads to the beat of their up-tempo song. They sit with relaxed body language watching the entertaining spectacle of the mistral show with pleasure. I have to acknowledge the obvious and uncomfortable fact that minstrel performance endured because it is pleasurable. The historic convention is so charged, so taboo, it is rarely enacted. It is too easy to hold the archive at arm's length, forgetting that the repertoire was popular because it was *fun*. The performance includes many horrible stories of oppression wrapped in song, painted in blackface, and in this way made pleasurable for the audience's consumption.

In post-performance discussions, audience members almost always articulate antiracist sentiments or ask real, messy questions as they try to understand their own responsibility within a structural system of power from which they benefit. Nobody appears to have chosen to come see a play called *Trapped in a Traveling Minstrel Show* as a celebration of white supremacy. I am surprised that, in these antiracist public discussions, there is a conspicuous silence around the blackface performance convention. When it feels organic to introduce the topic in informal conversations after performances, I ask audience members directly, "What do you make of the blackface?"

The most common response I receive is, "I trusted the artists." Audience members report suspending a reaction of outrage and, as one white woman put it, "I just went with it" because the artists "know what they are doing" and so she "trusted them."

The art historian Miwon Kwon critiques an artistic landscape in which the artist becomes a commodity, their identity location an integral part of what is being sold.[11] David Krasner writes of black artists in the late nineteenth and early twentieth centuries donning blackface for minstrel shows and selling the authenticity of their black performance.[12] This scholarship helps explain why white audience members at the performance I have just seen "trust that it's OK"; that blackface is within bounds when it is authorized by black artists and produced by a respected theater company with a track record of productions critiquing racism. One white woman confesses to me that she knows the form is taboo but didn't know why and had as a child assumed the convention was related to the white face paint worn by circus clowns. "I don't know where white clown makeup comes from. I didn't know where blackface came from. As a kid I thought they were the same thing," she tells me, shrugging her shoulders in bafflement at the conspicuous gaps in her education as a white child.

This is not to say that nobody is disturbed by the production's use of blackface. A black boy, who looks perhaps ten, enters one performance late, accompanied by an interracial couple I assume are his parents. He stands in the aisle staring at the blackface performance in abject horror and surprise, his mouth dropped open, totally shocked that he's confronted with a live minstrel show.

The playwright Scruggs tells me, "I was really disturbed by seeing the blackface. It's really—for me, and I'm like—in my head, I'm like the last provocateur. But when they came out the first time in blackface, I was like, 'James, maybe you went too far.'" Late in the run, the artists tell me that at one performance I did not attend, an older black man who was identified to them as a pastor made a comment objecting to the blackface. In the next night's post-performance discussion, Scruggs responds to this critique by asking the audience about the convention more directly:

> I think there's a lot of shame, and I'm realizing from talkbacks, especially last night, that there are segments of the population who believe that some things that actually happened should not be—ah, it's not appropriate to talk about it. It's dirty laundry, or it's shameful. It's better off left in the past. And, blackface is one of the things.[13]

He asks the audience if in the opening moment, when the actors came out in blackface, people were "ashamed." Six hands go up. The raised hands belong to me, three black women identified during the talkback as students in a college class studying minstrel performance, a white woman who does not speak during the talkback but who sits with a cluster of audience members whose overheard conversation marks them university faculty members, and a white man who, a few moments later, directly responds to Scruggs's question about shame. He begins by quietly acknowledging, "I know a little about minstrel performance and the concept of love and theft," obliquely referencing Eric Lott's foundational scholarship on blackface performance before addressing the topic head-on:[14]

> We should be ashamed, embarrassed, and pissed off, and I thank you because this show—You know, access to all of that . . . There's this uncomfortability, and when these actors come on and beautifully move their bodies, you're watching that, and you know it's the most insidious tropes of our culture, but there's also a beauty in the celebration of the movement of the body, the timing. You see the art in it, and that kind of conflict that you set up early on in the play, I think, shakes up the shame. Like, the moments when you're laughing, and then if you know the history of the malapropisms, and what that built in terms of the ongoing narrative of blacks in popular culture, and how that's been constructed over time. But, it's funny. That sets us up, and then we get to the incarceration of the body, and the destruction of the body. At the end, so much of the shit of race in this country, and the shit of white supremacy, and the shit of terrorism in this country is based on the fear of the black body in so many ways.[15]

Scruggs later asks the audience who has seen blackface performance live before this; this man's hand is the only one in the air.[16] Based on my multiple low-focus conversations with audience members and this isolated high-focus exchange in post-performance discussion, I learn that while most white people know blackface performance is somehow *bad*, only white audience members who have formally studied blackface performance know to feel *shame* watching it.

## Fear and Black Bodies

Black Man (Jones) and White Man (Bryan), both in blackface, turn tragic stories into song-and-dance routines, emphasizing relationships between entertainment labor and labor in a coal mine to highlight exploitative labor practices. They each tell a different story, alternating between the two using an aesthetic marked by interruption and staged to emphasize rhythmic syncopation. Black Man tells of being hired out as a teenager to an affluent white family on Long Island for a weekend to entertain the teenage daughter

Fig. 3.3. Wesley T. Jones in *Trapped in a Traveling Minstrel Show*. Photograph by David S. Marshall.

and her friends, to "teach them cool black dances."[17] He tells the audience how the young woman comes on to him, saying, "are you going to be my big strong Mandingo warrior."[18] As Black Man speaks the text of her provocative advance, White Man stands behind him, crouching down low and peering out at the audience from between his legs. White Man cocks his head to the side, as if mimicking the body language of the girl. As Black Man voices the girl's charged question, White Man pops his head through Black Man's legs, manifesting the violation in physical metaphor. Black Man is visibly shaken and afraid; he tells the audience how he puts his hands on the girl's shoulders, urgently admonishing her not to put him in a position that would get him in trouble. It is dangerous for him to be the object of her desire. He puts his hands up in a gesture that conveys both "don't come any closer to me" and "I am unarmed, don't shoot" as footage from the original 1933 black-and-white *King Kong* movie plays behind him larger than life on the projection screen, the white actress Fay Wray's arms similarly upraised and her face expressing terror (fig. 3.3).

White Man (in blackface in-role as a black man) walks wearily across the stage, demonstrating his commute home after a long day of coal mine labor. He describes how, in his exhaustion, he does not step into the gutter to make way for a white woman walking down the street in the other direction, which makes her step into the gutter. On the projection screen behind him, *King Kong* footage continues to play. The audience watches Fay Wray struggle against her bonds on film, a monstrous hairy gorilla grabbing her with his enormous, powerful hand.

Both men walk backward, hands up in submission and fear in their eyes. They back into each other center stage under the image of the hulking gorilla. White Man tells us, "S'like time slowed down. That white woman, she stared me like I was a dangerous animal and looked like she was about to scream, I just froze."[19] Black Man finishes his earlier story, "But just when I grab her . . . her mother walks in and sees me with my hands on her shoulders and, I mean, I musta look pretty mad cause, I was."[20] His eyes are wide, his breath heavy.

This theatrical moment manipulates object and subject, drawing attention to the ways in which reception is context-specific and subjective. Fear and rage motivate the same externalized, observable tableau, facial expression, and breathing pattern. The audience knows that as a subject, Black Man's response is a rational reaction of fear to a legitimate danger. The superimposition of *King Kong* imagery imposes the unspoken gaze of the girl's mother—and indeed, US society—overdetermining Black Man's body as an object of fear. Complicating this moment is Black Man's explanation that he *does* respond to his own fear by getting angry—his anger is not misread. He is innocent of antagonistic intent, and in the full context of the moment, we know him to be the victim. Black Man's anger is a reasonable human response to the situation; his reasonable human response looks dangerous because his black male body is overdetermined as an object of fear. The theatrical moment forces audience members to confront a hard truth. Even within this clearly critical framework, Black Man's physical expression of anger still looks scary—even when we know better, he still *feels* dangerous in this moment.

The production leans into this tension, and the actors turn to the audience and make eye contact with white women in the house. They enter into the aisles to get physically close, "uncomfortable close," as they put it, to these audience members, turning them into scene partners. They invoke public spaces—the empty subway car, the quiet street:

> Just you, and me—
> And you don't know me
> You don't know what I'm gonna do—
> And you are . . . well . . . scared
> You've heard the stories and you don't want to be a victim
> And I've heard them too.
> Black man . . . white woman—alone . . . a scream—
> We both know what's at stake. You make a choice
> And you know that if you scream they will believe you . . . no matter what I say.[21]

This moment flips the script on the cultural narrative that black men are a danger to white women, taking a turn to emphasize the danger white women's fear poses to black men. I ask Michael Bryan later how the women he makes eye contact with in this moment respond. He tells me that "either the woman that I stare at breaks out into a nervous laugh or she stares hard back, very, very hard back. But other than that, usually they don't say anything or really do anything. One time, I had a woman nod at me when I was like, 'No matter what, if you screamed . . .' and she nodded." In this response, the woman seems to acknowledge the structural power she has as a white woman over a black man—she leans into the problem the moment invokes. The overdetermination of black male bodies as objects of fear places the onus on black men to constantly prove they are not a threat in ordinary situations in which they find themselves in the proximity of a white woman in public space.

This moment of performance draws an implicit parallel between the white woman who is afraid of being alone in public space with an unarmed black man's body and the police officer who pulls a trigger because he is afraid of an unarmed black man's body. This connection unsettles the ease with which politically progressive audience members—particularly the progressive white women who dominate mainstream theater audiences—can judge acts of excessive police force against unarmed black men to be abhorrent without recognizing how we participate in the structures enabling these atrocities to occur. It takes the blame—too easy to place elsewhere—and makes me face it.

## Racism Is Somewhere Else

White Man, in blackface, delivers the central argument of the minstrel show. He is alone onstage, directly addressing the audience that "the unflinching continuous task thrust upon me and my people from birth, [is] to be the 'thing' that makes the white man smile, to be an amusing distraction and confirmation of his great superiority."[22] Midway through this monologue, he speaks the phrase "the white man is a devil" and stops, looking up at the sky, mumbling under his breath. He takes off his curly black wig, revealing his shaved white head underneath. He cannot continue. "I just can't, this is . . . bullshit," he says.[23]

On opening night, the mouth of a college student sitting in the front row hangs open. She stares in amazement, checking in with the students next to her. I watch her try to figure out whether the show has really stopped. She grins from ear to ear. I am reminded of Carole Martin's book *Theatre of the Real*, in which she excitedly asks, is "this an unsanctioned outbreak of the real exploding the realm of theatre?"[24] Meanwhile, during this performance, from backstage, we can hear the other actors whispering anxiously, "He's gone up on his lines!" (At many performances, audience members whispered and gestured to each other, legitimately trying to figure out whether the disruption is real or rehearsed.)

This moment of rupture draws my attention back to the reality that we have all been politely watching blackface performance for forty minutes and have neither stopped the show nor walked out. Initially, I think White Man stops the show in protest of the erasure his performance enacts. But as White Man goes on, his discourse takes an overtly racist turn. "I mean—shit—I am so over the 'black man as victim.' Huh—more white people get shot by policeman in any given year than black people anyway, but you don't hear about that do you?"[25] White Man has crossed what Shannon Sullivan calls the "bright line drawn between good anti-racist white people and bad white supremacists."[26] He tries to remove his blackface, and under the paint we discover what appears to be a white supremacist.

White Man seamlessly transitions between moments openly acknowledging tensions inherent in white allyship and overtly racist tropes. His logic slides too easily from discomfort to disavowal. Some of his verbiage is lifted directly from contemporary alt-right political discourse—for example, he quotes the defense of slavery put forth by Ben Carson, the black former neurosurgeon appointed by Donald Trump as secretary of Housing and Urban Development in 2017, as "'not that bad,' three hots and a cot."[27] These moments mark White Man as outside the community of politically progressive, antiracist white people. But how many of what Sullivan terms the "good white people" who watch this performance in silence find a kernel of agreement when White Man says he feels "forced into silence [around issues of race] 'cause a silent empathetic look is about all that doesn't hurt?"[28]

Scruggs did not intend to render White Man a white supremacist; he wanted to explore the perspective of a white man who has good relationships with individual black people but has not delved deeply into history and social justice. We have watched White Man collaborate generously with two black artists for forty minutes; White Man tells us he has tried "walking around in the shoes/skin of a black man" for insight, but the experience has frustrated and angered him, ultimately supporting a belief in his own racial innocence.[29] Scruggs tells me he was "trying to get at all the things in white heads that we can't say," hoping to model a radical openness beyond the veneer of decorum imposed by white antiracist performance codes in order to facilitate a more nuanced, honest discussion. "I'm not so sure everyone who is espousing such woke language really feels all of it in their bones," he tells me. "If white people say what is on their mind—it might be racist but it isn't mean spirited—they get thrown into the vat with David Duke [an avowed neo-Nazi]."[30]

The bright line separating good white people from bad racists does not allow for ambiguity—as Scruggs points out, "to be branded a racist is easy—it just takes one ignorant comment."[31] As soon as White Man's text violates what Sullivan identifies as "proper race/class etiquette," audience members—including me—respond to him as a white supremacist.[32] This disconnect between authorial intention and audience response highlights the vehemence with which *good white people* police the boundaries of the antiracist white community, distancing ourselves from anyone who crosses the line.

Actor Michael Bryan delivers this monologue as a vulnerable confession. His performance is open and honest, the actor's vulnerability contrasting with the overtly racist-reading text to create a complex moment of performance. He tries to connect to and enlist white audience members to agree with him, as White Man goes on, "This race, racism thing is not solely the fault of white people—can't be . . . this shit makes me so mad—we . . . are not responsible. White people! Say it with me! 'We are not responsible! We are not responsible! We are not responsible!' "[33]

The audience sits in frozen silence.

At two of the four performances I attended, white men who appeared to be older than fifty answered White Man's call, responding, "We are not responsible!" as instructed. Both times, I then saw these audience members look around, surprised that they were the only ones speaking. The participatory convention of call-and-response is set up early in the show, and audience members have grown accustomed to repeating texts when prompted by the actors. It is not clear whether the audience members denying responsibility in this moment did so because they wholeheartedly believed what they said or because they were following the rules of the event by doing what an actor tells them to do. However, it indicates that these audience members most likely did not recognize that the actor asks them to break a code of antiracist white behavior. It seems they do not know how this speech act performs racism.

Most of the audience recognizes the taboo—good white antiracists take responsibility for the ways we continue to benefit from oppressive structural systems of power; disavowing responsibility for racism is racist. When audience members spoke at that moment at the two performances where I saw that happen, the people surrounding them averted their gaze. At one performance, a woman who appeared to have come to the theater with one of the men who spoke shook her head sharply, as if trying to get his attention and communicate that he should stop speaking. The people sitting near the audience members who responded that they "are not responsible" looked embarrassed for the people who, as Michael Bryan puts it, have perhaps been "duped" into speaking.

At one performance I did not attend, the audience refused to let White Man continue. Bryan told me the story of what happened:

> A few members of the audience were just not having it. They were calling me out on what I was saying, and they were like, "Would you do this if it was the Holocaust?" or, "Would you say these things if it was this way?" or, "Of course, white people are responsible because they've benefited from the system."

At this performance, the audience openly resisted the query, and Bryan needed to improvise and told me he "[did] not get through" the monologue as scripted. At another performance I did attend, audience members shook their heads no when asked to decry responsibility, folding their arms over their chests and making eye contact with one another in solidarity against the request. This audience silently collaborated to communicate resistance without any breach in etiquette that would disrupt the performance.

Through this monologue, White Man continues to try to remove his blackface. It smears, the dark makeup gets on his white gloves, and he is able to remove streaks so that the audience is hyperaware of his white skin under the blackface makeup. We are good progressives abhorred by his white supremacist text. We have also been politely watching this white man perform in blackface—naturalizing the convention, laughing at the jokes, and participating as prompted—for forty minutes. And now we push away the racist monster who has been here with us all along; we just didn't know what was lurking under the surface. It's an easy move, to push away the racist other in blackface—to feel the moral superiority of a more enlightened white person who knows better.

## Participatory Justice

Jacqueline O'Connor observes, "The justice system, designed to serve as a neutral platform for the resolution of private and public discord, often fails to achieve or maintain proposed neutrality, fostering skepticism about whether courtroom procedures and decisions can produce both just and satisfactory denouements during times of major social conflicts."[34] The third act of *Trapped in a Traveling Minstrel Show* uses the familiar theatrical conventions of a trial to judge the justice dispensed in real hearings exonerating police officers of killing unarmed black men.

White Man and Black Man, now without makeup, both wear simple white T-shirts and jeans. Their heads are both shaved. The white T-shirt on Black Man reads as simple and neutral—in a white T-shirt and a clean-shaven head, he is everyman. Every black man, that is, "dying over and over."[35] He is the plaintiff, here to prove an "intentional and continued attempt from white folks in power to terrorize black people 'to keep them/us in line.' "[36] In a white T-shirt and a clean-shaven head, White Man is a skinhead. The defendant in this trial, he is every white supremacist. Black Man frames the problem: "Today I am repeatedly shot for no other reason than my blackness made a police officer nervous as he legally kills me by using the phrase of exoneration 'I feared for my life.' "[37] Interlocutor Vienna Carroll serves as the presiding judge. The audience is impaneled as a jury and given red and green voting paddles and asked to evaluate the validity of the officers' fear.

O'Connor describes how "as trial proceedings are adapted for the theater, as they are moved out of the courtroom and into other public venues, the cases themselves are not reopened, but the cross-examinations are cross-examined and the decisions that emerged from them are scrutinized."[38] *Trapped in a*

*Traveling Minstrel Show* asks its audience to watch documentary evidence and hear testimony adapted from the real police officers who killed Freddie Gray, Michael Brown, and Walter Scott, judging the justice dispensed in their real trials. The evidence presented is fragmented and at times contradictory, representing the conflicting perspectives of police officers and victims. We are to vote green "if you believe the accused is innocent" and red "if you believe the accused is guilty of excessive force, manslaughter, or murder."[39] This staged trial explicitly highlights the disconnect between the legal standard for exoneration—an officer's fear—and a commonsense moral standard for guilt. With every vote, a sea of red paddles rises from the crowd. These officers were not convicted in real courts of law, and the audience formally registers disagreement with the structural system of power exonerating them.

Scruggs articulates a desire to "show both sides" in this trial, but it feels as if he instead puts white supremacy on trial.[40] One black woman described in a post-performance discussion how, to her, there are not "two sides" to this issue:

> It's not a game for me to vote to say if the police officer was right or, you know, if the dead black man was right? The dead black man was right, in my mind. That's it. There is no vote and there's no need for me to show anyone my vote. You should know what my vote is. My vote says that one man is alive today, and then one is dead. And that didn't need to happen.[41]

The moments in which the audience casts their votes were, on the surface, nearly identical at every event. The actors speak the same lines from the same positions onstage. Audience members raise red paddles. In the post-performance talkback on closing night, the three actors discuss watching audience members look around to see how others are voting before casting their votes. Michael Bryan describes this as a collective moment in which, after looking around, the audience appears to silently agree, "Okay, we're all raising our reds."[42] But at each performance event, the manifestation of this phenomenon in the theatrical moment operated in a distinct manner.

On opening night, the woman sitting in front of me turns around after the show. "What did you think?" I ask. She responds that she felt like the act of voting "correctly" reinforced audience members' sense of moral superiority. At performance events I attended in which the audience was mostly white and voted unanimously, the moments of voting could feel a little hollow.

On closing night, at another performance with a mostly white audience, one white woman responds to a direct question the actors ask about why audience members look around before voting. She comments, "You want to do the right thing—you want to do and say the right thing. We as the jury, we wanna do and say the right thing and I want to teach my children to do and say the right thing, but sometimes there's more than one right thing."[43] White audience members gauge the right thing in these moments by looking to see what others are doing and then they do the same. The moment of hesitation manifests an ambivalence some white audience members may feel about condemning white police officers' violent responses to fear—fear the production may have shown them they share. When audience members look around to see what others are doing, they reveal how the right choice is not sufficiently obvious to everyone, exposing a noticeable undercurrent that perhaps the *wrong* choice could be an acceptable option.

The moment is pedagogical, as the group ultimately reinforces its own sense of *right*, conforming to the collective norms reinforced by this moment of participation in the theatrical event. By voting the right way, white audience members perform their status as *good white people* for each other and for the actors, confirming their participation in a temporary community that does and says the right thing. That is not without political impact. The goodness of the audience contrasts with the evil of a real justice system that sanctions the murders of unarmed black men. It alienates the "good" from the state's version of "just," agitating for systemic change in a status quo that is actively evil.

The same moment of voting operated slightly differently in the one performance event I attended with a racially integrated audience. At the final Saturday matinee, the house is packed with a diverse audience. Most audience members are adults in their thirties through sixties, and some school-age children are also present. Throughout the play, black audience members participate audibly in a call-and-response with the performance, uttering um-hums in agreement or derision. During one moment of the minstrel show involving a variation of "the dozens" staged as if on a racquetball court, a black woman behind me whispers to her companion, "I should not be laughing at this."[44] The audience laughs raucously whenever White Man is slighted from early on in the play, and Carroll as the Interlocuter (who facilitates many moments of audience interaction) plays up this humor for their benefit throughout the performance. Such jokes provoke laughter at most performances, but black audience members vocally treat the spectacle of a white man in blackface as an object of humor and derision. One black man seated behind me laughs out loud at White Man's overtly racist statements during the final part of the play. With their laughter, black audience members appear to reclaim the blackface minstrel as an object to scorn and mock, inverting the historic resonance of the form. The white audience members laugh, too, but not as much, and the moments at which they laugh are moments that get laughs at performances with mostly white audiences. In examining this difference now, I draw on Colbert, who argues, "African American drama returns to the scenes of crimes to interrupt historical processes used to render black people objects and offers performance strategies that not only keep the dehumanizing force of objection at bay but also enable the performers and audiences to object by reconfiguring the historical order."[45] Black audience members' reception of the blackface minstrel reconfigures the historical order in this way.

With a diverse audience at the final Saturday matinee, the trial portion of the play is particularly intense. When White Man utters the sentence of exoneration "I feared for my life," a black woman sitting behind me speaks it with him. One black woman leaves the room during the video of the killing of Walter Scott, and she explains why in the talkback:

> That disturbed my soul, for me, taking that in. It just disturbed me to just see you telling it was just the injustice done on our black men, that we just clearly see it on tape. It just disturbed me. I couldn't take it. I had to step out. For me, I don't know about anybody else, but I had to take a breath, and step out. It was just too much.[46]

Several black women surrounding her chime in and augment her response. The woman who had left during the video had an aisle seat in the front row and was able to easily access the exit. I wonder as I listen to her comment how many other audience members had wanted to leave and felt as though they couldn't.

When asked during the performance to vote, one black woman holds up her red paddle high before Carroll finishes giving the audience instructions, and several audience members respond to her gesture with um-hums of agreement. In a diverse audience, the moment of unanimous voting carries a different resonance than it does in audiences that are mostly white. It still creates a morally good "us" in opposition to a system committing evils in the name of justice. But the diverse audience creates a racially integrated Greek chorus to reject the exonerations, a "utopian performative" of a diverse society in complete agreement.[47] United, we judge the court's standards of guilt and innocence unjust and evil. Whatever else may divide us, we perform our agreement that a socially ingrained fear of black male bodies should not give the state license to kill in the name of that fear.

## Dissensus and Pedagogical Space

Every performance of *Trapped in a Traveling Minstrel Show* is followed by a post-performance discussion. Director Mark Rayment, who is white, observes, "Race is hard to talk about in a mixed group. Plus, there's people walking on eggshells, 'What if I say what I really mean? I'm not really a racist, but I feel this way. How much trust can I—?' It's a real dance."[48] The post-performance events often operate as pedagogical spaces as white audience members work hard to understand the complexity of race relations in the contemporary United States. The National Endowment for the Arts found that the two most important reasons people attend performance events are to socialize and because they want to learn new things.[49] The audience for *Trapped in a Traveling Minstrel Show* comes voluntarily to see the performance to grapple with racism, and large portions of the audience stay to talk about it. The full cast and artistic team participates in every post-performance discussion, and the intimate performance marked by many moments of audience participation builds a degree of trust between artists and audience that allows for vulnerable, substantial discussion. Audience members in many discussions thank the artists for creating a live, public space in which they can navigate the complexity of racism with other people, referencing the ways in which social media have become the principal public sphere in which they access these issues. As one white man who appears to be in his forties puts it:

> The capacity to hold the terror and the trauma is so importantly done by having space and by having each of you hold us to things I can't otherwise look at. These videos, for example, are all over Facebook; I couldn't watch them. I could watch them, though, together. And, I could hear the different stories together being held in a public space. I thank you very much for doing this hard work, because it's—it is traumatizing to live it, and it's traumatizing to witness it, and it takes your creativity to help us sit with it and try to figure out what do we do. One of the things we can do is sit here together.[50]

He invokes the experience of sitting alone with a screen, scrolling through videos and op-eds and commentary describing tragedies and horrors that somehow feel both distant and immediate at the same time. Of feeling the impulse and desire to do something to right the wrongs and having no idea what concrete steps to take to help.

Learning is not always easy and not always comfortable. Because *Trapped in a Traveling Minstrel Show* gets under the veneer of civility we need to minimize conflict in diverse society, the post-performance discussions are not always polite affairs. Early on, director Mark Rayment tells me, "I'm interested for them to have debate." Debate differs from open antagonism; at one post-performance discussion in particular, the gloves come off and the event dissolves into what Sleeping Weazel artistic director Charlotte Meehan, who is white, later calls "a shit show" marked by privilege callouts.[51]

Actor Wesley Jones, who portrayed Black Man and is a black man in in his twenties, comments on excessive police force; this comment is similar to ones I have heard him make at earlier post-performance events:

> I think what we need to do is, number one, work with our police officers and where they train these policemen. And, I think it is also our responsibility as the black community to sit down and have conversations with their black children and with—because I've had conversations with my parents.

A white man who appears to be in his twenties in the audience critiques Jones's framework that black people have a responsibility to obey police commands and act in a way that won't get them killed. His critique is blunt but respectfully framed, rooted in a belief that responsibility should be placed on the shoulders of police perpetrators of violence rather than the black community:

> I 100 percent agree that cops—that they need to be trained better, but it's fucked up that I never had to have a—like, my parents never had a conversation with me that if you get pulled over, make sure you don't mouth off to a cop, make sure you don't—like, that you keep your hands constantly visible because you might be dead. I never had that conversation, and I don't think it appropriate, fair, just, and equitable to say black people need to have this conversation with your parents—with your kids, so that way they don't get shot in the street by the cops that are supposed to be paid, by our tax dollars, to defend them.

An black man in the audience who appears to be in his fifties chides Jones, echoing this critique that it shouldn't be on black people to act deferentially to avoid being killed and police just shouldn't kill people:

> I wanted to speak to the point of the saying of we need to teach our black children how to treat police officers. That is the most ridiculous thing I've ever heard in my life. We do not have to teach our kids how to treat police officers; police officers need to treat everybody correctly. There shouldn't be a certain way that we have to act as black people because we are black, if a police officer pulls us over. Police officers need to be trained.

A white women who appears to be in her fifties then critiques the construct of an armed police force:

> I have to say that I am terrified of police. And, I don't really—honestly—I feel like it's true that black kids have it worse, and probably black boys have it worse, but I really don't see how it can ever be right for a bunch of people to be going around with guns, when the rest of the population doesn't have them.

She continues in this vein for some time and begins to ramble, and Meehan as the facilitator gently steps in to end her extended comment. Meehan redirects the conversation to defend Jones from the critique of his initial comment, pointing out how black parents fear for their children and lay down rules so as to not get them killed:

> Of course it's wrong that an African American or a darker-skinned child is going to be treated this way, or the parents have to raise them to just almost go dead when there are police around. However, one has to realize in the culture we're living in, the mother, the father, is saving the child's life by trying to do that.

The conversation turns in another direction, but about ten minutes later, a white man who appears to be in his thirties brings the topic back up in an aggressive manner, decrying the appropriation of black parental fear and calling out both Meehan and the other white woman as racist:

> I guess I got a little triggered by the two of you talking, because it feels so weird to me to have, like, a couple of white women talk about what a black mother must be feeling.[52] And, I feel like that's one way that we shift the conversation away from us, is we start, like, talking about, oh, well, this black mother has to do it this way. It's like, we have no idea, we have no idea what a black woman—

Meehan tries to intervene:

> So, you know what you can do, is at Thanksgiving, when your racist uncle is ranting on, you can interrupt him.

He refuses the offer of resolution:

> I'm interrupting right now, because I feel like that was a racist dialogue where we talk about what black people think and feel, and we don't have any idea. Like, to me, that was a racist dialogue. And, I just—we find ways to shift the conversation off, but what we do—the culture is the way it is because we want it that way.

Phoebe Maltz Bovy characterizes the "privilege call out" as an insult often deployed in the direction of "poorly worded or otherwise naive attempts at *challenging* privilege" rather than overtly oppressive actions. It shifts the conversation from a focus on structural oppression to focus on the identity location of the individual being challenged.[53] This "privilege call out" is a white racialized performative, policing the boundaries of the antiracist white community.

Everyone participating in the conversation in this particular post-performance discussion appears to agree that undue burden is placed on black people to navigate dangerous landscapes in which armed representatives of state power are given impunity to act violently in response to racist fears. The point of disagreement within the initial conversation hinges on the difference between Jones's belief that there are things black people can do to help keep them safe—a belief instilled in him by his parents that if he follows a set of behavioral codes, he will be all right—and a commitment held by progressive white people and authorized by the black man in the audience that the power structures requiring Jones to hold these beliefs are oppressive and evil. This is fundamentally a disagreement of framework—the artists operate within a pragmatic framework of individuals navigating the unjust world as it currently exists; the audience members operate within a structural framework of how systems of power should operate in the better world we want to create. The individualist framework isn't wrong, though the structural critique fits more easily into prevalent antiracist discourses.

The man performing the "privilege call out" does so, ostensibly, as a critique that Meehan's shift of the framework to insert her own understanding is an act of erasure and appropriation, displacing the absent actual black mother. This critique is not fundamentally different from Saidiya Hartman's critique of the limits of empathy when she asks the rhetorical question, "Can the white witness of the spectacle of suffering affirm the materiality of black sentience only by feeling for himself?"[54] But as Bovy points out, there's a difference between a critique of systemic oppression and a personal accusation, and the man in this post-performance discussion appears to perform this critique as a way of asserting that he is a better antiracist white ally than the white women are.[55]

This man had sat in the front row during the performance and was within my field of vision through the show, and I saw the same audience member who called out appropriation in the talkback laughing, smiling, and looking relaxed through the blackface minstrel show. The erasure baked into the cake of the theatrical convention did not appear to provoke in him the same outrage as a (far less charged) set of comments in talkback. These elements of the performance event cannot be disconnected—the performance peeled back the veneer of civility and as such provoked an uncivil response to the discomfort.

Director Rayment cuts the man off, ending the false debate by personalizing the issue:

> I don't know what a black mother or a black woman feels, but I do know that living with a dark-skinned, tall, big, African American man [*he leans over and tenderly touches Scruggs on the shoulder*] that I kind of worry every time he leaves the house. And, I know that if we're [out in a car together] and if I'm driving and we get pulled over, I don't have to necessarily put my hands out of the window.

Rayment can end the conversation by authentically claiming the contested perspective as his own. He does so in a way that both validates the original story the actor told and honors the critique of appropriation. His husband is a black man, and this is his story, too.

Other audience members are visibly uncomfortable through the altercation, and I watch people cross their arms to close off their bodies and shift their gaze away from the man performing the "privilege call out." A white woman who appears to be in her thirties sitting near me makes eye contact with me and tilts her head, opening her eyes wide in incredulity that we are witnessing this spectacle of conflict. These gestures distance audience members from the speaker—they are similar gestures to the ones performed by audience members in response to the people repeating "I am not responsible" for racism at White Man's request during the performance proper. One white woman who appears to be about thirty calls out the callout in the final comment of the evening, "I want to just touch on your comment of, like, how uncomfortable we felt. And, I did. And, I'm so okay with that. And, I think that white folks, as a race, we need to fucking learn to lean into that discomfort." By the end of her extended comment, tears stream down her face. "I'm crying. I'm fine. But, like, we got to fucking lean into it, guys."[56]

The radical pedagogy of this dissensus-filled post-performance discussion teaches contradictory lessons. The callout reinforces an argument White Man makes during his white supremacist rant, that "a silent empathetic look is about all that doesn't hurt" and white people perhaps should remain "silent" on matters of race lest we be called racists.[57] Conversely, the audience's response to the callout teaches that open conflict is as undesirable as speech acts unintentionally violating the codes of *good white* decorum, rejecting the man's aggressive response to his own "triggered" discomfort.

After this volatile event, Sleeping Weazel adjusted the post-performance discussion format so that Vienna Carroll facilitated the discussion, extending her role as Interlocuter in the minstrel show and Judge of the trial into Facilitator of the final portion of the evening. It also allowed her to use the weight of her gravitas as an elder, expansive stage presence, and authenticating blackness in the service of maintaining order in the talkback. More formal rules for the discussion were established—audience members were reminded that the material is volatile, asked to speak only from their own experience and perspective, told each person will only be called on once to allow many people to speak, and asked not to comment on one another's comments.

A tension exists between the desire to open up spaces for radical learning and the desire to avoid conflict. Too much conflict will cause many participants to shut down, foreclosing the possibility of learning. Structure gives facilitators more control over message, but too much structure can devolve into polite consensus, becoming a space in which learning does not take place—in which audience members perform their capacity to supply right answers, rather than ask tough questions. A balance must be struck. The more structured discussions following performances of *Trapped in a Traveling Minstrel Show* largely found this balance. The clear ground rules maintained the degree of order required to avoid the open conflict that can foreclose the possibility of learning. The panel of artists asked the audience some of the direct, tough questions I discussed in earlier sections of this chapter—for example, Scruggs asked audience members about feeling shame watching blackface, and Carroll and Bryan asked them why they looked around to see how other people vote. These challenging, specific questions focused audience members on their own experiences interacting with the charged performance event, continuing to unsettle them even after the most provocative aesthetic portions of the evening had passed. This process was particularly effective with a diverse audience present, as audience members with a range of lived experiences and interpretations responded to specific prompts, listening to one another grapple with tough questions in a respectful, generous space of learning.

## Chapter 4

✦

# Outrage and the Boundaries of Community

This chapter differs from the others in this volume. Most of this book interrogates moments of audience response to theatrical events that Lauren Berlant might describe as *situations* in which, "something that will perhaps matter is unfolding amidst the usual activity of life."[1] Situations fit within the bounds of ordinary audience behavior. Those moments of tension or conflict stay safely within the framework of performances and organized post-performance events; they do not assert themselves into the real world outside of the performance space.

In this chapter, I turn my attention to a pair of scandals surrounding critical engagement with theatrical events at Chicago's Steppenwolf Theatre: *This Is Modern Art* in 2015 and *Pass Over* in 2017. I focus on digital performances, analyzing social media comments from audience members and published reviews from professional critics rather than using participant observation to examine the embodied performances of live audience members. I do this because so much contemporary activism and discourse surrounding race and racism takes place in digital spaces. People perform differently online than they do in person, and as such in this chapter I attend to digital performances in response to theatrical events. These case studies straddle a particular nodal point in recent US history: the 2016 ascension of reality television star and real estate mogul Donald Trump to the presidency of the United States. On the surface, both events appear similar: high-profile white theater critics wrote reviews of productions focused on the experiences and perspectives of young men of color in ways revealing uninterrogated biases and reflecting patterns of white spectatorship I discuss throughout this book. Members of the theater community used social media to push back against these reviews in a targeted (and at times, enraged) manner.

Theater critics are professional audience members, tasked with rendering lived experiences of theatrical events into language for imagined readers. Newspaper criticism is a specific genre, operating primarily as a consumer guide for newspaper subscribers.[2] Veteran critics writing for major newspapers know their readership to be dominated by the same older, affluent, white people who dominate mainstream theater audiences; they write reviews to help these imagined readers make informed choices about how to spend their time and money. Newspaper criticism has a secondary function—within the theater community, it documents, legitimizes, and draws attention to artistic work. In the scandals I describe in this chapter, these two functions collided as artists protested the frameworks white critics use to inform the theatergoing choices of their (predominantly white, older, affluent) readership.

I consider these events to be "theater scandals," borrowing Neil Blackadder's use of the term to refer to "a perceived affront that provokes a demonstration of opposition that itself generates a counterdemonstration."[3] Blackadder studies late nineteenth- and early twentieth-century theater scandals, in which audience members protested live in the auditorium and their counterprotest became part of the theatrical event. Much twenty-first-century oppositional behavior is digital in nature, fought through posts in the public square of social media. These digital performances become part of the theatrical event by shaping audience members' horizon of expectations to view their performance attendance as a facet of collective activist action. Like the live demonstrations of historic theater scandals, Blackadder observes, "evidence abounds of the protesters' complicity in the uproar: clearly many of them wished to participate in a theater scandal, and enjoyed doing so."[4] Participation in a theater scandal binds an individual to a camp, enacts belonging, and calls community into being by drawing a line differentiating *our* shared values from *their* distasteful, rejected ideas.

John Fletcher argues that the ultimate triumph of an activist movement is for "a group's values to gradually become integrated into a society's political 'common sense,' becoming so taken for granted that no one seriously questions it."[5] That is, activist victory is for a group's values to become hegemonic—obvious, invisible, assumed as the way things should be. Fletcher borrows Kwame Anthony Appiah's concept of a "moral revolution," in which a society shifts its collective consensus as to what it considers honorable. To win a moral revolution, a party must "monopolize notions of honor" while its opponents' stances are "branded as contemptible."[6] In the activist performances powering the theater scandals I describe in this chapter, a community binds together over a project to create a hegemony of antiracist theater criticism. This chapter examines the role antagonism plays in community building, as it digs into the ways communities bind together over the project to *stick* dishonor to a distasteful *other* for activist ends it considers honorable. It examines the community binding in an antiracist project alongside the community binding in resistance to it, emphasizing the ways the same social mechanisms can operate in pursuit of opposing political ends.

Ernesto Laclau and Chantal Mouffe define *antagonism* as "the negation of a given order is, quite simply the limit of that order"; to paraphrase Laclau and Mouffe, *I cannot be me if you exist*.[7] The collaborative, mediated activist performances comprising the bulk of these particular theater scandals offer case studies of the power of antagonism to bind community. These scandals on the surface appear similar, but the differences in their contours provide a window into a moment of dramatic social and cultural change.

Humans are social beings; we need to feel like we belong to groups, and we take pleasure in group belonging. Communities are comprised of diverse individuals with disparate interests, needs, and values who agree to bind themselves together as a group around a common aspect of their identity. Anthony Cohen argues that the common elements around which groups coalesce are symbolic, and symbols can be interpreted in multiple ways. This slippery aspect of symbols makes space for people to belong to the group without subsuming their individuality within a "tyranny of orthodoxy."[8] They facilitate a reconciliation between individuality and commonality. Cohen highlights how "the boundary encapsulates the identity of the community and, like the identity of an individual, is called into being by the exigencies of social interaction."[9] These boundaries are not imaginary, for they are performed and enacted in the real world, but they are symbolically constructed and maintained through the manipulation of symbols. In moments of scandal, social interactions around the interpretation of symbols articulate (and sometimes redraw) the boundary of a community. Victor Turner highlights how "the concept of threat or danger to the group . . . is one of the chief ingredients in the production of existential communitas."[10] The shared threat binds the group in "communitas"; crisis temporarily dissolves the usual structures and hierarchies to form the collective bond. That threat may be real in an immediate and material way (e.g., soldiers fighting in a platoon), but frequently it is symbolic.

Laclau and Mouffe highlight how all discourse attempts to dominate an interpretative process, fixing a symbol's meaning in a way I'm going to refer to as *sticky*. They argue that every social practice is, on some level, articulatory, as groups make and agree on shared meaning. In the scandals surrounding the events discussed in this chapter, competing "camps" work to stick opposing meanings on the same action or symbol.[11] Once a symbol becomes a *nodal point* for antagonistic conflict, it cannot be stripped of that status. *Sticking* meaning activates antagonism. Sara Ahmed explains, "Hate may respond to the particular, but it tends to do so by aligning the particular with the general; 'I hate you because you are this or that,' where the 'this' or 'that' evokes a group the individual comes to *stand for* or *stand in for*."[12] The hated aspect or action operates as a metonym; it comes to symbolically define the whole of the object. Laclau argues that the hated nodal point of antagonistic conflict "is not simply one more, neutral element but an *excluded* one, something that the totality expels from itself in order to constitute itself."[13] All other differences become unimportant as the act of differentiating the group from the rejected difference takes focus. As no real, fixed totality comprises any group, the act of exclusion helps forge group identity.

Ahmed identifies *disgust* as the feeling powering a social act of abjection. Indeed, throughout the scandals, social media commentators use the language of disgust to express their repulsion—for example, "The racial bias on display in [Hedy Weiss's] reviews are dangerous and disgusting. The Chicago community that makes art and consumes art deserves better."[14] Ahmed describes, "Disgust reads the objects that are felt to be disgusting: it is not just about bad objects that we are afraid to incorporate, but the very designation of 'badness' as a quality we assume is inherent in those objects."[15] Disgust requires proximity: it is a response to a bad object coming too close. Ahmed identifies the way this feeling produces "a rage that the object has got close enough to sicken."[16] This rage powers generative communicative acts demanding witnesses. In the scandals I describe in this chapter, these acts include Facebook posts, tweets, comments on articles, blog posts, and comments on a Change.org petition. They generate a community of witnesses who repeat condemnation, sticking disgust (rejection, abjection) to the expelled objects—in this case, biased theater reviews and the critics who authored them. Ahmed describes the way this community of witnesses, "comes into being as 'sticking together' in the shared condemnation of the events, a sticking together, that not only spits out the word 'disgusting,' but also 'stands for' the spitting out of the bodies of those who become stuck to the word itself."[17] This is an affective process, rooted in feelings of similarity and otherness. A clean *we* congeals in opposition to a rejected, contaminated *other*.

Audre Lorde argues, "Anger is an appropriate reaction to racist attitudes, as is fury when the actions arising from those attitudes do not change."[18] Such anger becomes a method of connection, with social media providing a vehicle for people to find others sharing their fury. Donatella Galella writes of bonding with a group of young women of color over sharing similar reactions to a moment of yellowface performance, highlighting the pleasure she feels in pointing out how cultural products socially reproduce hierarchies.[19] These scandals demonstrate moments of this pleasure amplified in scale, as thousands of people band together in a similar act of community binding.

Individuals look to other people whom they consider *like them* to help them interpret symbols and form judgments. Meghan Sutherland examines how audience members watch a potentially transgressive spectacle, "but only as they watch the reactions of other audience members for signs of their differing responses."[20] Sutherland describes how a nineteenth-century audience for a blackface minstrel show affirms the normalcy and acceptability of their collective and repeated affective responses. A similar affective process takes place within social media circles, as participants watch the reactions of acquaintances and tastemakers to circulating cultural texts (memes, images, objects). In the virtual public square, posters and respondents teach and enforce the social rules of any given microcommunity by modeling decorum and flaming responses of outrage to transgressions.[21]

Cass Sunstein describes the ways group opinion can polarize within this virtual public square. He describes how people who begin a discussion within similar opinions on a matter are more likely, by the end of the discussion, to agree on a more extreme version of the position with which they began. Sunstein argues that this process is amplified by the way in which "reputational considerations" lead people to adjust to a position that seems dominant so that other people whom they respect will think favorably of them.[22] On social media, these phenomena can combine to create a *cascade*. Individuals look to other people they consider to be like them—people they respect in their community—to interpret an action or a symbol that becomes a nodal point of conflict. This creates a mass movement of interpretation, as consensus builds around the positions taken by an initial, influential few.[23] In a cascade of antagonism, hatred is stuck to a repellent object, and a community rallies online as a *we* to expel the rejected *other*. This process plays out in the theater scandals I describe in the following sections, as the Chicago theater community used social media to bind together in opposition to biased criticism of first *This Is Modern Art* and then *Pass Over*.

## *This Is Modern Art*

The premiere production of Kevin Coval and Idris Goodwin's *This Is Modern Art* was directed by Lisa Portes and produced at Steppenwolf Theatre Company from February 25 to March 14, 2015, as part of the Steppenwolf for Young Audiences series. It tells the true story of the graffiti crew who "bombed"—that is, painted a large-scale unauthorized public work—on the Renzo Piano Modern Wing of the Art Institute of Chicago on February 20, 2010. In fourteen minutes, during a snowstorm, a crew painted an unauthorized 44-foot-long mural bearing the text "This Is Modern Art," critiquing the elite institutional framework of the museum. The play *This Is Modern Art* utilizes hip-hop aesthetics to argue for the artistic legitimacy of graffiti as a form, critiquing the power held by elite institutions to determine and proscribe what is beautiful and culturally worthwhile. Seven, the leader of the graffiti crew, argues "high art, fine art, street art, museum art—whatever whatever. Institutions are built on them. They need these to justify their existence."[24]

Productions in the Steppenwolf for Young Audiences series are performed primarily for student audiences in weekday matinees, opening up to public audiences for a handful of weekend performances. The weekend performances include many teenagers and families, drawing in a more diverse audience in terms of race and age than is typical of most mainstream productions at institutional theaters. The series takes theater for young audiences seriously, producing sophisticated fare for young adults. The target audience for this production is, therefore, a diverse audience of teenagers from all over the city, and young people respond to the production with enthusiasm.

*This Is Modern Art* operates as a primer on the specificity of graffiti's history and artistic processes, consciously defining terms for uninitiated audiences;

as one character comments, "Seriously, this is like, crash art school."[25] The play argues that it takes training, talent, and skill to create a "piece"—short for "masterpiece," or complex work of graffiti art; the characters teach the audience the difference between a "tag" of the sort used to mark gang territory and the kinds of pieces graffiti crews create. The play addresses the consequences of the graffiti bombing on the crew. Should any of these young people be found out, they face substantial jail time and a million-dollar fine. Their fun comes to a screeching halt when their work draws the attention of the news media and law enforcement. The working-class boys of color in the crew disband and go into hiding; the middle-class white girl who has been the crew's driver and lookout rebuffs her parents' urging to speak with a lawyer and ultimately leans on her class privilege to leave town. These asymmetrical consequences are central to the play's critique of the ways structural systems of power work to limit the opportunities available to young, working-class people of color in Chicago.

This hip-hop play about young people of color carving out spaces for artistic expression in opposition to institutional power was critiqued by Chris Jones of the *Chicago Tribune* and Hedy Weiss of the *Chicago Sun-Times*, the most prominent theater critics in the city, as not engaging appropriately with the destructive nature of graffiti as vandalism. Jones's and Weiss's reviews both focus on these white critics' own experiences of feeling unsafe in graffiti-covered public spaces in New York City in the 1970s and 1980s. Both critics argue that the production should not focus on graffiti as art but instead define graffiti purely as criminal vandalism. Jones argues, "Graffiti had the effect of making people feel unsafe in the city. It terrified people. It was only when public officials declared themselves determined to wipe it out that cities finally came back to life, with broad benefits."[26] Weiss, too, understands graffiti as "a warning sign that a neighborhood was dangerous, infected with crime, on the decline, and a bad place to set up a business."[27] In their reviews, Jones and Weiss both demonstrate unrecognized biases as they misrepresent the perspectives of affluent and middle-class white adults as universal, characterizing neighborhoods devoid of affluent white people as devoid of life. This view of graffiti may, perhaps, be shared by many subscribers to the *Tribune* and the *Sun-Times*. Jones's and Weiss's reviews operate as consumer guides for this imagined readership, meeting them within frameworks these critics assume their readers share. The "people" graffiti terrifies are not represented in *This Is Modern Art*, and with good reason—the play centers the perspectives and experiences of working-class young people of color, pushing the perspectives of middle-aged, middle-class white property owners to the margins. As Bear Bellinger comments on Jones's wall on Facebook, "graffiti makes people like you feel unsafe, but for those of us who grew up surrounded by it, it makes us feel at home and that is who the show is talking to."[28] The play highlights artistic processes through which working-class people of color mark spaces as *theirs* in the absence of the capital to join the class of property owners.

Jones and Weiss both target, in their reviews, the educational mission of the Steppenwolf for Young Adults series and its audience of teenagers. They each in their own way contend that theater for young audiences requires, to use Jones's words, a "moral obligation" to teach the dominant perspective alongside the resistant.[29] This reflects an assumption that a central purpose of Theatre for Young Audiences is to teach dominant, normative values. Weiss takes this argument a step farther, contending, "No amount of classroom discussion will scrub clean the irresponsible ideas promulgated in this play," claiming that direct discussion of the ways in which minority teens are "shut out of opportunities and earmarked for prison" reinforces stereotypes and "deepens and solidifies racial and class divisions and a sense of hopelessness among those who need to dwell on possibility."[30] Weiss, in essence, argues that naming structural inequality directly reinforces it. Ahmed describes how "when you name something as sexist or as racist you are making that thing more tangible so that it can be more easily communicated to others. But for those who do not have a sense of the racism or sexism you are talking about, to bring them up is to bring them into existence."[31] Weiss cannot see, from where she stands, that "those who need to dwell on possibility" can clearly see the ways racial and class divisions marginalize their access to opportunities. For Weiss, the play appears to call them into being.

A social media firestorm erupted as Jones's and Weiss's reviews drew the attention of members of the Chicago theater community as well as national commentators on equity, diversity, and inclusion in the American theater. Many critiqued the ways the reviews reflect race- and class-specific assumptions about young people of color, art, and education. Much of the commentary contains critical pedagogical feedback for the mainstream reviewers. For example, Mica Cole replies to a comment Chris Jones makes on Facebook, "your review does what is done everyday by the white middle-class power structure in our city, which is to lecture and police any expression of young people of color's self-determination that does not fit into your idea of respectability."[32] Commentary is at times heated, and insults are targeted at the critics, such as Ellen Chambers's tweet at Hedy Weiss, "Are you that bigoted? #racism."[33] On Facebook, Lisa Portes, the production's director, calls for civility: "Name-calling shuts the conversation down. . . . This revolution is about opening space."[34] The community largely heeded her call, and rage and disgust powered a robust conversation on the role of theater criticism in an era of diminished resources for arts journalism and the power that institutional gatekeepers hold to marginalize artistic perspectives differing from their own.

When commentators defend the reviews—and there are far fewer defensive comments than condemnations—they do so in defense of definitions of artistic greatness that transcend cultural specificity. Jones, on Facebook, fights back against the notion that

> to be a critic—one who was young once but has aged—is to be constantly told that you don't like something, or get something, because you are other than the artwork—of a different ethnicity, perhaps, or some other way in which you cannot get it as you were not the target audience. It's an easy hit. Hard to defend. There is some truth in that, but not as much as you think, if all minds are open.[35]

To be fair, in his decades of reviewing, Jones has demonstrated his capacity to like and get plenty of culturally specific work. He has lauded the work of August Wilson, advocated for a League of Resident Theatres (LORT) African American theater company in Chicago, and championed the work of artists of color such as Nambi Kelley, whose adaptation of Richard Wright's *Native Son* he called "one of the most important works ever written in the city."[36] However, the camp rallying to Jones's defense did not draw on his body of work. As this community came together, its members rallied around a more extreme version of Jones's initial position, rejecting entirely the idea that spectatorship is subjective and culturally specific. They avoided direct engagement with issues of race and class and stayed away from topics that might open up opportunities for opponents to *stick* to them accusations of racism. They instead advocated for the notion of universal artistic greatness or, as Keith Jackewicz puts it, art that "completely transcend[s] such petty things as time and culture," by referencing works that they consider to transcend cultural specificity.[37] Many of these works are from the traditional Western canon, but many commentators also referenced works from non-Western cultures and works created by artists of color. For example, Jackson Hawley argues for artistic criteria that "allow one to see equally the merits of a Tu Fu as one would a Robert Frost."[38] This counterdemonstration does not take on the features of antagonism. Members of this small camp do not *stick* dishonor to its opponents; they instead work to recruit opponents to join their camp. They rally a community around the value of universal beauty, and the debates surrounding their counterdemonstration revolve around the specifics of their aesthetic tastes.

It is perhaps not surprising that most of the people with a stake in a battle over institutional gatekeeping of artistic legitimacy are well versed in artistic canon. Those criticizing the reviews also frequently referenced a wide range of artistic works. They argue, as Alex Huntsberger does, "We would absolutely NOT be seeing these kinds of hand-wringings expressed by major theater critics if it was a show about, say, Shepard Fairey or Banksey."[39] They joke about direct transference from theatrical action to audience behavior, as Mia McCullough tweets, "If you see a Shakespeare or McDonagh drama, do you criticize the artists for glorifying/condoning murder?"[40] They reference critical theorists, as Lisa Yun Lee tweets at Weiss, "unable to grasp how criminality functions as a component to black political consciousness in graffiti—read Frantz Fanon."[41] Most comments engage canonical or critically acclaimed works as evidence in arguments targeted toward readers with sophisticated cultural knowledge. Some comments stray far from the race- and class-specific issues at play in the larger controversy and seem to primarily operate as performances of a commentator's cultural distinction. Across them all, this pattern of commentary highlights the cultural capital of both the participants in and audience for this controversy. The battle is over the legitimacy of forms of expression owned by young working-class people of color, but it is fought within the context of an interracial community of highly educated adults.

Full time critics for daily newspapers wield cultural power. They select the productions they review in the most prominent venues; their attention legitimizes theater companies and artists. In Chicago, glowing reviews from Jones can result in an uptick in ticket sales. When artists critique the critics, they punch up. All the social media commentators posted under their real names, taking credit for their contributions in the public square of social media. For some artists, doing so risked that Jones and Weiss might retaliate by ignoring or panning their work. Many of the strongest voices in the debate came from artists who make culturally specific or experimental theater in smaller venues in working-class neighborhoods who do not expect the most prominent critics in Chicago to attend their productions. Their rage is powered, in part, by the way in which the targets of their critique gatekeep artistic legitimacy in ways that largely exclude them. Like the piece on the wall of the museum, manifestos and quips in the public square of social media draw attention to artists and critics of all races who do not have access to venues legitimated by legacy sources of cultural authority. They draw on the moral rightness of their position as an alternate source of cultural authority, binding together as a community in disgust to expel the symbols of an old, white, classist regime that devalues culturally specific artistic work designed to be of interest to working-class people of color. In a moment in which social media followings can be leveraged for career opportunities, such attention is valuable.

Coval, who is white, and Goodwin, who is black, responded to the reviews and the surrounding social media conversation immediately. Coval says, "What I'm not surprised about is old white people, critics for these dying papers, don't want to celebrate stories about youth culture who have been systematically denied agency." Goodwin considers the negative reviews to be "satisfying in a way" as they have sparked debate within the theater, arts, and youth communities. "It's like, that's the point y'all . . . the crew was trying to wake people up, to get people talking, and the play is doing the same thing."[42] The artists welcomed the debate and the attention, and they enjoyed the irony that the critical response to their play mirrored the events they depict and amplified their central argument. Halle Gordon, the artistic and education director of Steppenwolf for Young Adults, weighed in online with a formal institutional response on HowlRound Theatre Commons a week into the scandal:

> It is precisely this capacity to debate—even in a heated fashion—that leads me to conclude that the show is achieving its purpose. I believe that *This Is Modern Art's* educational aim—real education, education intended to make you question what you're seeing and the wider world—is spilling out from our intended teen audience to include many more voices and perspectives from across the region. In fact, it's worth emphasizing: the sold-out public performances for this show are attracting exactly the kind of economically, racially, and geographically diverse crowds that the field is desperate to attract.[43]

The scandal over *This Is Modern Art* largely drew attention to the production and amplified its message. Following the scandal, Jones responded to social media comments and participated in events with Coval discussing the role of the critic and the ways artistic value is assigned and legitimized. The scandal over *This Is Modern Art* did not permanently stick to Jones, who as of early 2020 remained the most powerful theater critic in Chicago. However, two years after *This Is Modern Art*, Weiss found herself at the center of another, similar scandal.

## *Pass Over*

The world premiere of Antoinette Nwandu's *Pass Over* was produced at Steppenwolf June 1–July 9, 2017, under the direction of Danya Taymor. *Pass Over* is about two young black men, Moses (Jon Michael Hill) and Kitch (Julian Parker), trapped on a purgatorial street corner, plotting and yearning for escape to the promised land. They are visited by a lost and entitled white man, Mister, and an antagonistic white cop, Ossifer (both played by Ryan Hallahan). The play riffs on *Waiting for Godot* while gesturing to Exodus, painting an absurdist landscape in which the men are overtly trapped by multiple manifestations of white supremacy.

*Pass Over* does not ask the spectator to imagine social turmoil through the rubric of conflict—that is, a rubric of problems that can be solved through individual will—but instead uses an allegorical, absurdist dramaturgy to imagine it through the rubric of antagonism, to borrow Frank Wilderson's definition, "an irreconcilable struggle between entities, or positions, the resolution of which is not dialectical but entails the obliteration of one of the positions."[44] In the world of *Pass Over*, there are no good white people; black liberation is not possible without the obliteration of whiteness. The double casting of a single white actor in the roles of Ossifer and Mister clarifies the pervasive power of white supremacy.

Early on, Moses and Kitch reference how the threat of police violence keeps them on the block. Several scenes later, when Ossifer does appear in the flesh, he clears his throat. At the sound of his approach, Moses and Kitch dive for the ground, lying prostrate with their hands spread on the ground above their heads. They look terrified. "You goin' somewhere?" he asks. "Got word you were going somewhere, but I said, no, no. Not my n*****s."[45]

Ossifer orders the prostrate men to put their hands behind their heads. They comply.

"Now I know you like to think of yourself as some kind of ringleader. Some kind of alpha dog. [*He barks at Moses.*] So we're going to do this nice and gentle just like we always do. Who are you?" Ossifer prompts.

"Stupid. Lazy. Violent. Thug," Moses responds, defeated and in submission.

"Good. That's good. And where are you going?" Ossifer queries.

"Nowhere," Moses replies.

"What's that, n*****?" Ossifer snaps.

"Nowhere, sir."

"All right boys," Ossifer allows, smiling. "Let's keep it that way." He whistles Dixie as he walks away. As he leaves, Moses and Kitch, who continue to lie facedown on the asphalt with their hands behind their heads, breathe a sigh of relief. They have survived.

This allegorical moment grounds itself in the fear that Ossifer inspires in Moses and Kitch, as the threat of violence hangs over the encounter. Throughout the play, Moses and Kitch cower from the sound of distant bullets, referencing and mourning other young black men the police have killed. Ossifer's gun and badge give him all the power; they have none. Ossifer demands submission to remind Moses of his degradation—to punish him for thinking he might have any kind of power or status. On this purgatorial street corner, they have enacted this scenario many times before. Fear of police aggression is woven into the fabric of Moses's and Kitch's lived experience.

Hedy Weiss's review of the play in the *Chicago Sun Times* calls the premise of the play "inspired" and praises it as "brilliantly acted." However, she argues that "this play distorts the full story" as she understands it of "senseless, endemic violence in Chicago," taking issue with the allegorical play's archetypal characterization of a racist white cop as "clearly meant to indict *all* white cops."[46] Weiss focuses on "the look of relief when the police arrive on the scene," as represented in "news reports about recent shootings (on the lakefront, on the new River Walk, in Woodlawn)," as evidence that the play's structural critique of a police state is "wrong-headed and self-defeating."[47] In this critique, Weiss reveals the disconnect between many white people's experiences of the police and the play's representation of the black characters' experiences of the police. Weiss interprets this disconnect to mean *the play is wrong*; her review instead exposes the limits of her own lived experience and understanding. Her interpretation is in line with patterns of white spectatorship demonstrated throughout this book, as she places her own lived experience at the forefront of her interpretive process.

Ike Holter, Kevin Matthew Reyes, Tony Santiago, Sydney Charles and Sasha Smith, five respected artists of color, formed the Chicago Theater Accountability Coalition (ChiTAC) primarily in response to Weiss's review of *Pass Over* and partly in response to blogger Katy Walsh's use of the N-word in her review of the play.[48] They stated, "These reviews have brought harm to the theater community and have caused an overwhelming response from artists who are ready to act toward creating a safe, healthy, inclusive, and intersectional environment to practice art free from prejudice and damaging language."[49] ChiTAC asked the Chicago theater community to stop offering free tickets to reviewers who "routinely review theater through a sexist and racist lens," and specifically to create a petition on the website of Change.org to "Stop Inviting Hedy Weiss to Your Productions."[50]

Two days after the petition went live, actor Bear Bellinger publicly circulated a letter he sent to the Goodman Theatre. He had been cast in a developmental workshop production at this large institutional theater, and he had written to artistic leaders that he would not be comfortable performing for Weiss to review. In this letter, Bellinger frames the issue as one of workplace protection:

> We do not have the typical structure of a work environment, but that does not, ethically, remove us from the burden of extending the same protections the 1964 Civil Rights Act has attempted to grant to employees since its implementation. We look for a fair, safe, and equitable work environment; one free of discrimination on the basis of gender, sex, race, religion, orientation, age, or disability. To act as if critics are not a part of our arrangement, and therefore absolve ourselves of any blame, is irresponsible to the community we attempt to cultivate and the work in which we participate.[51]

As with the scandal over *This Is Modern Art*, the uproar over Weiss's review took place over social media. Theater community members of all racial and ethnic backgrounds were infuriated. Critics of the critic circulated the review, introduced by enraged comments such as Kelly Ann Parker's tweet, "Chicago doesn't need anymore [*sic*] racists and she must be stopped."[52] The *Hawk Chicago* theater blog compiled a list of inflammatory, biased comments Weiss had made over the course of her career, which was then circulated widely on Facebook.[53] A storm of angry tweets and Facebook comments to the *Chicago Sun-Times* called for Weiss's dismissal.

The ChiTAC petition gathered 3,766 supporters. Roughly 800 of the signatories wrote comments as they signed the petition. These comments can be examined as evidence of a process through which a community utilizes antagonism to redraw its boundaries. More than half of the comments reflect a desire for an inclusive community free of discrimination, such as Maddie Martin's comment, "I'm signing this petition, because I believe in a safe positive theatre world in which all artists regardless of race, sexual orientation, appearance, etc. can create and collaborate without the fear of being judged unfairly."[54] These comments focus on the positive values signatories want to define their community—what the *we* should signify. More than 250 of the comments expel or reject the behavior at the heart of the controversy, decrying racism, such as Jay Easton's comment, "Racism is not acceptable—not in theatre; not anywhere else."[55] These comments expel racism as an abstract concept, symbolically ejecting it from the community. Finally, more than 200 of the comments target Weiss with personal insults, such as Nic Park's comment, "Hedy Weiss is a racist dinosaur."[56] These comments stick the expelled concept to the figure at the center of the scandal, rejecting and punishing her as the symbolic act through which the community rids itself of racism.

Steppenwolf Theatre's artistic director Anna D. Shapiro and executive director David Schmitz responded to the scandal in a statement denouncing Weiss's review for failing to "acknowledge the very systemic racism that *Pass Over* addresses directly" and revealing "a deep-seated bigotry and a painful lack of understanding of this country's historic racism."[57] The *Chicago Tribune* published the Shapiro and Schmitz statement as part of its reporting on the scandal. Four days later, the *Tribune*'s editorial board defended Weiss with a snarky editorial, "Hey Steppenwolf: Critics Gonna Critique," which frames the controversy as a theater company complaining over an unfavorable review: "*We denounce her viewpoints!* says Steppenwolf. *She's not willing to work with us to create a positive environment!* reads an online petition from members of the theater community."[58] The editorial board resequenced events to signal to the casual reader that Steppenwolf incited the petition, erasing Holter, Reyes, Santiago, Charles, and Smith from the narrative. In doing so, the Tribune rebranded a protest initiated by artists of color into a fight between a high-status white institution and a lone white critic. The fight may be over racism, but as the *Tribune*'s editorial board frames it, it is a fight among powerful white people.

The *Tribune*'s editorial endorses Weiss's analysis of the production, stating, "Weiss watched the play, considered the context of Chicago's policing problems and decided the play's final 10 minutes didn't work. She wrote in part that because much of the city's gun violence is perpetrated within the community on itself." It endorses her interpretation not only of the play but of the social problem the play critiques. The *Chicago Tribune* is a conservative-leaning newspaper; its statement of principles describes the publication's core beliefs as including "the traditional principles of limited government; maximum individual responsibility; and minimum restriction of personal liberty, opportunity and enterprise. It believes in free markets, free will and freedom of expression."[59] The editorial board aligns with a conservative or libertarian camp; in this instance, it rallied that camp to Weiss's defense. If ChiTAC, the signatories on their petition, and theater community members commenting on social media focus on Weiss's review as the symbol of abjection, the *Tribune* editorial board reclaims the review and Weiss. Weiss becomes an avatar of freedom of expression, bullied by a mob of liberal snowflakes who cannot tolerate her conservative political viewpoint. The op-ed emphasizes this angle, invoking members of the theater community who expect "that Weiss should be a cheerleader" and demand "campus-style intellectual coddling."[60] These tropes draw on anxieties already circulating in conservative circles that conservative voices are censored and marginalized. They push back against the activist project to create an antiracist hegemony on the grounds that hegemonic formations are coercive. To borrow from Fletcher, the losing side of a moral revolution faces marginalization and, they fear, discrimination.[61]

The *Tribune* published three articles about this scandal within the span of a week, and its editorial board stoked the fire with tweets such as, "Complain too much, theater people and you look like crybabies, especially if you also accept praise."[62] It pushed back against the activist project to create an antiracist hegemony by drumming up support for its camp, working to prevent its opponents from achieving consensus that shutting down biased reviewers makes *common sense*.

The editorial board of Weiss's own paper, The *Chicago Sun-Times*, published a parallel editorial the following week. In it, the board members voiced support for Weiss, indicated she would continue to review for the paper, and asked readers to appreciate her thirty-plus years of work as a *Sun-Times* critic. The *Sun-Times* newspaper has a center-left bias, and in this instance, its editorial board placed itself within the left-of-center political camp by identifying Weiss's "failure to understand the facts of life about crime and policing in minority communities" and acknowledging that the paper "must do a better job of finding journalists of color to cover this work and all the arts."[63] These board members instead framed their defense of Weiss as a First Amendment issue, decrying a "mob-like effort to silence a critic."[64] They reconstructed the scandal as a lone journalist fighting for the First Amendment against a censoring mob.

These institutional responses to the scandal utilize antagonism to bind a camp in opposition to the one forming in support of the ChiTAC petition. They define freedom of expression as their camp's core value, rejecting censorship as the unwanted element they come together to expel. They stick this unwanted element to the rejected figures of the theater community members who seek to silence Weiss, reconfiguring them as an angry mob. Social media comments proclaiming participation in this camp are far fewer than those condemning Weiss and her review. Most include broad, straightforward statements of support for Weiss, such as Joseph Sikora's tweet "I support @HedyWeissCritic."[65] A number attack Steppenwolf, such as Elizabeth Johnson's comment on Steppenwolf Theatre Company's Facebook page,

"So disappointed in Steppenwolf's over-the-top response to the review. Not exactly the way to foster open dialogue. There was a way to address your concerns. This wasn't it. Shameful to malign Hedy in the way you did."[66] These comments appear to be responding to the scandal in relation to the *Tribune*'s construction of the story—they stick the unwanted element of censorship to Steppenwolf as a nodal point of antagonistic conflict. None of the comments defending Weiss or attacking censorship engage with any discussion of race, racism, or violence; they reframe a scandal about racialized bias in theater criticism as a scandal about censoring free speech.

As with the scandal for *This Is Modern Art*, the increased attention on *Pass Over* may have helped to boost ticket sales and raise the national profile of the play. The most significant legacy of the scandal is that Weiss's position at the *Sun-Times* was eliminated in February 2018, eight months after the scandal. The scandal made Weiss a nodal point of antagonism. To borrow from Ahmed, Weiss had "become sticky, or saturated with affect, as [a] site of personal and social tension."[67] At the time of this writing, the *Sun-Times* had not hired a replacement full-time theater critic, leaving Chris Jones at the *Tribune* as the only full-time theater critic employed by a daily newspaper in a city with more than two hundred theater companies.

These two theater scandals took place two years apart, and they played out in fundamentally different historic contexts. Nationally, the divisive presidential election of 2016 activated a progressive resistance movement. Locally, the Chicago theater community experienced the power of social media activism in 2016 following a *Chicago Reader* exposé of a pattern of sexual harassment and abuse at Profiles Theatre. The subsequent outrage led to the theater's closure, as the community rallied around #NotInOurHouse in support of women who had been abused and to advocate for safe working conditions free of violence, sexual harassment, intimidation, and bullying. Under the leadership of Laura Fisher and Lori Myers, Not In Our House developed the Chicago Theatre Standards, which are guidelines for workplace safety and communication that have been widely adopted by nonunion theaters across the city.[68] This productive campaign taught the Chicago theater community the power of its collective action and offered a template for ChiTAC's activist actions in response to *Pass Over*.

Examining the scandals surrounding *This Is Modern Art* and *Pass Over* side by side, many orders of magnitude differentiate the stakes of paint on the wall of a building from bullets in the bodies of black boys and men. The scandal surrounding *This Is Modern Art* appears tame and polite when examined in relation to the one surrounding *Pass Over*. The scandal surrounding *This Is Modern Art* consists of a community coming together in an attempt to educate its two most prominent critics. Its fundamental action is critical pedagogy. Much of the discourse is heated, and some personal insults are thrown, but the community binding together for activist action self-regulates to focus on nuanced critiques of institutional power and the ways in which art is structurally legitimized. This extends the central message of the play far beyond the reach of the sold-out limited run consisting mostly of school matinees. The creators directly engage with the controversy and welcome the way in which it amplifies the message of the show, as the critical crucible mirrors the play's content.

Two years later, the fundamental action of the scandal surrounding *Pass Over* is to force a change of regime. It takes place in the context of a movement resisting the conservative regime of Donald Trump, whom progressive activists have less power to oust than a theater critic producing biased reviews. There are no calls for civility. Within twenty-four hours, local artists consolidate and focus feelings of rage and disgust into the coordinated action of the online petition, which in turn gives the social media cascade a point of action-oriented focus. Weiss's review activates existing nodal points of conflict that are already hot within the context of Black Lives Matter, and ChiTAC activates a resistance movement already in progress. Theater community members of all races enthusiastically participate in the cascade, binding together in a multiracial collective in opposition to a hated cultural authority.

At the heart of both scandals is a community engaging in a process of exclusion in order to forward values of inclusion. The affective processes of community binding through antagonism are neither inherently good nor inherently bad. Disgust and rage are constructive pieces of a progressive political project. But I am wary: these are the same social processes in operation when children bully a classmate they decide is different, the same processes at play when social conservatives vilify immigrants. In the heat of the social media cascade, an attack that is fundamentally about, as Kevin Coval puts it, "culturally white theater spaces and the white critics who preserve systemic inequality" becomes a personal attack against a representative "white person aligned with whiteness, no surprise there."[69] Antagonism obscures the larger structural issues at the root of a biased review. Critics of the critic drew attention to moments in Weiss's long career in which her writings displayed unconscious biases; no one drew attention to moments in which she championed the work of artists of color, such as the way she has lauded the work of the Black Ensemble Theater as having "the ability to restore your emotional health and lift your joyfulness quotient straight off the charts . . . [which] tends to be the effect of pretty much all of the company's productions—shows that also manage to forge a connection between audience and performers that is close to foolproof."[70] I am less inclined to read Weiss as an irredeemable overt racist than as a white audience member, displaying patterns of white spectatorship I describe throughout this book.

There is pleasure in belonging to a tribe, pleasure in having your interpretation reinforced as *morally good*. In the theater scandals I have described in this chapter, this pleasure incentivizes building a world in which racist speech acts are not permissible. That is a good thing. Spaces free of racist speech acts are legitimately more racially inclusive than ones in which racist speech acts are tolerated. A hegemony of antiracist speech acts makes *common sense*. However, the catharsis of expelling an unwanted element brings with it a feeling that a problem has been solved. Sianne Ngai identifies an ambivalence at the core of "ugly feelings," resisting the easy urge to reduce them to expressions of resentment or valorize them into therapeutic solutions to the problems they target.[71] And in this spirit, I am deeply ambivalent about the way these scandals stick hate to a scapegoat to symbolically expel racism. If, to follow Shannon Sullivan, racism is understood as evidence of an individual's moral badness, a racist opponent is by definition a contemptible one.[72] Antiracist activists win the battle for hegemonic dominance by equating individual racism to dishonor and moral badness; antiracism is the only honorable and morally good position. The difficulty with this activist tactic is the way in which it reinforces racism as an individual moral failure rather than a structural system of power in which we are all embedded. An individual can be expelled from a community as a symbolic act representing group values, but this does not fundamentally alter the material conditions supporting the larger, existing structural system of power. Expelling Weiss did not create more racially equitable and accountable cultural institutions or increase the diversity of critical voices employed full-time in the city's most prominent cultural platforms.

The systems legitimizing cultural representation continue to be dominated by whiteness; despite many calls for a more diverse corps of critics in elite venues, the situation was not altered by the scandals surrounding *This Is Modern Art* and *Pass Over*. The expulsion of Weiss acts as an object lesson, teaching white critics all over the United States to be more mindful when tackling discussions of racism. But I fear it can also have the opposite effect, discouraging white critics from covering culturally specific productions, avoiding direct discussions of race and racism. Smaller, culturally specific theaters are most at risk of having their work ignored or avoided by white critics who are afraid to review theatrical events tackling culturally specific topics. As I will discuss in greater detail in the conclusion, smaller culturally specific theater companies are frequently better positioned to use theatrical events to intervene in racism than large, institutional theaters are. As access to the platforms legitimizing artistic work and driving audiences to theater shrinks—while continuing to be dominated by whiteness—the theaters proving most effective at intervening in racism have the most to lose.

Further, both of these scandals raise important questions regarding the nature and function of newspaper criticism. The reviews at the heart of these scandals are primarily designed to be consumer guides for the older, affluent, white people who dominate both newspaper subscription bases and theater audiences. As such, they are written for readers imagined to share the biases they display. These biases are *bad* for a pluralistic society—of this there is no question. However, they are not uncommon within the world as it currently exists. If newspaper criticism's primary function is as a consumer guide, should it operate within frameworks that imagined readers already hold, or should it educate readers to be better prepared to meet artistic work within the frameworks held by their creators? Where are—and should be—the lines between newspaper criticism and dramaturgy?

# Part 3

✦

*Decolonizing Gazes and Spaces*

# Chapter 5

✦

# Maintaining White Racial Comfort

I'm squirming in my seat, trying not to make a scene. I've just finished watching Steven Simoncic's *Broken Fences*, directed by Ann Filmer and Ilesa Duncan at 16th Street Theater in Berwyn, Illinois, and we are in the midst of a post-performance talkback in 2013. The play is about gentrification, and the production shows the complexity of the problem and highlights how good intentions cannot mitigate privilege. And yet in post-performance talkback, middle-class-looking white audience member after middle-class-looking white audience member regales the room with anecdotes about how cheap the rent used to be in the Wicker Park neighborhood of Chicago, back when it was dangerous. How great the block parties were, back before the neighborhood got so expensive. I am wondering, *Did we just watch the same play?*

Most white people in the contemporary United States live in segregated majority-white neighborhoods and send their children to majority-white schools. The features of white spectatorship described throughout this book insert themselves into performance events tackling the quotidian ways in which middle-class white people sustain white supremacy through gentrification and the maintenance of systems supporting de facto school and neighborhood segregation. These are domains in which middle-class white people *can* exert individual agency to disrupt the status quo but frequently choose to structure our actions in tacit support of oppressive systems. Within these domains, we reveal contradictions between antiracist white discourse and middle-class white action. By examining the ways white audience members maintain racial comfort through resistant readings of theatrical events critical of such contradictions, we can see the interpretive processes at work that facilitate them and enable white people whose actions support gentrification and segregation to understand ourselves as antiracist *good white people*. In this chapter, I draw examples from theatrical events I attended and wrote about during the two years (2013–15) I worked as a critic for HowlRound Theatre Commons, writing a monthly column analyzing plays produced in Chicago as part of their NewCrit initiative.[1] I am embarrassed to admit that, as a white participant in theatrical events, I did not notice patterns of white spectatorship until I began to write about mainstream theater productions on a regular basis for this part-time job. The things I saw audience members do—and some of the things I now realize I did—planted the questions fueling this book.

The 16th Street Theater's 2013 production of Steven Simonic's *Broken Fences* offers a nuanced and sophisticated look at gentrification. It focuses on the Garfield Park neighborhood of Chicago, located perhaps six miles from Berwyn, the close-in suburb in which the midsized professional theater company makes its home. The 16th Street Theater has been much lauded, winning awards from Broadway in Chicago, *Chicago* magazine, and the American Theatre Wing, producing world premieres in its intimate theater in the basement of the Berwyn Cultural Center. Ann Filmer, the company's artistic director, who is white, collaborated on the project with its codirector Ilesa Duncan, who is African American. The press release the company sent out explains that this collaboration was essential to representing the texture of the diverse neighborhood and handling the complexity of the issues the play raises.

The play opens with a white couple, Czar (Scott Allen Luke) and April (Kirsten D'Aurelio), moving into their new home in a racially diverse neighborhood. They've sold their condo and, five years into marriage and expecting their first child, are both excited and scared to own a house. "A condo isn't a home," Czar explains, "A house is a home." While single-family homes do exist in the affluent, predominantly white neighborhoods on the North Side of Chicago, an area that real estate agents call "the Green Zone," they are out of the price range of most middle-class families. When Czar and April outgrew their condo, they were faced with a choice: move to either the suburbs or a more "adventurous" neighborhood in which they could afford the home of their dreams.

Choice, is, of course, the province of privilege. Their African American next-door neighbor D (Krenée A. Tolson) points this out: "People from this hood are here 'cause they *have* to be, not because they want to be." D and her fiancé Hoody (Daniel J. Bryant) live in the house Hoody inherited from his mother, who inherited it from her mother before her. It is "almost paid off" and is the only home either of them has ever known. They get by on Hoody's job at Jiffy Lube while D studies to be a hair stylist. We learn of tragedies in their past, but in the present, they are a hardworking middle-class couple grasping for the brass ring of the American dream.

When Czar and April move in next door, Hoody and D are wary but welcoming. D gives April a quilt square—a neighborhood tradition symbolizing the beginning of a new venture. But the neighborhood is shifting under Hoody and D's feet. A Starbucks has opened. Hoody's half brother Marz (Eric Lynch) has started teaching "boot camp" exercise classes to white people in the local park. And with the upscale renovation and sale of the house next door, Hoody's property assessment has gone up—and so his property tax bill has tripled. While Marz identifies the rising property values as an opportunity to sell high and get out, Hoody and D just want to figure out how to pay their property tax bill to stay in their home.

*Broken Fences* treats gentrification with nuance. The white couple is well-meaning, and April, in particular, wants to integrate into the community. They value the neighborhood's diversity. Czar explains, "We thought it'd be good to actually try and find a real, diverse community in Chicago—with the kid coming we wanted him to grow up in a place where people didn't all look . . . exactly the same." The audience is given their friends Spence (Bradford Lund) and Barb (Tasha Anne James) as a foil—white folks who chose to move to the suburbs, and while much humor is found at Spence and Barb's expense, Czar and April are pretty clearly *not* terrible people by comparison. But the presence of Czar and April, however well-intentioned, causes real hardship and disruption for the neighbors they genuinely want to befriend. Their newly renovated dream home raises Hoody and D's tax bill beyond what they can afford. By moving into the neighborhood, Czar and April are inadvertently forcing Hoody and D out. Czar and April cannot reconcile this tension.

This complex approach to the issue of gentrification is subtle and nuanced, and the production clearly illustrates the damage white people who value diversity can do to communities of color. However, in a post-performance talkback, this message seemed somewhat lost on the audience of mostly middle-class-looking white people. When asked for responses to the play, audience members regaled the actors and the playwright with stories of their own experiences of gentrifying neighborhoods—highlighting moments in which they felt afraid and moments in which other white neighbors who had also moved into their diverse working-class neighborhoods just didn't try hard enough to "get" neighborhood norms. In these stories, audience members framed themselves as open-minded and "adventurous" inhabitants of diverse neighborhoods. I was disappointed they could not see how power and privilege enabled them to have choices their neighbors did not seem to have. White spectators read their own stories into *Broken Fences* and could not seem to get past their own good intentions to take responsibility for the ways in which the characters in the story legitimately did more harm than good.

Jacques Rancière argues in *The Emancipated Spectator*, "There is no straightforward road from the fact of looking at a spectacle to the fact of understanding the state of the world."[2] Audience members' stories demonstrate a pattern of understanding focused on differentiating between white people who embrace living in diverse communities—open-minded, sophisticated, adventurous, well-intentioned—and those who choose to live in places previously established as bastions of whiteness—closed-minded, provincial, uncool, quietly racist. Meghan A. Burke emphasizes the ways that white residents in diverse communities "embrace a personal identity that is appreciative of diversity in part by living within a community that embraces it" but "often unintentionally act in ways that may undermine it."[3] White people reveal and reproduce a *white habitus*—that is, a framework of unexamined assumptions upholding white privilege—in part by developing identity locations relying on the consumption of diverse culture. Both the white characters in *Broken Fences* and the white audience members in the talkback structure discourse and action in this way.

From their stories, audience members demonstrate that they identify with Czar and April, having needed to make similar choices about housing or property ownership. Such choices are framed within the production and the talkback as material actions informed by the intersection of personal preferences and financial resources; the play is designed to encourage audience members to recognize these choices as representative of larger racialized and class-based social patterns. Audience members, however, appear to understand them primarily as decisions made by unique individuals with autonomous agency.

Western ideology emphasizes individualism, and most people understand themselves as individuals with autonomous agency making independent choices in relation to the material conditions of their individual lives. John Meyer and Ronald Jepperson argue, "The modern social system at present is imagined to operate via fully realized and unfettered actors pursuing their goals (if under institutional 'incentives' and 'constraints,' understood as background conditions)."[4] This way of understanding the world encourages people to make choices in their own self-interest while sustaining a larger ideology of individualism. Such choices frequently adhere to a narrow set of culturally mediated patterns, which Meyer and Jepperson consider "scripted."[5] These include choices we make to forward our material interests and the ways we act to reinforce our identities and membership in particular groups.

In *Broken Fences*, April and Czar make a choice to accrue wealth through home ownership, prioritizing living in a newly renovated single-family home. This choice supports their financial self-interest. Home ownership is a fairly common way middle-class families build wealth, and both the play and the audience treat it as such. However, both the characters and the audience members responding in talkback also understand April and Czar's choice of neighborhood as one freely made by individuals with autonomous agency. It has to be an independent choice if it is to support and reflect their identities as antiracist good white people who appreciate diversity, in contrast to the other, kind-of-racist bad white people who move to the suburbs. This choice forms the nodal point of white audience members' interpretations of and verbal responses to the play.

The play highlights the contradiction at the heart of this choice: the action sustaining the identity of the morally good antiracist white people materially oppresses the people of color who already live in the diverse community. Nevertheless, the play does not seem to be able to get white audience members to question the justness of actions with which they identify. Instead, white

Fig. 5.1. Tyrese Hall, Leah Aberman, and Esme Ayvar-Perez in *Forgotten Future: The Education Project*. Photograph by Anna Sodziak.

audience members interpret the play in ways consistent with their own sense of moral goodness. April and Czar's choices are well-intentioned, but they inflict substantial pain upon Hoody and D. To maintain white racial comfort, white spectators ignore the adverse impacts of well-intentioned actions.

## Meritocratic Blinders

Audience members sit at tables and desks in an interactive classroom, an immersive performance space designed to evoke a K–12 classroom. Blackboards are covered with homework assignments and test reminders, posters with test-taking tips and motivational quotes such as "For success, attitude is as important as ability." This production of *Forgotten Future: The Education Project* begins as an interracial, intergenerational ensemble of actors enters the space chanting and waving signs reading SAVE OUR SCHOOLS and SUPPORT OUR SCHOOLS: DON'T CLOSE THEM in protest of Chicago's dysfunctional public school system (fig. 5.1). Some wear red T-shirts, and several are clad in the real-life protest T-shirts worn during the school closure protests and the teachers' strike during the 2012–13 school year. The audience soon claps and chants along, "There's no power like the power of the people and the power of the people don't stop" (clap, clap). Adult actors playing parents and teachers give speeches in between the chants. The kids in the ensemble try to speak, but the adults run right over them. By the end of the rally, the kids are standing off in a corner of the space, forlorn and ignored, while the adults yell on their behalf without ever asking for their perspective.

*Forgotten Future* was produced by Collaboraction, a twenty-year-old theater company based in the Wicker Park neighborhood of Chicago, as part of its 2014–15 season.[6] The play was conceived by Sarah Moeller, cowritten by Moeller, Adam Seidel, and Michele Stine, and codirected by Moeller and John Wilson, using theater as a platform for community discussion of the dysfunction plaguing the Chicago Public Schools (CPS). The play as a whole tells the intertwining stories of three families—a Latinx family on the West Side, a black family on the South Side, and a white family on the North Side—examining their distinct problems and highlighting sharp inequalities within the CPS system.

African American fifth grader (Tyrese Hall) has just had his school closed. We watch his mother (Ebony Joy) review the complex, specific route he needs to take on his thirty-minute walk across gang lines to get safely to school. Once he is there, he suffers from bullying, and his white veteran teacher (Susie Griffith) tries her best (in her now-overstuffed class of forty students) to connect with him.

A white eighth grader (Leah Aberman) is under tremendous pressure from her father (Nathaniel Swift) to get a perfect score on every assignment and every standardized test to win a coveted slot in the most elite selective-enrollment high school. "Your test scores need to be perfect, your future is determined by what high school you go to; you have to go to Northside Prep." She struggles with depression and perfectionism as her Latinx teacher (Angelica Roque) battles against the incessant demands of standardized testing that act as an obstacle to actual teaching and learning.

A Latinx eleventh grader (Esme Ayvar-Perez) who got horrible scores on the pre-ACT tests and because "tests determine the ACT and the future" has given up hope, is determined to drop out. Her well-intentioned mother (Jasmin Cardenas) is supportive and hopeful for her daughter's future but doesn't entirely know how to help, and her white history teacher (Scott Merchant) is in his first year of teaching and stymied by the school's lack of simple resources—forget computers to prep kids to take the digitally administered ACT, the school doesn't even have pencils and paper for practice or unbroken windows to keep in the heat during the brutal Chicago winter.

*Forgotten Future* examines each family's distinct problems and highlights the sharp inequalities within the CPS system. It reflects the lived experiences and social realities of young people—a group whose voices aren't often heard in the public/political sphere—from three distinct communities in a segregated city in which there isn't much exchange among disparate worlds. Moeller is herself a teacher, and her motivation for creating *Forgotten Future* was to educate audiences about the issues plaguing CPS. She observes that many people who do not have school-age children have no idea how schools are funded or what the recent conflicts are actually about. In addition, while debates in the media highlight the voices of politicians, Moeller told me that she and her team "wanted to focus on the voice of the students, rather than the adults in the room."[7] They engaged in an extended process of interviewing teachers and students identified through snowball sampling, sifting through stories, identifying the gaps, and heading back into the field to conduct more interviews to fill in conspicuous silences.[8] The draft of *Forgotten Future* that I saw in October 2014 underwent multiple major revisions through its development as new stories and perspectives were added, edited, and removed for both breadth and clarity.

Public schools are funded by property taxes, and in a racially and economically segregated city such as Chicago, this system reinforces and exacerbates inequality. In the fall of 2012, a seven-day teachers' strike was followed by a wave of school closings in the spring of 2013 that was concentrated in poor neighborhoods on the South and West Sides. Collaboraction highlights these substantial hot-button local issues in this production. Creator Sarah Moeller's explicit goals for the production were to "incite people to at least be more aware of what's going on around them" and to "incite change."

Returning to the performance I attended, the audience is specifically framed as students in a classroom; we sit at desks and the production's staging in the round enables us to see one another sitting at desks. The production design and the setup of the performance event evoke multiple layers of meaning: We are there to learn. We are asked to imagine ourselves in the shoes of the real students represented in the play. We are part of the story and not separate from it. The space was set up to reinforce a sense of what Victor Turner calls "communitas" and common ground by physically locating the audience in a classroom and spatially framing these three stories as happening in the same classroom in which we are all the students.[9] These aesthetic choices encourage audience members to identify with the characters onstage. They unify a set of diverse "personal" problems and tell an overarching story about the common structural and political problems at their root.

Preshow projections scroll through statistics showing the total annual spending on education by country and international test scores, placing the United States in a global educational context—we spend more money and get poorer results than other nations. An audio track from a *PBS News Hour* segment on the school closures plays on a loop, including interviews with Mayor Rahm Emanuel and Karen Lewis, president of the Chicago Teachers Union. Lewis's argument that "the status quo is rich people get richer, beautiful schools, and poor people get bad schools; we are against the status quo" echoes through the space. This highlights the realness of the problems represented in the play. In the opening rally and at other points through the play, we are encouraged to chant and clap along, as we would in a real rally. It certainly isn't required, but I clap and chant along, as do the other audience members I see next to me and across the space from me. We are fellow protesters—from the beginning, we are incorporated in the play's activist agenda. The production assumes that we agree with the message of the play. And that's probably true. Who comes to see a play explicitly about the problems with the school system who doesn't care about the school system? Chicago's public school system is highly dysfunctional, and there is a lot of press surrounding this dysfunction. It is unlikely that anyone paying attention to the schools or the local news would *not* think there are problems with the school system.

The Sunday matinee I am attending has an intergenerational audience—about half the desks are filled with middle-school students. In the post-performance "town hall discussion" it becomes clear that many of the adults in the audience are their parents. In later interviews, Moeller confirmed that the production routinely attracted an intergenerational audience that included public school students, parents, and teachers.

By using real kids—real CPS students (fig. 5.1)—the production foregrounds and highlights how they are at the center and yet totally marginalized in a contentious policy debate. The realness of the kids (and of the documentary audio track) highlights the realness of the story. In her *Theatre of the Real*, Carol Martin explains how "performance of the real can collapse the boundaries between the real and the fictional in ways that create confusion and disruption or lead to splendid unplanned harmonies in the service of the creation of meaning."[10] The presence of these real kids is particularly useful in collapsing these boundaries. At the performance I attend, half the audience members are present to support actor Leah Aberman (see fig. 5.2), a white middle-school student who in real life has gone through the rigorous and stressful testing process to be able to attend a selective-enrollment school. These audience members read the fictional story as a thin overlay of their lived experience of the actor's real life. Martin highlights how theater is live and happening and therefore both real and not-real at the same time. The production intentionally highlights this overlap, and in the performance of this story line at this particular performance event, the real and the not-real overlap and blur. These audience members empathize and identify with the real girl as they watch her character's story line.

Moeller indicates that "it helps having youths in the play because they bring their friends." Putting real kids in the play convinced friends and families from their disparate communities to come see the play. The audience I experience is full of people who might not otherwise take time out of their busy lives to come see a play. This diversity seems to offer the potential for genuine dialogue among community members in a segregated city who, as the play points out, do not routinely interact. Sonja Kuftinec highlights theater's capacity to create a transactional space in which dialogue is possible, and I want this piece to be able to activate theater's potential to create an encounter among people whose points of view might not otherwise have opportunity to come into dialogue.[11] However, at the performance I attend,

Fig. 5.2. Leah Aberman (center) and the ensemble of *Forgotten Future*. Photograph by Anna Sodziak.

the audience is predominantly white: only Aberman's friends and family—that is, white middle-school students and their white parents from the more affluent, predominantly white North Side. This audience focuses exclusively on the white North Side narrative, to the exclusion of inequalities that are clearly present in the play and highlighted by the talkback facilitator. Even when the facilitator pushes audience members to recognize the inequalities, they cannot get past their own stories to see them. As a result, the "town hall meeting" after the show amplifies the divisions the production attempted to bridge. It distorts a theatrical event about a system of interconnected dysfunction into one about the problems of middle-class white families.

Moeller told me that "the [post-performance town hall] discussion oftentimes was driven by the audience members that were there, what their personal experiences were, what their takes on things were and that's completely what drove things." At the performance I have just seen, many audience members have lived the story of the white student applying for a slot at a selective-enrollment school. They identify with that character, are excited to see this grueling experience represented onstage, and want to talk about it.

A young white girl is the first audience member to speak up at the start of the discussion. "I could definitely really relate to Leah's character's comments on the stress of the selective enrollment process," she said. The discussion evolved to clarify that all of the young people in the audience (and the actor in the production) went to a selective-enrollment elementary school ending in sixth grade and went through the process to get into a seventh-grade academic center last year. The stress over this process begins, they say, as early as fourth grade.

Moeller, who is cofacilitating the discussion, offers context—selective-enrollment high schools take 5 percent of students who apply, and selective-enrollment seventh- and eighth-grade programs are even more selective.

A woman in the audience introduces herself as Leah's former teacher and comments that she teared up at points—the girl who had worked herself to the bone to get into the selective-enrollment high school was "not necessarily going to be ok." The discussion continued to focus on this story line. A parent says, "It's unlike anything you could ever imagine. And it's grueling." A student tells us, "The day my letter came, I ran downstairs every fifteen minutes to see if the mail had come." Another student chimes in, "All of us were going to a different place; you weren't going to be with your friends."

The discussion facilitator attempts to refocus the conversation to engage with the larger narratives of inequality in the play, asking, "What does it mean that we live in a society where education is viewed as a privilege rather than a right?"

No intervention on the part of the facilitators can get this audience to engage with either the problems of the black and Latinx students or the larger structural problems plaguing the system. I quote this talkback at length to provide evidence that despite this production's goals, audience members structured discourse in ways that supported a white habitus—a framework of unexamined assumptions upholding white privilege. Even when facilitators tried to refocus the discussion on the larger landscape of inequality, I watched the white audience members continue to focus on elements of performances that reinforced their lived experiences as middle-class white people and existing worldviews shaped by that experience.

I did not want to assume that every town hall discussion mirrored the one I observed, so I asked Sarah Moeller to tell me stories of performances I did not see where the audience was more diverse and audience members with differing lived experiences were present at the same performance. She told me about town hall meetings where some audience members were focused on their experience of trying to get into selective-enrollment schools while others were saying, "My school doesn't even have textbooks."[12] In these mixed audiences, Moeller told me, audience members talked past each other; they could not hear one another over the noise of their own lived experience:

> I think it was hard for them to see each other's perspectives because we are all innately selfish, even if we don't want to be. Especially when it involves our own children. That it's hard to hear each other. I do think people would try to hear each other but everybody's individual problems run so deeply personal that more so we would end up having two completely different conversations.[13]

Martin warns that presented with evidence reflecting their existing views, "people can remain convinced of their own views without having to entertain, let alone understand or agree with, the views of anyone else."[14] Moeller's observation takes this argument a step further—even when presented with evidence of alternate perspectives, people can remain convinced of their own views. *Forgotten Future* connects the dots among diverse problems plaguing the Chicago Public Schools, highlighting the ways that structural systems of power hurt everyone as they reinforce existing social inequalities. Even when explicitly prompted by facilitators, audience members had trouble pushing past their own stories to engage with these larger structural problems.

Spectators select and interpret, making sense of what they see based on knowledge they already possess. Signs can have any number of meanings—for them to be read in the ways artists intend, audience members must share a body of knowledge with the artist to make desired meanings legible. Rancière argues that images of intolerable injustice derive their power "from the obviousness of theoretical scenarios making it possible to identify [their] content and from the strength of political movements that translated them into practice."[15] That is to say, audience members must already have a framework to understand a problem in order to make critical meaning of a representation of that problem. Those frameworks come from cultural currents beyond the theatrical event.

Audience members at the *Forgotten Future* talkback I described do not appear have an ideological framework to critique the methodology of meritocracy peeling resources away from the many to create functional schools for the high-testing few. Meritocracy operates within a larger framework of color-blind racism to obscure the racialized nature of inequalities and naturalize their existence.[16] The production depicts an interconnected landscape. The middle-class white girl is obsessed with preparing for the tests that will gain her access to the elite schools in which she can be buffered from the experiences the working-class kids of color must survive. The kids are not only linked through large and abstract systems of capitalism and white supremacy, they are concretely embedded within the same public school system. Lara Nielsen and Patricia Ybarra highlight how neoliberalism operates as an ideology in which "with the rhetorical emphasis on 'choice,' rising inequality is recalibrated away from the concerns and social goods of the welfare state, toward the optimization of difference in which the market functions as the final arbiter of value."[17] In the talkback I observed following *Forgotten Future*, audience members critique the pressures placed on middle-class kids by a system optimizing difference through standardized tests, but they do not critique the value that difference should be optimized. They appear to accept the overarching ideology of a meritocracy governed by standardized tests. They benefit from the system as it is currently structured, sifted into an elite through a painful process designed to convince the advantaged that they deserve more because they are better than those who have less.

The middle-class, predominantly white audience members do not seem to have an ideological framework to imagine the possibility of a system that is less punishing for everyone because the neighborhood schools are properly resourced and not institutions anyone need scramble to escape. Instead, they focus on the stress of getting *their* kids out of failing schools—schools that are, implicitly, just fine for the working-class black and brown students whose problems they do not want to talk about. White racial comfort relies on an uninterrogated framework of white superiority and white entitlement.

## Writing Good White Intentions In Where They Are Conspicuously Absent

The white racial frame is powerful, and I am not exempt from it. I unwittingly manifested my own white racial frame in my published review of the Next Theatre Company's 2014 production of Kirsten Greenidge's *Luck of the Irish*.[18] I resurrect and reexamine it here as an example of a way white spectators displace represented perspectives of people of color in favor of imagined white perspectives. The productions I described in the previous sections include sympathetic white characters for white audience members to identify with and focus on. *Luck of the Irish* does not—and so white audience members (including me) maintained our white racial comfort by writing ourselves into the story in a different way.

*Luck of the Irish* is a multigenerational drama revolving around a house that is "ghost-bought" in the 1950s by the working-class Irish American Donovan family for the affluent African American Taylor family. Ghost buying was a real estate transaction in which a white family formally purchased a home in a segregated area on behalf of a black family; it was a strategy that marginalized groups and their allies used to bypass prejudice. In *Luck of the Irish*, this transaction goes horribly awry. The narrative jumps back and forth in time between the 1950s and the present day, as the Taylors' granddaughter and her family move back into the house in a still mostly white suburb.

An implicit argument of *Luck of the Irish*, directed by Damon Kiely, may be that class mobility is a myth. In the 1950s, the black, upper-middle-class Taylors have money to buy a nice home in an upscale suburb not only because Rex (André Teamer) is a doctor but because the father of his wife Lucy (Mildred Marie Langford) had the resources to sell some land to give them enough money for a down payment. Lucy wears pearls and quotes Robert Frost; both she and Rex are clearly college educated. They speak in fluid Standard English, in clear contrast to the working-class Boston accents of the Irish American Joe (Chris Rickett) and Patty Ann Donovan (Cora Vander Broek). The Donovans need money; a third party introduces them to the Taylors, who need a white family to help them buy a home in a white suburb. Patty Ann, in particular, resents both this arrangement and that a black family could have so much more than her family.

Two generations later, the upper-middle-class black Taylor family is still upper-middle-class—their children and grandchildren have graduate degrees and white-collar jobs, and most important for this story, they own an inherited home. The working-class white Donovans have not raised their standard of living in fifty years. Patty Ann Donovan needs to feel like her lot in life has improved—like she has gotten up a rung on the ladder of the American Dream. She has spent fifty years stewing in rage over every holiday fruitcake Lucy Taylor sent her. The Taylors have more than she does; Patty Ann can no more afford to send annual fruitcake to casual acquaintances than purchase a large home in an upscale suburb. Patty Ann's bitterness leads her to harass the Taylors in the present day for having, in her view, cut in front of her in the line to prosperity.

Next Theatre is no longer in operation, but it was for more than twenty years a midsize professional theater located in Evanston, Illinois, a racially integrated, politically progressive suburb just north of Chicago. Evanston is known for its excellent public schools and close proximity to the city; it is one of the towns affluent young families relocate to when they want to retain access to both diversity and city resources while avoiding the Chicago Public School system. In the 2010 census, Evanston was reported to be approximately 65 percent white, 18 percent black, 9 percent Asian, 9 percent Latino, and 4 percent multiracial (the latter accounting for a total greater than 100 percent). Larger percentages of the black and Latinx populations live in a handful of neighborhoods on Evanston's west and southwest sides, but those neighborhoods still have large numbers of white and Asian families and are far more integrated than most neighborhoods in the city of Chicago proper. As a result, Evanston has a reputation for diversity. Within this context, Next Theatre's production of *Luck of the Irish* seems to implicitly pat Evanston audiences on the back for their choice to live in this diverse enclave, in which a family like the Taylors would never feel so isolated as they do in the all-white suburb of Boston in which the play is set. At intermission, I overhear the white women in their sixties sitting behind me talking about how much they appreciate living in the diverse community of Evanston as they tick off how many of each of their neighbors are black, Latinx, and Asian.

Next Theatre's production of *Luck of the Irish* makes for a comfortable viewing experience for me as an upper-middle-class white audience member. I watch a family who speaks much as mine does, wearing sweatshirts emblazoned with the name of their alma mater as we do, eating miniature cupcakes as we do. I recognize the present-day Hannah Taylor's absurd and mundane daily struggle to get children to eat dinner and go to bed. It's easy for me as a white audience member to identify with the upper-middle-class black characters—who in educational attainment and consumption patterns perform identities Bryant Keith Alexander might describe as enacting positions and behaviors presumed culturally "white," regardless of the races of the bodies performing them.[19] Within this framework, the black characters in *Luck of the Irish* could be considered to perform "whiteness" better than the working-class white characters do.

Shannon Sullivan in *Good White People* highlights how "the production and display of white middle-class moral goodness" is "achieved by establishing the moral badness of poor and lower-class white people," as middle-class white people blame lower-class white people for continuing to act in racist ways and perpetuating "lingering racism in our enlightened times."[20] In Patty Ann Donovan, *Luck of the Irish* gives audience members a white, working-class, overtly racist antagonist from the 1950s to hate. I can think how the Taylors would be welcome in my affluent, diverse town and feel good that I may be white but am not a bad, racist white person like Mrs. Donovan. I can be glad that people like her—*other* people, people from a different generation—are dying out and leaving me my racially integrated world of cupcake-eating, craft-beer-drinking, college-educated neighbors. This sentiment hinges on what Joyce Bell and Douglas Hartmann identify as "assimilationist assumptions" that white people view diversity as positive as long as it excludes "political or linguistic deviations from American mainstream culture" and continues to support "a social system and set of practices dominated and defined by whites."[21] In giving white audience members African American protagonists for whom we can root and a white antagonist from whom we can distance ourselves, *Luck of the Irish* offers a comfortable experience for white audience members. The play premiered at the Huntington Theatre Company in Boston and subsequently received a high-profile production at Lincoln Center—both predominantly white institutions—and it is written in a way that doesn't make white people uncomfortable.

However, the racial politics of the play are not so simple. In the present day, Hannah Taylor (Lily Mojekwu) is hyperaware of the family's blackness in a sea of suburban whiteness; it threatens to drown her. Her husband Rich (Austin Tally) and ten-year-old son Miles (Mesiyah Oduro-Kwarten) do not appear at all fazed to be living in a place in which theirs is the only black family. Miles is hyperactive, as are many ten-year-old boys, but he exceeds at athletics and appears popular. However, he has problems: he bites another child and is suspended from school. Patty Ann's harassment sends Hannah into a spiral of anxiety as she fears she has made a terrible mistake moving her black family back to this white place.

In the review of this production I published on the HowlRound Theatre Commons website in 2014, I identified Miles's problems as seeming "quite ordinary." As a white audience member and critic, I dismissed Hannah's anxiety; I assumed the character was being overly sensitive and overreacting. I took my cues from the way her husband responds to her, ignoring how many of the tensions that cause her anxiety fall into the domestic sphere she is required to manage on a day-to-day basis, which he interfaces with only occasionally. There was enough ambiguity in the production to give me and other white spectators the space to interpret that Hannah is being overly sensitive, that contemporary upper-middle-class white people do not behave in racist ways, and that the legacy of racism is mostly in her head. In *The White Racial Frame*, Joe Feagin argues, "Holding [the dominant] racial frame in their heads, but trying to suppress some overt actions reflecting it, whites frequently send powerful nonverbal signals as their real feelings, the emotions central to their racial framing, leak out into cross-racial interactions."[22] It seems clear to me now that Hannah reacts to these nonverbal signals that she is being tolerated but she does not belong. The play is about the continuing impacts of racism and the nuanced ways it appears. It highlights some of the particular contours of the ways gender and race intersect as the pressures US society places on women and mothers and the stereotypes that same society places on black boys collide. Hannah's isolation in her anxiety is the product of the particular intersection of race and class that lead her to be raising a black family in an otherwise all-white suburb.

Since writing that initial review, some key experiences and learnings sharpened my analysis of the intersectional dynamics at play in Hannah's story. Engaging with critical race theory, listening to audience members of color respond to performances and fellow audience members, and paying close attention to the racialized dynamics of performance events taught me to listen to and believe Hannah. The concept of *microaggressions*—quotidian performances of unrecognized bias—was not one I was familiar with in 2014, but it was in common circulation by the time I revisited my review, and engaging with Claudia Rankine's *Citizen* as part of my work on this book helped deepen my understanding of them. Listening to women of color in Citizen Read events and *The White Card*'s act 2 (described in chapter 1), I came to better appreciate the ways in which the concerns of women of color are frequently dismissed as "overreactions"; Hannah's story resonates with their comments. Mourning with Jamel's mother in *The Bitter Game* (described in chapter 2) helped me better hear how Hannah fears for her son. Multiple viewings of *Trapped in a Traveling Minstrel Show* (described in chapter 3) helped me recognize the ugliness of my own white gaze. Carrying these experiences and readings with me, I move through my daily life thinking about white racialized performances. I pick up on the "dog whistle politics" at play when a white neighbor asks me if it is really safe to park my car in a commuter parking lot in a working-class black neighborhood.[23] (It is.) Pedestrian performances of racialized bias work to maintain social segregation, even within a relatively diverse place. Today, I can recognize that Hannah responds to such signs—and see how common they are in affluent, politically progressive spaces. They are what make such spaces *hauntingly white*.

## Staying Comfortable

Most white people want to make conscious choices to be a *good white person* rather than a *bad racist white person.* This binary relies on an ideology of individual agency framing racism as reliant on individual acts of ignorance and cruelty. Even when we understand racism to be a structural system of power in the abstract, many white people unreflexively retain attachments to this binary. Within this individualized framework, white people believe we can exempt ourselves from the generalized category of *white people*, a group whose racialized dominance created and sustains racism. Many of the social patterns forming the fabric of much middle- and upper-middle-class white life quietly sustain the dominance of affluent whites, including gentrification, de facto school and neighborhood segregation, and meritocratic systems relying on standardized tests.

All spectatorship relies on a process of selecting and interpreting signs. When white audience members see theatrical representations of the social patterns sustaining the dominance of affluent whites, we tend to interpret them in one of two ways: (1) we either identify with characters and rationalize their actions as good, selecting signs we recognize as *like us* to focus on, ignoring signs offering evidence of oppressive impacts, or (2) we recognize oppressive impacts and distance ourselves from the characters performing them, selecting signs marking them *not like us* and ignoring the things we have in common with them. This pattern of interpretation relies on and reinforces a definition of racism that is individual rather than structural. We interpret in this way because it retains our sense of racial comfort.

To borrow from Bridget Kiger Lee and Patricia Enciso, a problem needs to cause dissatisfaction, stress, or anxiety for audience members to be motivated to change.[24] Many productions look to provoke a degree of racial stress in white audience members with goal of motivating change. However, white audience members frequently rely on the interpretation patterns I have described in this chapter to insulate ourselves from racial stress. Theatrical representation of the stress and anxiety a problem causes for people of color may provoke empathy from white audience members, but it does not put enough direct pressure on us to motivate change—not when the problem represented reflects social patterns from which we benefit. When change would potentially *cause* an audience member stress and anxiety, we actively avoid it. As a result, white audience members interpret theatrical performances in ways supporting our existing worldviews, even if that requires ignoring substantial elements of the work we have seen. These patterns of white spectatorship fundamentally support white racial comfort.

## Chapter 6

✦

# Building Diverse Community

In Halcyon Theatre's intimate forty-seat theater on the third floor of Christ Lutheran Church in Chicago, a working-class Latinx teenager begs a resurrected river goddess to teach her the river's words that will give her the power to rebuild the broken world through which she moves. The run of Caridad Svich's *De Troya* through May and June 2018 coincides with the revelation of the Trump administration's policy separating and detaining migrant and refugee families at the southern border of the United States, ripping children from their parents and guardians and creating tent city detention centers that look a whole lot like internment camps for children. As two-thirds of the country screams bloody murder, and the news is full of images of crying toddlers yanked from the arms of their mothers, *De Troya* stages a world in which migration and family separation are common, leaving rifts and scars in need of healing.

Teenager Mara (Valeria Rosero) makes her case to the mysterious and powerful Raya (Isaly Viana) that she will use the river's words to help "us"—everyone who "knows what it's like to be told people like us aren't worth anything."[1] The diverse audience members assembled sit only a few feet away in the small thrust performance space. They shift in their seats, catch each other's eyes, sigh, or shake their heads in acknowledgment that their government enacts policies performing this very sentiment. This moment of audience performance rehearses interracial solidarity with both the fictional working-class Latinx characters onstage and the real Latinx actors playing them.

Halcyon Theatre is a small professional ensemble theater, founded in 2006 with a mission "to connect people across our communities, by sharing stories that reach through our past and imagine a new future."[2] It is rooted in the ethnically diverse, working-class Albany Park neighborhood of Chicago, home to substantial communities of immigrants from Mexico, Korea, Guatemala, Ecuador, the Philippines, Cambodia, Somalia, the former Yugoslavia, Pakistan, Iran, Iraq, and Lebanon; more than forty-two languages are spoken in the neighborhood schools. Through its radical hospitality program,

Halcyon provides no-cost access to all its productions, offering free tickets on a first-come, first-served basis for all performances.

In the introduction to this book, I posed the problem that most theaters are hauntingly white spaces, and most chapters contain moments describing unreflexive white racialized performatives sustaining their haunting whiteness. This chapter is different. It illustrates the ways in which audience members of many races engage with theatrical events in a theater led by white artists that is *not* a hauntingly white space. It highlights the long-term commitments through which a company can decenter whiteness, alongside the tensions and material challenges such commitments pose.

The histories of racial subjection in the United States differ across racial and ethnic groups, but their stories are linked. Moon-Kie Jung describes the United States as an "empire-state," a racial state of white supremacy. Empire-states are not homogenous and are hierarchically differentiated; their people are by law or by practice (or both) afforded different access to rights and privileges.[3] In the United States, many immigrants and descendants of immigrants suffer racialized violence at the hands of the empire-state. Much of Halcyon's body of work includes new and contemporary plays by artists of color focusing on stories directly engaging the experiences of the many immigrant groups living in Albany Park. Taken individually, most of these productions are not overtly interventionist in nature, but taken together they represent an overarching project using professional theater production to create an inclusive, equitable community in which artists and audience members can pierce through the segregated bubbles that comprise much of contemporary life in the United States. This chapter looks at eighteen months of Halcyon's programming through 2017–18, drawing evidence from audience response to three productions: Lloyd Suh's *American Hwangap* (which was coproduced with A-Squared Theatre, an Asian American theater company, and directed by Helen Young), Marisela Treviño Orta's *The River Bride*, and Caridad Svich's *De Troya* (both directed by Halcyon's associate artistic director Rinska Carrasco-Prestinary). They include stories of families, love stories, and coming-of-age stories focusing on the experiences of first- and second-generation immigrants.

Two of these productions explicitly explore dynamics within immigrant families to the United States—the middle-class Korean American family in *American Hwangap* and the impoverished Puerto Rican family in *De Troya*.[4] *The River Bride* is set in Brazil and uses magical realism to tell a story of migration in which the migrating Others are river dolphins transformed into men by true love. It is not an accident that these plays include no Caucasian actors, that their stories reposition whiteness as offstage and marginal to the narratives. Mainstream white US culture exists in *American Hwangap* and *De Troya*; both navigate the ways in which families manifest tensions surrounding assimilation to majoritarian culture. Artistic director Tony Adams, who is white, says:

> I try to program work that both reminds audiences what they love about seeing stories performed and show that more is possible. I think of it as giving our audience a magic mirror to see a different way forward, and to understand our history. One of the most powerful ways whiteness projects itself is by erasing the full array of people who make up our histories. Our present has more possibilities, and our past was much more vibrant than many of us learned. We work to expand the center of the stories that are being told by simply telling a wider array of them. We don't make a big deal of it, we just do it. By not treating stories that don't usually fall under the blanket of whiteness as something special, we hope it works to normalize the breadth of stories that have always existed in our community.[5]

I joined Halcyon as an artist-in-residence in 2013 and stayed on to become an ensemble member from 2014 to 2018. I have directed for the company and supported its work writing occasional grants, developing a teaching artist residency program, and developing program evaluation systems. Halcyon's interracial, intergenerational ensemble has, in the five years in which I have been involved with the organization, included white, Latinx, black, and Asian artists ranging from their early twenties to their early seventies. Most of the ensemble members who have been with the company for more than five years are from working-class backgrounds. Halcyon opened my eyes to the ways in which my professional artistic praxis had been highly segregated up to that point. I realized that I had frequently created artistic projects with racially diverse ensembles of artists who had all been trained in the same handful of elite programs. Regardless of origins, most artists trained in such ways who work in professional theater settings have absorbed and display professional-managerial-class habitus. Halcyon is different. Artists observe professional behavioral standards—for example, actors are on time to rehearsal and learn their lines and treat one another with respect—and artists from diverse backgrounds bring their full and honest selves into the space. Those full and honest selves reflect a polyvocal mix of habitus, which sometimes requires translation and navigation as part of artistic and operational processes. I have learned a great deal from collaborating in an ensemble in which I have needed to adjust my affect and expectations, recognizing them as race- and class-specific and at times unhelpful.

This diversity is the ensemble theater's biggest strength, but I do not want to paint too utopian a picture—it is not without its tensions. Discourses of diversity in the United States frequently focus on the positive benefits *difference* brings to members of dominant groups, often subsuming discussions of inequality. Degrees of assimilation to majoritarian middle-class culture, use of dominant and marginalized languages, and visual demarcations of race all provide differential access to safety and to opportunity. Audience members' lived experiences inform how they respond to particular aspects of Halcyon's productions, and as I will discuss later in this chapter, their polyvocal responses do not always create a harmonious utopia. In addition, the economic challenges present in most small professional theater production contexts are exacerbated by the economic diversity present in Halcyon's ensemble. Some of the operational and material tensions Halcyon faces may help explain why, in an era in which diversity is much lauded, the theater industry continues to be plagued by persistent attachments to a hauntingly white status quo.

Many small professional and fringe theaters perform to audiences containing many friends and family of artists, and Halcyon is no exception. Caroline Heim distinguishes "integral" audience members—critics, friends, theater professionals—from "ordinary" audience members.[6] At Halcyon, "ordinary" audience members do not dominate performance events; many audience members arrive with preexisting relationships to the theater or its artists.[7] I examine this phenomenon as a *feature* rather than a *bug* of small theater production, examining how this feature can operate to bridge social divides. Halcyon's core ensemble is legitimately diverse, drawing together people to make theater who would otherwise not encounter one another in a city of largely race- and class-segregated neighborhoods and cocareer workplaces. Artists circulate through separate worlds, drawing friends and family who are similar to them in various ways with them to the theater to support their artistic work or to join them for social events. The nature of ensemble theater is to create long-term artistic relationships, and so the audience members drawn to the theater by personal relationships frequently attend many events including informal game nights and concerts at the theater in addition to formal performance events. The ensemble theater as a project brings together a diverse community supported by many points of contact. The productions described in this chapter draw in additional guest artists, each with their own personal network of friends and family who come to see their work for the same reasons, which draws in new people for each performance run, creating temporary communities that are distinct to each production but still rooted in Halcyon's core base of friends and supporters.

Halcyon received a $50,000 grant from the Arts Work Fund for Organizational Development to study our audiences through the 2017 and 2018 seasons; this chapter draws on data collected as part of that larger self-study initiative, for which I operated as the principal investigator.[8] This project relied on using front-of-house staff as researchers. It is always important to Halcyon to hire diverse front-of-house teams, and this research made it imperative that these teams include individuals attuned to culturally specific details of reception.[9] For *American Hwangap* and *The River Bride*, the front-of-house staff filed nightly "snapshot" field notes, describing a moment of audience behavior that stood out to them and interpreting what they thought this behavior meant. Each front-of-house staff member also filed a longer weekly analytic memo synthesizing patterns and making sense of what they were learning about how audiences were receiving the production. Artistic leaders and I occasionally posed specific queries to the front-of-house/research teams, asking them to keep an eye on particular aspects or moments of performance or themes that were emerging. For *De Troya*, the actors joined the front-of-house staff in filing nightly "snapshots." Heim posits that "actors are the audience's audience," and we explored that dynamic by having them formally articulate the informal learnings about audience response that actors routinely incorporate into their work.[10]

This research methodology was designed to primarily operate as practitioner research—snapshots are not intended to provide the full picture of the theatrical event in the manner of a qualitative researcher's full field notes. Our goal was to build a system that made it easy for practitioners to conduct self-study and to home in on their audience's experience in a reflective and organic way.

Through all three of these productions, I attended select performances, collecting more exhaustive qualitative data as a participant observer. I used these understandings to contextualize the nightly snapshots researchers were filing, leaning heavily on their weekly analytic memos to understand what sense they were making of what they were seeing.

## Connecting

As Gloria Anzaldúa writes, "Borders are set up to define the places that are safe and unsafe, to distinguish *us* from *them*."[11] Halcyon's mission is to dissolve such borders preventing human connection, specifically by creating a culture in which strangers are encouraged to talk to each other. Barry Freeman theorizes "the threshold that distinguishes the stranger from the *neighbour*—who is nearby and may share certain values or belong to a shared community—or from the *other* who has been marked as 'outside.'"[12] The stranger, to Freeman, holds the potential to become *neighbor* or *other*. Sara Ahmed reminds me how the image of the stranger is frequently racialized.[13] Within a consciously and intentionally interracial space, contact can transform the stranger into a neighbor, dissolving the border defining that person as *other*.

Halcyon's front-of-house culture is distinct and designed to highlight the things people who do not know each other have in common, quietly transforming strangers into neighbors by amplifying the potential of the theatrical event to create social connections. Jenn Adams, the director of community engagement and special events and the company's cofounder, house manages the productions as if hosting a party at her own home. She welcomes every patron to the forty-seat space, remembers audience members she has met before, and finds points of connection with everyone who walks in the door. She introduces audience members to each other, seeding conversations by pointing to things people might have in common. After the performance, actors mingle freely with audience members, greeting their guests and talking informally with audience members they may not have already known. Halcyon rarely hosts formal post-performance discussions, instead creating an informal atmosphere in which people can socialize and discuss what they have seen. Gillian Sandstrom and Elizabeth Dunn found that casual social interactions among people with weak social ties foster feelings of belonging.[14] This kind of informal pre- and postshow conversation is intended to do just that, forming temporary communities among the small, diverse audiences at performance events.

Halcyon's radical hospitality program erases economic barriers to entry and—in a move that places its theatrical events within a gift economy—removes financial transactions from the act of acquiring tickets. Audience members may purchase tickets, but this must be done online and in advance. At the door, any available tickets are free. Lewis Hyde argues, "Social proximity becomes social life through an exchange of gifts."[15] An exchange (in Halcyon's case, a performance in exchange for two hours of time) "sanctions another exchange—conversation—and a whole series of trivial social ties unfolds."[16] As I mentioned earlier, many audience members at Halcyon events attend because they are friends or family of artists. As a result, it is common for audience members to discover that they know people in common or have shared other experiences, which amplifies the sense that fellow audience members are *neighbors* rather than *strangers*.

Research assistant Jamie Kreppein noticed how, in this spirit, audience members at Halcyon's events seemed to want to connect with one another:

> In one of the performances where the audience ended up in isolated groups, I watched a woman, who had arrived by herself, look for a moment of communion with someone, anyone, in the audience every time she laughed. Unfortunately, no one was close enough to her to even notice. Arriving alone was not the problem, evidenced by the performance during which I sat next to another single audience member. I laughed at a subtle facial expression by one of the actors, and the woman next to me laughed, too. We made eye contact, laughed some more, and had a really pure moment of communion between strangers.[17]

When audience members are attending a performance to support a specific actor, they tend to respond to that actor in distinct ways. Frequently, friends and family of an actor laugh more frequently and have more audible responses to early moments of that actor's performance. This behavior gives the rest of the audience permission to laugh and respond audibly, saturating the performance event with audible, energetic moments of audience response. Because Halcyon's house is small, a small group of friends and family can make a difference—even three or four people audibly engaging with the performance can infuse a night's performance with energy. When an actor draws a large crowd, it makes for a lively performance event.

*The River Bride* draws on Brazilian folktales of the *boto*, a mystical river dolphin that shapeshifts into a man, weaving a tale of star-crossed lovers in world saturated in magic realism. The play takes place before and on the wedding day of Belmira (Sophia Tew), the youngest daughter of the Costa family. Helena (Flavia Pallozzi), the eldest, has been in love with Belmira's future husband, Duarte (Jonathan Nieves), since they were children—at least until Moises (Nate Santana), a mysterious and charismatic stranger, is fished out of the *Amazonas* by Señor Costa (Johnny Garcia) and Duarte. Moises needs to find true love before he transforms back into a dolphin. Moises begins to court Helena, but Belmira's jealousy and the mystery of his past cause Helena to second-guess her feelings, leading the lovers to a tragic end.

Director Rinska Carrasco-Prestinary's nonverbal storytelling foregrounds Moises's dolphin nature, as he swoops and dives through transitions, transforming from man to fish and back again. Scenic designer Eleanor Khan, projection designer Smooch Medina, sound designer Jeffrey Lavin, and lighting designer Cat Davis (who received a Joseph Jefferson Award for her work on the show) create an evocative, immersive world of the village that surrounds the banks of audience seating. The space is dominated by a blue floor—the river—which operates as both central metaphor and material center to the fishing village and the story, with playing spaces on wooden boardwalks and fishing docks surrounding and jutting into the river. A canopy of vines frames the entire theater, running over the heads of audience members.

One weekend of *The River Bride*, ensemble member Tamika Lecheé Morales replaces Ana Maria Alvarez as Señora Costa, the mother of Helena and Belmira. Morales is a charismatic and energetic performer and a master of public relations. She brings a crowd of friends and family to support her whenever she is in a production. Because, as an understudy, she is only scheduled to perform one weekend of the run, the attendance of her supportive network is concentrated into only a few performances. They pack the house. These audience members interact freely with one another, recognizing one another from other events they had attended in support of Morales both at Halcyon and elsewhere. They form their own community, even if they don't know one another, because they begin to develop a consciousness of their shared, ongoing participation in Morales's performance events and life. During the performance itself, they respond audibly and frequently to the comedy present in the early scenes of the play, making for high-energy, supportive performance events. The research team dubs this phenomenon "The Tamika Effect," when a single actor's friends and family pack the house and raise the energy of the performance.

This phenomenon is not distinct to Morales—once we are looking for it, we see it when other performers bring groups to performances. On another night we observe this effect when Flavia Pallozzi brings five friends, and we realize that in a forty-seat theater, even a small group of vocal supporters can transform a performance event. In response, Halcyon creates an "alumni night" for its next production, intentionally drawing a crowd of supportive insiders with relationships to artists and the theater on a weeknight midrun when attendance is typically sparse. This promotion creates a similar effect, albeit one at which certain audience members have varying levels of familiarity with certain collaborating artists. Audience members at this event are aware of one another as fellow "alumni" and working artists. They build a party-like atmosphere before the performance, finding shared points of connection, and they feed this energy into the performance proper. The actors feel it and it fuels them.

Freeman describes how audience members navigate their relationships to characters throughout the plays they watch and, with the accumulation of dramatic actions, make decisions about just how strange the stranger is. In much narrative drama, including *The River Bride*, audience members respond to characters with empathy; the stranger is not so strange. Postshow, the distinct front-of-house culture Halcyon cultivates encourages audience members to talk to the actors, who do not seem so strange after watching them take the journey of the play. The actor an audience member has come to see introduces her family and friends to the other actors, who in turn reciprocate introductions. These informal interactions can turn into extensive post-performance discussions as audience members discuss what they have just seen, or they can transform into tangential conversations about topics audience members and artists discover are of mutual interest, or they can remain minimal and casual. It is not unusual to see a cluster of audience members and artists of mixed races and ages socializing in the middle of Halcyon's performance space fifteen or twenty minutes after the end of the play.

## Empathy

*American Hwangap* is about the Chun family gathering to celebrate the *hwangap*, or ritual sixtieth birthday, of Min Suk (Joe Yau), its absent patriarch. Min Suk left his wife Mary (Cheryl Hamada) and his children David (Gordon Chow), Esther (Helen Joo Lee), and Ralph (Jin Kim) to return to Korea approximately fifteen years prior to the start of the play, broken after being let go from his job as a nanotech engineer for being "obsolete." He has been an alcoholic mess in his absence; the rest of the family has moved on. He returns to reunite with his family, setting off the events of the play. The play begins a day or two before his *hwangap* and is interspersed with inner-monologue toasts given by each member of the family, a tradition of the *hwangap* celebration.

Halcyon's intimate space is configured in a thrust around Andrea Healy's abstracted rendition of the kitchen and basement of a middle-class-looking

American house. In the background, a climbable tree stretches into the sky in front of a backdrop of desert mountains. The play is about homecoming, and a sound design heavy with acoustic indie-rock helps make the production as a whole feel warm and cozy.

Audience members respond to this narrative family drama full of sympathetic characters in empathetic ways—they appear to identify with and care about the characters. Audience members of all races engage in conversations with members of the front-of-house staff/research team in which they draw personal connections to members of the family. These range from trivial similarities (such as sharing a birthday with a character), to humorous stories of trying to wrangle relatives for family events, to more profound personal stories of estranged relatives. People frequently stay in the theater for an extended time after the end of the show participating in these sorts of conversations.

Helen Young, the production's director, asks the research team to keep an eye out for differences between the ways in which Asian audience members react to the play and the ways non-Asian audience members react. We find a few culturally specific differences in reception in relation to moments referencing the characters' Koreanness. For example, in an early scene in which Min-Suk awkwardly gives his grown daughter Esther dating advice, he comments, "You are date somebody, is he Korean?" in a setup in which one expects him to press her to date Korean men, only to have him flip the expectation and warn her, "Korean people are kind of fucked up." She responds sardonically, "Yeah, I already know that."[18] This joke consistently gets laughs only from Asian audience members. The research team does not know the ethnic heritage of every audience member who appears Asian, but because they talk to a lot of audience members and many audience members have come to support artists working on the production, they have more information about the details of audience members' ethnic heritage than would be typical at most theaters. They identify that people who they know are Korean or Korean American often laugh at this joke, and on occasion they see Asians who are not Korean laugh too. The joke is funny and resonates with the lived experience of many people whose relatives have at one point or another badgered them about dating within their ethic group. But joking at the "fucked up"-ness of an ethnic group to which one does not belong could cause offense; we interpret non-Asian silence as a gesture of cultural respect. On nights with an audience full of people the research team knows to be Korean or Korean American, the joke is a big laugh line. On nights without such critical mass, the joke lands as one of many awkward attempts Min-Suk makes to connect to Esther in the scene.

That said, audience members' visible and audible reactions indicate patterns of empathy tracking more reliably with intersections of gender and age than with race. For example, the morning after Min-Suk succeeds in seducing his estranged wife, Mary, she makes it clear that she does not intend to restore or resume martial relationship with him and that he must not take last night's sex as an indication that they are back together. Mary asserts:

> This old house might seem familiar, but it's mine now, see? We paid the mortgage you left us with, me and the kids, so it's our roof you're under, and you don't get to just jump in and suddenly call this home. . . . I live a different life here, without you, I'm nimble and I'm out in the world, I have a life. . . . I am not at home in the wait with a hot meal and a pair of slippers. . . . If you think you can just roll up in here lookin' all sexy and turn me back into some do-it-all darn-your-socks kimchee-burying melon-cutting *ah-joo-mah* well you've got another thing coming, understand?[19]

Audience members of all ages and genders lean in; the scene is engaging. Women of all races over the age of fifty or so visibly and audibly respond with applause, vigorous nods, audible um-hms and whoops of pleasure to the moments when Mary asserts her ownership of the house and her life. When women in the audience perform these responses, they frequently check in with one another, making eye contact or sharing knowing nods. Lindsay Cummings uses the term *dialogic empathy* to describe "a provisional process that involves thinking and feeling, imagining the other in the other's situation, allowing his or her affect to resonate with us, and communicating our interpretations back to the other whenever possible for feedback."[20] Cheryl Hamada as Mary plays off the responses of women in the audience, adjusting her timing to incorporate their performance of solidarity and amplify an experience of dialogic empathy. The pleasure and strength she takes from their audible support affirms their responses, reinforcing a feedback running from actor to audience member, from audience member to audience member, back to the actor, back to the audience. In this moment of dialogic empathy, the women "of a certain age" in the room create a temporary, interracial community of support focused on shared aspects of their lived experience.

Irene Hsiao's review of this production describes Mary as a "successful American struggling to reconcile with traditions from another place," highlighting the ways in which the production and performance text emphasize similarities she shares with other American women, inviting them to identify and empathize with her.[21] Women who do not share Mary's experience as a first-generation immigrant subsume the culturally specific differences between their lived experiences battling patriarchy in US culture and Mary's fight against Korean gender norms. To follow Rancière, they "develop their own translation in order to appropriate the 'story' and make it their own story."[22] This translation minimizes the culturally specific aspects of Mary's story for many audience members. Suh's text encourages US-based audience

Fig. 6.1. Cheryl Hamada and Joe Yau in *American Hwangap*. Photograph by Marivi Oritz.

members who are not Korean to find similarities to the family at the center of the story through Mary's emphasis on her Americanness. The independence Mary insists on relies on assimilated US ideas of contemporary middle-class womanhood—the "here" where she has built a new life differs culturally from the "there" whence Min Suk has recently arrived in significant ways. She posits Americanness as a metonym for independence. The self-determination the audience and Mary celebrate uncritically characterizes her assimilation as an entirely positive thing. This interpretive maneuver, on one level, supports the white supremacist empire-state, emphasizing the happiness assimilation offers.

That said, empathy has the capacity to make the strange familiar. In a national political context actively antagonistic toward immigrants, highlighting the ways in which immigrant families are *American* families can operate as a strategic, productive tactic for advocacy. To return to Freeman, empathy can make strangers into neighbors. The dialogic empathy I describe in this section creates a feedback loop across women of many races who are about the same age, highlighting a lived experience they have in common and minimalizing differences that might emerge in other contexts. They perform solidarity with and for one another, taking pleasure in a moment in which they can feel heard and understood.

## Language

Marvin Carlson reminds me that language is socially constructed, and historical commercial, political, and cultural forces contributed to the dominance of the "standard" languages spoken in contemporary geographic areas. In the United States, Standard English may be the official language, but it is but one of many competing dialects and languages in use. Alternate ways of speaking are marked as subordinate to the "standard" dominant one in mainstream cultural contexts.[23] Multilingual theatrical events create moments in which that dominance can be destabilized.

As Anzaldúa puts it, "language is a homeland."[24] All three of the productions discussed in this chapter are written to resonate in specific ways for audience members who speak, respectively, Korean (*American Hwangap*), Spanish (*De Troya*), and Portuguese (*The River Bride*). These plays all blend linguistic forms, reflecting the hybrid languages spoken by immigrant communities. Carlson uses Mikhail Bakhtin's term "heteroglossic" to describe plays such as these that incorporate distinct languages and dialects.[25] The bulk of the narrative of all three plays takes place in English. Each incorporates linguistic variations, including moments in which characters code-switch from English into a second language, using that second language for emphasis, for humor, or to emphasize bonds between characters. These are, often, realistic uses of hybrid language reflecting the ways people in the communities the plays represent actually speak. Producing plays in hybrid languages that are typically marginalized in mainstream US contexts centers and welcomes the people who speak those languages.

This phenomenon plays out in all three productions and is particularly pronounced in Caridad Svich's *De Troya*. An urban fable about resilience and renewal, *De Troya* uses magical realism and poetry to explore faith, rebellion, and relationships between teenagers and the family members who care for them in a violent, desolate landscape of poverty and blight. *De Troya*'s characters speak, as Svich describes it, "an English laced at times with words, phrases and more in Spanish. It reflects who they are and how they live between languages and cultures."[26] Anzaldúa writes, "as long as I have to accommodate the English speakers rather than having then accommodate me, my tongue will be illegitimate."[27] Halcyon's production of *De Troya* creates a world in which a hybrid blend of English and Spanish is the default mother tongue and non-Spanish speakers must adjust to accommodate it.

In the wake of a highly abstract, climactic scene in which a forest erupts out of the concrete jungle, Lupe and Grandpa, two lonely older people who are in the process of building a relationship, respond to the sudden emergence of a forest in the city:

> GRANDPA: And over there, a forest. Puro trees.
> LUPE: Like the maleza back home.

GRANDPA: Cual?

LUPE: La maleza where people would get lost. The maleza huele mal, mi abuela would say—a algo malo. Don't go near the maleza. If you do, it will swallow you whole.[28]

The forest is offstage and the audience cannot see it, so this passage carries crucial exposition, helping to stabilize audience members' understanding that a forest with dense underbrush has just sprouted out of the concrete. This scene includes enough English for non-Spanish speakers to get the gist of it, but in performance, non-Spanish speakers sometimes appear a bit bewildered by the combination of theatrical abstraction and Spanish language. Lisa Jackson-Schebetta describes the challenge non-Spanish-speaking artists had to face in a production process in which the stage manager ran bilingual rehearsals, speaking Spanish first and English second. She describes how "it disoriented, it empowered, it disempowered, it challenged presumptions of privilege and destabilized the center and the margin."[29] Moments like this one in *De Troya* function similarly. Non-Spanish-speaking audience members need to work to make sense of the bilingual moment. This interpretive labor causes a degree of discomfort for native English speakers who do not speak Spanish; many are unaccustomed to linguistic discomfort, as the dominance of Standard English in public spaces in the United States goes unmarked.

Jorge Huerta describes the artistic decision to produce theater in a mixture of English and Spanish that reflects the "linguistic particularity" of its audience "a subversive act that [leaves] non-bilingual audience members out of the narrative," centering the bilingual and marginalizing the monolingual.[30] In centering hybrid language in this way, *De Troya* carves out a public space resisting the empire-state's insistence that all must assimilate to dominant ways of speaking and hearing. The linguistic specificity is essential to the production's intervention in white supremacy, but at times it amplifies the divide that the production wants to bridge.

The actors feel a palpable difference on nights with a critical mass of Spanish-speaking Latinx audience members. On these nights, they comment, "You could feel a deeper connection to what was happening. There would be little nods and smiles at things the aunts would say to each other, at the relationship moments between Lupe and Grandpa, and what felt like a familiarity to the story." For audiences recognizing the linguistic particularity of the play as reflective of their lived experience, culturally specific textures invite them to come closer. The actors point out the importance of having a critical mass of such audience members to receiving the production, commenting, "Without a language barrier, and with the support of knowing that others in the audience also felt the same way, audience members felt more relaxed to respond to things that were happening." Audience members who speak both Spanish and English—and in particular, audience members who speak a hybrid blend of the two—are energized by and relax into the production centering *their* language.

Implicit in actors' comments is an observation that absent a critical mass of Spanish-speaking audience members, audience members are less relaxed and they respond less. The most overt difference between the ways Spanish-speaking and non-Spanish-speaking audience members respond to *De Troya* is through laughter. Relaxed and energized audience members laugh more easily than audience members feeling discomfort as they work hard to interpret a challenging piece of theater. Some of the biggest laugh lines in the play are in Spanish, and so Spanish-speaking audience members laugh at jokes while non-Spanish-speaking audience members work to puzzle out their meaning. When a critical mass of Spanish speakers is present to laugh at the jokes, the event feels lively and full of energy. The actors are attuned to audience laughter as a marker of their engagement; when they do not get laughs, it feels as though the audience is not with them. And so when there are not enough Spanish speakers present to laugh, the play feels heavier and the actors feel less connected to the audience.

Audience members who speak one but not all of the languages incorporated in a heteroglossic play find themselves faced with moments of linguistic disorientation, in which they *do not understand* a moment. These moments of disorientation often cause mild stress and discomfort. Experiencing mild stress within a context otherwise structured to feel welcoming and inclusive can help audience members learn to tolerate discomfort. Halcyon's culture of informal post-performance discussion supports this project, encouraging audience members to ask questions in low-focus settings about moments they might not have easily understood, to take pleasure in the challenge of interpreting a challenging work, and reinforcing that individuals who might not have understood a moment of performance nevertheless belong in the theater and its created community.

After a performance of *De Troya*, a non-Spanish-speaking audience member addresses the linguistic specificity with a member of the front-of-house team. They share that they appreciate and enjoy the Spanish-language moments and cultural specificity. This audience member seems to welcome the productivity of a space in which they can practice tolerating a degree of discomfort. Robin DiAngelo identifies that white fragility is a product of expectations for racial comfort and a low capacity to tolerate racial stress.[31] Linguistic discomfort differs from racial stress, but they both emerge in disruptions to the dominant. Whiteness and Standard English do not march in lockstep. Halcyon's audience includes people of color for whom Standard English is their mother tongue and white people who did not grow up speaking Standard English. That said, many white people in the United States who speak only Standard English spend much of their lives as insulated from linguistic discomfort as they are to racial stress; cultural and racial dominance offers the twin privileges of linguistic and racial comfort. A heteroglossic theatrical event offers a live, social space in which white people who speak only Standard English can practice tolerating discomfort born of dominance's disruption.

Fig. 6.2. Flavia Pallozzi in *The River Bride*. Photograph by Tom McGrath.

## Policing the Boundaries of the Culturally Specific

After a performance of *The River Bride*, an audience member self-identifying as a "proud Tejano" looks over at Flavia Pallozzi, who plays Helena, and comments to our team member Jenn Adams, "That actress over there . . . the one with the red hair . . . What's her stock? I mean, I know you said it is an all-Latinx cast, but . . . I mean, I was just wondering . . . she looks pretty Irish . . ."

Adams, who is white, tells him, "She identifies as Latinx and is from Uruguay, but I don't know more than that."

He responds, "No one is really *from* Uruguay," and offers Adams a lecture about migration patterns and colonization.

"I can't speak to that, but I know there are many cultures that make up the Latin American experience," Adams responds, uncomfortable with the exchange. She later recalls, "I basically just tried to be polite and noncommittal, as I wasn't sure where he wanted the conversation to go and I didn't want to say anything disrespectful to him or about any of the artists involved."

He waves his hand and says, "I'll just go ask her." He marches up to Pallozzi and says, "So you're from Uruguay, is that right?"

Pallozzi launches into fluent Spanish to answer his question, performing her cultural identity through linguistic fluency. She later mentions to me that she has experiences like this with some frequency, in which people question her ethnicity because of her appearance.[32] If, as Anzaldúa argues, "Ethnic identity is twin skin to linguistic identity—I am my language," Pallozzi performs her ethnic identity through linguistic fluency.[33]

As an actor of Uruguayan descent, Pallozzi has been cast as a Brazilian character within mainstream Pan-Latinx casting conventions. These casting practices broadly conform to a principal of *racial congruity*, which Brian Herrera defines as "the principle that performers should, in some meaningful way, be of a kind with the character being portrayed, and that such congruence (of gender, race, physicality, ability, etc.) necessarily amplifies the aptness of the subsequent performance."[34] Pan-Latinx casting conventions operate from the principle that an actor's Latinx heritage authenticates their portrayal of a Latinx character. Within these mainstream casting conventions, this authentication operates regardless of the alignment between an actor's ethnic heritage and the specific ethnicity scripted for a character. Pallozzi's Uruguayan heritage differs from the Brazilian ethnicity of her character, but the audience member does not question this conflation. His resistant interpretation of Pallozzi's body insists on what Herrera calls "the nonwhite raciality of the Latina/o performer."[35]

This conflict demonstrates the inconsistent ways in which the terms *race* and *ethnicity* are understood in the contemporary United States. Angela Pao explains:

> As far as the fundamental distinction between race and ethnicity goes, theatrical practice has on the whole been consistent with current general usage in English-speaking society, where "a physical feature is taken to indicate that an individual is to be assigned to a racial category while a cultural feature is taken as a sign that the individual is a member of an ethnic group."[36]

Race and ethnicity are frequently conflated, and Latinx racial identity is constructed, as Herrera puts it, "occupying the borderlands of racial distinction marking whiteness apart from blackness, Nativeness, and Asian-ness."[37] Under this rubric, Latinx people whose physical features might mark them white are constructed as racially nonwhite, highlighting the slipperiness of racial categorization.

Pao highlights how casting practices "reveal the simultaneous resilience and arbitrariness of ethnic and racial categories. When a company requires a particular racial background, very often the criterion reverts to a genetic definition."[38] This is how Halcyon casts, in keeping with current panethnic casting conventions. The tension between racial categories and ethnic identities crystalizes as a point of contention in this moment of resistant reception, as the Latinx audience member polices the boundaries of the culturally specific. Ju Yon Kim points out, "Beliefs about the body are crucial to structuring the world, and even dated or contradictory beliefs (those that empirical or historical study could potentially discount) can have important effects."[39] Pallozzi is ethnically Latinx, and her body is marked by physical features that would often be assigned a white racial categorization. But the audience member is so invested in his preexisting understanding of *Latinidad*, or Latinness, as racially nonwhite that he is unsettled and distracted by the way Pallozzi's body violates his expectations. He polices the boundaries of *Latinidad* based on his beliefs, forcing Pallozzi to authenticate her cultural identity on linguistic terms. As Herrera points out, "The appearance of authenticity always lay in the eye of the beholder."[40]

This audience member attends *The River Bride*—a production written, directed, and performed by Latinx artists—to participate in an event centering *Latinidad*. He expects the event to center his culture and his identity, which he holds up as a point of pride. When faced with whiteness, embodied by a leading actor violating his expectations of *Latinidad* as racially nonwhite, he feels betrayed—a space he expects to be absent whiteness instead appears, to him, to feature it. Throughout this book, I highlight instances in which white audience members interpret details of performances in resistant ways supporting their preexisting understanding of their own identities. This audience member engages in the same interpretive action—albeit with a different relationship to dominant power structures—exposing the *stickiness* of audience members' preexisting ideas about the way the world does and should work. In this moment, the audience member creates an artificial division, policing the boundaries of *Latinidad* in a way that excludes Pallozzi's body, undermining artists' intentions for the theatrical event to bridge cultural divisions. Pallozzi attempts to use her linguistic fluency to mitigate the rupture, but she is only able to do so after the performance proper. The stickiness of the audience member's racialized understanding colors his reading of the performance, and Pallozzi and Adams do not believe they succeeded in bridging the divide he created.

## Operational Friction

Hans Abbing explains how "the exceptional economy of the arts" hinges on a unique relationship between the gift sphere (donations and grants) and the market sphere (ticket sales) in arts funding.[41] This relationship is particularly clear at the level of institutional budgets, and Abbing argues it ripples down into a landscape in which artist stipends are treated as symbolic gifts rather than market-rate wages for labor. He points out how "artists and others employed in the arts give large amounts of money to the arts by funneling income from second jobs, allowances, or inheritances into the arts," allowing arts organizations to hire skilled labor that is cheap or temporary because those workers find other creative ways to make ends meet while making themselves and their labor available.[42] Danielle Rosvally calls this the "love or money" model, in which an artist "gives and receives time and resources on the basis of love" rather than the expectation of a living wage.[43]

As a small professional theater, Halcyon makes good-faith efforts to prioritize artist salaries, hiring some Actors' Equity Association actors and paying fees for nonunion actors, directors, designers, playwrights, and technical and front-of-house staff that are more generous than many theaters of its size. They do this by relying on minimally stipended administrative labor, as do many small theater companies. As Jesse Green highlights, in Chicago storefront theater, "idealism and sacrifice on all sides keeps the prices down and the work vibrant."[44] Tony Adams as the company's artistic director for a time receives a salary as the theater's only full-time employee, and the theater's associate artistic director, literary manager, production manager, company manager, and director of community engagement receive minimal monthly stipends for labor that amounts to substantial and sustained part-time jobs. All staff members are also ensemble artists, hired on a per-show basis for artistic contributions when they act or direct in the production season.

Most of the midcareer artists of color who participate in the ensemble long term work full-time jobs while raising families. The ensemble's culturally specific programming regularly includes roles for them, and as members of Halcyon's ensemble they are able to sustain full lives that include continuing artistic engagement. The theater consistently draws diverse audiences by creating a long-term artistic community of diverse artists who sustain deep connections to their neighborhoods, churches, families, and friends from outside the theater community. This is no small accomplishment, and it operates as a productive intervention in the hegemonic, haunting whiteness pervading the theater industry.

However, artists working full-time jobs and raising families do not have available time to do the minimally stipended long-term administrative labor required to run a theater company. Many theaters in Chicago are interested in producing culturally specific theater, and good actors of color have opportunities to perform elsewhere. Most of the actors of color who are not currently raising children take advantage of opportunities to act all over the city; many are ensemble members of other companies in addition to Halcyon. These ensemble members sometimes take on administrative projects for Halcyon on a project-to-project basis, fitting service to the ensemble in and around artistic commitments to other companies, but the majority of their contributions to the company are artistic.[45]

The ensemble members with the flexibility, availability, and inclination to take on the bulk of the company's administrative labor are mostly white women in their twenties of middle-class origins. Most of these women act; some also hope to build careers in playwriting or directing. Kay Krohn and Mariah Schultz conducted a study of gender parity in the Chicago theater community, focusing on the 250 plays produced at 52 theaters in the 2015–16 season. They found that 25 percent were written by women, 36 percent were directed by women, and 43 percent of actors hired to perform in them were women.[46] There are far more white women graduating from training programs and moving to Chicago hoping to write, direct, and act than available artistic opportunities with established theater companies.

The Chicago theater community includes many ensemble theaters. On a practical level, many companies select their seasons, hire their artistic staff, and cast their roles from their core ensemble of long-term collaborators and fill in roles and artistic positions around those core teams. The most reliable way for an actor to get to play substantial roles is to be a member of an ensemble (or multiple ensembles) for casting priority. Playwrights and directors join ensembles for access to developmental artistic opportunities with a hope that they will lead to mainstage slots. Artists trade volunteer or minimally stipended labor in exchange for this priority. This is framed as a gift economy, building artistic homes and communities. The exchange feels equitable when most of the labor the company requires from an artist lines up with their larger career goals or when the totality of an artist's labor across multiple jobs provides enough compensation and allows for enough leisure time to feel comfortable and sustainable to that artist.[47] Each artist has their own idiosyncratic sense of "comfortable" and "sustainable," and these definitions shift through an artist's life cycle.

There is a tension between Halcyon's diverse representational ethos and its material need for the cheap labor these young white artists provide. The eighteen-month period of production I cover in this chapter included no mainstage roles for non-Latinx white actors, and through this period the company hired no white directors and no white playwrights. In an ensemble devoted to showcasing the voices of artists of color, there is not a surplus need for white actors—and even less need for early-career white directors and playwrights seeking their first professional credits.[48] The early-career white women artists cycling through minimally stipended staff positions at Halcyon such as literary manager, company manager, and production manager all played at least one principal role in a mainstage production—their labor did result in artistic opportunity—but such opportunity is neither sustained nor sustainable. The exchange of two or three (or more) years of labor for one juicy role is asymmetrical. Priorities shift. The exchange of time-intensive labor for artistic opportunity ceases to appeal when an eighty-hour week no longer feels like fun and artistic opportunities rarely arise.

The gift economy of small professional theater production presupposes that the material conditions underpinning artists' lives materialize from somewhere. It can be sustainable for artists whose cocareers are both flexible and relatively high-paying, or whose artistic career is underwritten by a partner's salary or inherited wealth. For artists of working-class origins, such supports prove elusive. An ensemble boasting a racially diverse ensemble including many artists of working-class origins is not one in which many artists are able to provide ample volunteer labor in addition to artistic labor on top of the cocareer labor required to bring in the material resources to support their families.

Early in this chapter I described the ways in which a diverse ensemble of artists can draw together a legitimately diverse community in an organic way. Artists bring their families, their neighbors, their friends, and their colleagues to the theater, where they anchor diverse audiences. This support network creates inclusive conditions of reception for culturally specific theater, in which, to borrow from Quiara Alegría Hudes, the characters in the plays would be able to afford tickets and would not feel out of place in the lobby.[49] But it takes time and energy to maintain relationships—time and energy that are in short supply in lives packed with cocareer labor, artistic labor, and domestic labor. Many ensemble theaters and theater communities concentrate social energy; artists live and breathe in a tight-knit world intertwining the social and the professional. Halcyon's ensemble spreads across the city with tendrils in many neighborhoods and communities. To do that, many ensemble members dedicate less time to their commitment to the theater, which operates as a nodal point in but not the center of their lives. The thing that makes the company strongest is simultaneously the thing that undermines its operational stability, which makes Halcyon a productive example of a professional theater that resists white supremacy and simultaneously a case study of the material conditions underpinning a status quo that remains hauntingly white.

## Conclusion

✦

# More Work to Be Done

In this brief conclusion, I synthesize patterns appearing across case studies to identify some of the specific theatrical and operational tactics that seem to make the most impact in dismantling white supremacy, offering recommendations for artistic leaders, dramaturgs, and community engagement staff to consider when tackling antiracist projects, tips for white audience members on strategies to begin the process of decolonizing our white gazes, and questions for future study.

The theatrical events described in this book are produced by mainstream theater companies with predominantly white leadership teams, and they share common structural features: actors of color perform material often (though not always) written by playwrights of color, in productions frequently (though not always) directed by white directors, watched by audiences in which most of the spectators are white. The fictional worlds center the experiences of people of color, and many of the productions draw attention to the dynamic of white people watching people of color perform onstage to emphasize the ways in which white audience members are complicit in the structural systems of power the performances depict. Many performance events attempt to use formal post-performance discussions to get audience members to reflect on and personalize what they have seen; these often end with invitations for audience members to move these reflections into actions in the real world outside the theater in the days and weeks following the show.

The artists creating these projects share a common desire to challenge audience members to recognize and act on the injustice of a racist status quo. Keith Wallace highlights the artistry required to navigate white fragility to achieve such goals:

> I want it [theater] to be truthful and honest and transparent and challenging, but it can't be so much so that it could completely shut down conversation or makes people who are actually here feel like they can't engage. It's a really delicate balance, and I'm not sure that there is a balancing point where that actually exists at all.[1]

I have confidence that this balancing point does exist—I have described moments in which artists (including Wallace) appear to achieve it at multiple points throughout the book. That said, it often proves elusive. The delicate balance facilitating brave engagement might only coalesce a few times across multiple performances of the same production. Part of theater's appeal is its ephemeral nature, the way the chemistry of the audience cocreates each theatrical event in an idiosyncratic way. I highlight some of the actions artistic leaders, dramaturgs, and facilitators can take to help increase the likelihood of striking this balance, in full recognition that there is no silver bullet.

## Disrupting De Facto Segregation

Ongoing de facto segregation sustains white supremacy, buffering many white people from racial discomfort by allowing us to ignore, in our day-to-day lives, the ways racialized power structures operate. Many of the case studies I include in this book look to use theatrical events produced in predominantly white spaces to make an impact on individual white audience members' intellectual and emotional understanding of the ways we benefit from these power structures. They create fictional worlds centering the lived experiences of people of color, inviting white audience members to begin to understand perspectives we cannot directly access from within white segregated lives. They then frequently ask those white audience members to stay and reflect on what we have seen in post-performance discussions. These events are designed to be one-off interventions in segregated white lives.

Racism is sustained through continuing de facto segregation; the haunting whiteness of formal theater production is part of—and therefore supports—the structure underpinning white ignorance. Disrupting segregation requires many points of contact over extended periods, making spaces in which interracial relationships and trust can be built. A single event cannot disrupt segregation by itself—a moment of productive communication in a temporary diverse community is no substitute for sustained interracial relationships. That said, if people come to the theater to socialize and to learn, theatrical events have the capacity to operate as equitable, inclusive spaces in which people of color feel heard and seen, white audience members can listen and learn, and a diverse temporary community can participate in a short-term experience of racial solidarity. Across this project, I saw many theatrical events attempt to configure such events and very few succeed, stymied by the haunting whiteness of mainstream theater spaces. When most theater companies sell tickets to subscribers and single-ticket buyers, they mostly attract white patrons; when they host discussions after performances with mostly white audiences, they configure events in which whiteness is the norm. Even when that whiteness is marked—and in such discussions, whiteness is always named—it is still centered because of its ubiquity.

When I saw mainstream, white-led institutions that do not revolve around stable, racially diverse artistic ensembles draw racially integrated audiences, they did so through partnerships with majority-minority institutions. On a practical level, smaller productions were able to configure robust interracial performance events by bringing a group from a single partner to an event—a twenty-five person group from a black church or a majority-minority community college class fills half of a fifty-seat black box. In such events, whiteness is *not* the norm. These events require white audience members to navigate the mild racial discomfort of being in a space in which their whiteness is hypermarked; they extend an invitation for white audience members to practice tolerating this racial discomfort. In racially integrated post-performance discussions, facilitators do not need to work as hard to center the voices of audience members of color as they do in majority-white events, and pressure is not put on isolated audience members of color to represent entire racialized groups. When white bodies do not dominate an event, I watch white audience members speak with less frequency, do more listening, and structure speech acts in ways revealing fewer uninterrogated biases. Such reception conditions help encourage white audience members to consider the impact of their words and actions on the people of color who surround them.

In smaller, culturally specific performance events, whiteness is not the unstated norm. These are frequently produced by underresourced small companies in spaces that do not inherit legacies of haunting whiteness. Such events are better positioned for racial integration—in many cities, white theater patrons will independently travel to working-class neighborhoods to see productions legitimized by cultural authorities (such as high-profile newspaper critics or awards committees) more readily than working-class people of color will travel to elite cultural institutions in affluent neighborhoods. White theater patrons build cultural capitol valued within many professional-managerial class contexts attending culturally specific theatrical events in working-class neighborhoods. Working-class people of color frequently cannot afford tickets to see productions at elite cultural institutions and are in danger of being misrecognized in affluent neighborhoods. This asymmetry of comfortable mobility is a feature of white supremacy that an individual theater would be hard-pressed to dismantle in isolation. White artistic leaders of well-resourced cultural institutions who are serious about intervening in white supremacy would do well to collaborate with and feed resources and attention to these smaller, culturally specific companies, whose work frequently goes unnoticed by cultural authorities.

## Activist Impacts of Aesthetics

Regardless of a theatrical event's aesthetic mode, white audience members tend to interpret what they see in a way consistent with their own sense of themselves as morally good. However, across case studies I observed aesthetic conventions having particular activist impacts.

Many white audience members live in segregated white bubbles and as such do not understand how and why people of color experience daily life in the contemporary United States differently than white people do. Realistic performances of sympathetic characters of color experiencing unjust dangers helped white people empathize with and start to understand some of the most dramatic ways racism causes trauma for people of color in their day-to-day lives. These performances seemed to have the greatest activist impact within theatrical worlds marked by a degree of abstraction—the characters at the center of the productions feel *real* as they navigate worlds marked by a degree of aesthetic distance. For example, *The Bitter Game* and *Pass Over* (discussed in chapters 2 and 4, respectively) both seemed to get white audience members to understand how and why black men carry fear through quotidian activities such as driving and waiting in public spaces, while white people do not need to think twice about such acts. *The Bitter Game* achieves this insight as a solo performance in which one actor plays multiple roles in a fragmented narrative; *Pass Over* achieves it as a multicharacter allegory. In both of these productions, audience members come to care about sympathetic black men who ultimately suffer from racialized violence. The power of white supremacy in both productions is theatrically rendered unnatural; white audience members recognize it as absurdly unjust.

Realistic narrative dramatic conventions create interpretive conditions in which many white audience members can leave the theater without interrogating their own complicity in white supremacy, feeling secure that they are *good white people*. When white characters are present in realistic narrative drama, white audience members find ways to interpret their specificity either as proof of their own moral goodness (by identifying with good intentions) or proof of their own moral superiority (by distancing from racist others). As Bertolt Brecht and Augusto Boal each have critiqued, realistic narrative drama tends to individualize structural problems.[2] In doing so, it exacerbates the problem that many white people understand racism as individuals consciously acting cruelly, motivated by racialized hate. As a result, white audience members watching realistic narrative dramas such as *The White Card* (discussed in chapter 1) misrecognize realistically drawn white characters who perform their whiteness in ungraceful, hurtful ways as *bad, racist white people* and find ways to distance themselves from these characters. They identify these characters as idiosyncratic individuals and cannot read them as representatives of a generalized class of white people, which is how these characters are frequently read by audience members of color. The gap between the ways white people tend to interpret the characters and the way people of color tend to interpret them exacerbates the divide that productions frequently aim to bridge, reducing their activist impact.

## Post-Performance Events

Many of the performance events I studied included some form of post-performance discussion. At their best, these public discussions provide platforms for audience members to reflect on performances and the issues they raise in vulnerable and respectful ways, creating engaging spaces for collaborative interpretation. Such events are relatively rare and marked by common features drawing on core principles of equity, diversity, and inclusion in workshop facilitation.

In the most productive discussions, facilitators lay out clear ground rules to structure the conversation. Martine Kei Green-Rogers offers a set of sample ground rules she uses when she facilitates post-performance discussions for productions tackling controversial subject matter:

1. Respond with "I" statements instead of "you" statements.
2. If you are responding to a question posed, attempt to avoid veering off topic with your answer.
3. If you are responding to the answer of someone else, please identify what idea you are responding to but not the person who originated the idea.
4. Always feel free to share what is on your mind. (Emphasis on your!)
5. Foster a spirit of non-judgement and respect.[3]

Green-Rogers suggests disseminating such ground rules in a production's playbill, thus giving audience members easy and ongoing access to guidelines and providing participants with a common framework they can reference to recognize when rules are violated.

Frequently, open-ended questions such as, "What struck you in the performance?" prompt white audience members who are well steeped in antiracist discourse to perform what Maurya Wickstrom might call an "appropriate affectual condition," supplying responses marking them *good white people*.[4] These conversations are often comfortable events in which white audience members say all the *right things* but do not seem to let themselves be vulnerable or grapple with new ideas in potentially messy ways. Questions about specific aspects of the production (for example, about *3/Fifths Trapped in a Traveling Minstrel Show*, discussed in chapter 3, "Who felt shame watching blackface?") frequently lead to more productively challenging events. This specificity challenges audience members to use the aesthetic distance of the theatrical event to reflect on specific spaces of discomfort. In these events, facilitators have the flexibility to adjust their questions and format in response to the specific needs of the group, reading the room, identifying conspicuous silences, and probing into specific areas of discomfort to intervene in too-comfortable conversations.

When post-performance events find the elusive balance of challenged engagement, facilitators working within clear ground rules and asking specific questions are met by audience members who arrive at the theater with a strong framework in place to recognize the problems posed by the production and the vocabulary to with which to discuss them. In essence, these robust post-performance conversations operate as intermediate or advanced seminars, using the pre-text of the performance as a focal point to discuss complex concepts with audience members prepared to be vulnerable in a challenging conversation.

At their worst, post-performance events reinforce the white dominance of the theatrical event as white audience members demand that the event center on their needs. A lifetime of cultural messages compounded by conspicuous silences upholding a racist status quo leave gaps in white people's understanding of the racialized landscape in which we live. We are sometimes not sensitive enough to the ways the legacy of white supremacy resonates through our bodies and actions. As playwright James Scruggs puts it, "You can't go from ignorant to woke without waking up, and the process of waking up is ugly."[5] In such events, white audience members for whom a production has introduced new ideas use the post-performance event as a space to try out new vocabulary and grapple with new concepts. Sometimes, they are able to do this in a way in which they take responsibility for their ignorance; audience members of all races frequently respond to vulnerability and honesty with critical generosity. But sometimes white audience members reveal their biases by putting their white ignorance at the center of the event, expecting the people of color who are present to operate as racial representatives. This assertion of white dominance frequently annoys, frustrates, and offends the people of color in attendance, reinforcing the haunting whiteness of the theatrical event. It simultaneously provides examples of *bad, racist white people* other whites can feel superior to and, in so doing, avoid focus on their own complicity in the problems the productions present.

These moments are messy—good intentions yield hurtful impacts. Facilitators work hard to honor the white audience member's good intentions, assist with their learning process, and simultaneously mitigate the moment's power to hurt performers and audience members of color. To offer a representative example, at a discussion following *Trapped in a Traveling Minstrel Show*, a white woman commented:

> So, I'm a white person, and I was wondering—I hope it's okay to just share a little bit. I was wondering—So, I kind of—I understand that the white person in this play is kind of, like, portrayed as, like, the bad guy, a little bit, but I kind of don't feel that I was responsible . . . and I kind of want to know, do black folks who are my age—I'm 30—do they feel that they were enslaved? To the same regard that I don't feel like I was a slave owner, do they feel like they were enslaved? How much of it is still carrying on as a young person?[6]

A tense silence descends. The white people sitting around the woman who asks this question shift in their seat, angling their bodies away from her. Some white audience members avert their gaze, studying their programs or their shoes or their hands. Some look to the stage, to the one young black actor in the cast, and he visibly tenses his body as the white woman who asks the question gazes at him, waiting for a response.

In this example, the woman demonstrates that she does not understand how the legacy of slavery continues to resonate in the contemporary United States. It is the subject of her question (she knows she does not understand it) and also manifests in its form (she does not understand contemporary racial dynamics well enough to ask the question in a way that does not cause discomfort to the artists of color onstage and the people of color in the audience). This white audience member reveals uninterrogated biases. She does not recognize the ways she, as a white person, benefits from the legacy of slavery. She asks an actor to speak for all young black people, treating him a representative of a generalized class. Her question clearly makes the actor uncomfortable. The comment catalyzes a number of silent performances of rejection from other white audience members, as they use nonverbal signs to communicate with one another and with the black artists onstage that they are a different kind of white person than she is.

The audience member implicitly directs her question at the young black actor onstage, but the white facilitator steps in to highlight how the legacy of slavery continues to inform contemporary race relations. She honors the audience member's intent to ask a brave question digging "deep into all of our unconscious moments and lives," acknowledges the discomfort the question appeared to cause, and redirects the question toward "what we should feel responsible to do" to change "the attitudes that come forward through history."[7] This response redirects the audience member's focus toward her own responsibilities, takes focus off of the targeted actor, and gives all the artists on the panel some time to decide whether and how they want to respond. The actor to whom the question was directed does not choose to answer, though other, older black artists choose to respond with examples of the ways racialized imbalances of power continue to play out in their lived experiences, highlighting how patterns of oppression track across distinct human experiences.

Moments like this one appear with some frequency in post-performance discussions, and facilitators know it is their responsibility to intervene. Green-Rogers suggests, "If someone shares a thought that causes any emotional response from you, you must acknowledge it and move forward, remembering to address the idea or comment, not the person."[8] Operating from the principal of "responding with 'I' statements," facilitators can use their platform to model discomfort when unrecognized biases arise, working from a place of transparency and in a spirit of openness. Navigating such moments is a specific professional skill, and it is particularly helpful for facilitators of discussions like these to have training in equity, diversity, and inclusion facilitation, either locally or through a national organization such as artEquity.[9]

Teaching and learning about equity, diversity, and inclusion requires trust built over time, and twenty minutes of conversation in a room full of strangers is not a particularly productive format for teaching white people to tolerate racial discomfort. A key principle of equity, diversity, and inclusion training is *knowing your audience*—and frequently, in post-performance settings, facilitators do not know and cannot control audience members' prior exposure to and experience with courageous conversations about racism. When it is possible, preperformance programming might help prepare audience members to receive a production, help facilitators get to know audience needs as they prepare post-performance programming, and deepen audience members' engagement.

Talk might not be the best way for all audience members to reflect after a performance. Matthew Reason highlights how, when audience members do not have the language to describe their responses to what they have seen, they can use drawing to reflect on their experiences, feelings, and memories.[10] Visual-arts based reflection might help white audience members who have not yet developed the vocabulary to productively offer public feedback a method to reflect without language. It might also unsettle white audience members for whom a mastery of social justice language provides too-easy right answers, offering a novel way to refocus on their own ongoing learning process. Laurie Brooks offers another alternative, suggesting that post-performance events infused with dramatic activities might carve out spaces for embodied reflection. She suggests using techniques drawn from Theatre of the Oppressed to enable audience members to create dialogue with the characters through carefully structured activities maintaining the aesthetic distance of the play.[11] Many theaters hire teaching artists to design and facilitate arts-based post-performance workshops for school groups; these existing applied and educational theater practices might be adapted to create spaces for arts-based reflection in lieu of the traditional post-performance discussion. There is a need for more study of how arts-based reflection might affect audience members in these contexts.

## Decolonizing the White Gaze

White audience members arrive at theatrical events embedded in white racial frameworks, carrying unconscious biases in our heads. I speak to my fellow white audience members when I insist that it is our responsibility to do the hard work of dismantling these frameworks. This is an ongoing process and not an end point. I watched white audience members engage in a number of productive strategies to work on decolonizing the white gaze throughout this study, and I experienced some moments that aided me in my own ongoing learning process:

1. *Make the familiar strange, recognizing white experiences as racially specific.* When a white audience member of *The Bitter Game* remarks at the unnaturalness of the ease through which he navigates a traffic stop, he makes his own familiar lived experience strange. He takes responsibility for engaging critically with this experience, seeing it as racially specific and reflective of a particular set of privileged relationships with structural systems of power. When watching performances onstage and in everyday life, white people can ask ourselves critical questions about the texture of racialized performances, recognizing the status quo of white supremacy to be strange.
2. *Empathize, with open eyes.* Ethical white spectatorship of racialized performances requires recognizing key gaps across racialized experiences of the world. Lindsay Cummings suggests, "Rather than latching on to what strikes us as similar in the other, we remain as receptive as possible to our sense of both similarities and differences."[12] Empathy need not erase critical engagement with the reasons why racialized experiences differ, and indeed, caring amplifies the stakes of needing to understand why inequalities exist and what can be done to dismantle oppressive structures. Furthermore, when sympathetic white characters' actions have unintended, negative consequences, we can attend to the distance between intention and impact and engage critically with the reasons for that distance.
3. *Interrogate the distancing impulse.* Some white audience members attending *The White Card* identify their impulses to distance themselves from the white characters performing unconscious biases, recognizing the desire to place themselves in the camp of *good white people* in opposition to a camp of *bad, racist white people.* They catch themselves in the act of responding with outrage to other audience members' problematic performances of whiteness, flagging the desire to distance themselves from racism. They are curious about the impulse and work to counter it, consciously flipping the instinct to insist "I am not like that" to instead ask, "How am I like that/how am I complicit in that?"
4. *Own discomfort as necessary for learning.* When *Trapped in a Traveling Minstrel Show* explicitly connects fear I have felt as a white woman walking alone at night in proximity to bodies of black male strangers to the fear powering acts of excessive police violence against black men, I find this parallel upsetting and uncomfortable. To learn the lesson the moment offers, I need to

> lean into the productive discomfort it provokes. Pushing it away would allow me to avoid complicity and in so doing maintain my white racial comfort. But in letting the discomfort in and accepting the offered lesson, I am able to better understand my own white gaze, enabling me to better catch myself in moments in which I instinctively look with it in everyday life.

## What Theater Can Do

Theater spectatorship is live, embodied, and collective. Race lives in our bodies and we read race on one another's bodies. Theatrical events, in their liveness, can draw our attention to our own racialized bodies as we watch. This attention can help white audience members start to recognize the bodies of knowledge we may or may not have amassed in our white bodies, learning about the racialized specificity of our own white experiences. The collective nature of live theatrical events works to socialize our racialized responses—we see, hear, and feel how the other people around us are responding, and we react in relation to those responses. This process helps audience members solidify how race is understood within our immediate, live community. It can, as I highlight throughout the book, emphasize the ways in which white supremacy endures—but it can also socialize the unacceptability of acts revealing uninterrogated racial biases.

Mainstream theater decorum insists we turn off our cell phones and cease multitasking to focus our attention on a complex story or theme for a period of ninety minutes to three hours, depending on the duration of the event. Blocking out those other stimuli opens up an opportunity for more focused engagement with the nuances of aspects of racial injustice than many other media can offer. It makes some space for reflection needed to transform white habitus. It takes work to get to the theater—audience members frequently make advance plans to see a production and physically travel to a performance site. This planning and effort heighten the significance of theatrical events as *special*. White audience members attending antiracist plays make an effort to carve out time and space to focus on learning about racial injustice. This desire presents an opportunity for public critical pedagogy, as theatrical events work in concert with other parts of a larger cultural landscape.

Some of white supremacy's most traumatic impacts are painful to engage with. White privilege includes the luxury to decide when and how to engage with racialized tragedies. A generation or two ago, social injustices played out on the nightly news, and families gathered around the television to witness and be changed by the spectacle. In our contemporary media landscape, we encounter most of our news of public events solo, through digital devices. A white audience member thanks the artists of *Trapped in a Traveling Minstrel Show* for making space in which he can focus on excessive police violence live, as part of a group—for not letting him scroll past things he does not want to see. Mainstream theater decorum insists we stay in our seats and watch. This is a double-edged sword—the survivors of trauma are often trapped in their seats alongside people who would often rather not look at it—and so aesthetic distance and mechanisms to opt out are key. Theatrical events' collective nature can operate as a supportive structure through which to examine painful truths, bearing witness as a group.

Many artists want to disrupt the haunting whiteness of theater to create inclusive, equitable, pedagogical spaces disrupting racism at a material level within the industry, puncturing de facto racial segregation, bringing together communities to obliterate racism through risky art. This work is fundamentally material, requiring deeper institutional changes than can be addressed by programming antiracist plays or reconfiguring the format of post-performance events. Disrupting whiteness requires *disruption*, unsettling the status quo in ways that will cause a degree of discomfort to those whom the status quo benefits.

I do not, in this book, engage with solutions to the ways white dominance haunts the theater industry that I did not see enacted—for example, strategies for hiring and retaining diverse staff, developing pipelines of young working-class leaders and critics of color via youth theater programs, and building long-term reciprocal collaborations between arts organizations and culturally specific organizations, all of which are beyond the purview of this study. However, these kinds of material changes are necessary to build inclusive institutions and industries. As I collaborated with artists and theaters to collect the data incorporated into this study, I found that many institutions are hungry for participatory action research projects to develop diverse audiences, facilitate community collaborations across multiple tour sites, and develop models for post-performance events striking the perfect balance between challenge and comfort. There is a need for collaborations between theater companies who want to develop innovative solutions and scholars who have the luxury of reflective space to collect and analyze data and disseminate findings. There is much discussion of equity, diversity, and inclusion in the theater industry, and yet many of our institutions remain dominated by whiteness. Internal silos and hierarchies—between industry and academy, between mainstream and applied theater—prevent us from collaborating to develop solutions to urgent problems. As we take a clear-eyed look at the spaces in which we fall short of our ideals—in which we want to do better—we know there is more work to be done to dismantle white supremacy on our stages, in our houses, and in the world beyond the theater. In the words of Augusto Boal, "Theatre can help us build our future, rather than just waiting for it."[13] Let's get to work.

## NOTES

### Epigraphs

Bryant Keith Alexander, "Black Skin/White Masks: The Performative Sustainability of Whiteness (With Apologies to Frantz Fanon)," *Qualitative Inquiry* 10, no. 5 (2004): 647–72, quotation on 650. Copyright © 2004 by SAGE Publications. Reprinted with Permission of SAGE Publications, Inc.

Shannon Sullivan, *Good White People: The Problem with Middle-Class White Anti-Racism* (Albany: State University of New York Press, 2014), 4. Reprinted with Permission of State University of New York Press.

### Introduction

1. Research assistant Pablo Hernandez Basulto was the young Latinx man in the breakout group witnessing this exchange; he recorded it in his field log, March 22, 2018, 68–70.

2. Black Lives Matter is a political movement founded in 2013 by Alicia Garza, Patrisse Cullors, and Opal Tometi in response to the acquittal of George Zimmerman in the murder of Trayvon Martin. It aims to end state-sanctioned violence against black people.

3. Shannon Sullivan, *Good White People: The Problem with Middle-Class White Anti-Racism* (Albany: State University of New York Press, 2014).

4. Caridad Svich, "Dispatches from the Field," in *Audience (R)Evolution: Dispatches from the Field*, ed. Caridad Svich (New York: TCG, 2016), xiii–xviii, quotation on xvi–xv.

5. Alan Brown, "All the World's a Stage: Venues and Settings, and Their Role in Shaping Patterns of Arts Participation," in *The Audience Experience: A Critical Analysis of Audiences in the Performing Arts*, ed. Jennifer Radbourne, Hilary Glow, and Katya Johanson (Bristol: Intellect, 2013), 49–66, quotation on 52.

6. Tammie M. Kennedy, Joyce Irene Middleton, and Krista Ratcliffe, eds., *Rhetorics of Whiteness: Postracial Hauntings in Popular Culture, Social Media, and Education* (Carbondale: Southern Illinois University Press, 2017), 4.

7. National Endowment for the Arts (NEA), *A Decade of Arts Engagement: Findings from the Survey of Public Participation in the Arts, 2002–2012*, NEA research report 58 (Washington, DC: National Endowment for the Arts, January 2015), 4.

8. NEA, *Decade of Arts Engagement*, 12; percentages in text rounded: actual figure for white is 80.4 percent. The study indicates that of the remaining 19.6 percent of theater attendees who do not self-identify as white, 6.4 percent identify as Hispanic, 8.5 percent as African American, and 5.5 percent as other.

9. National Endowment for the Arts (NEA), *When the Going Gets Tough: Barriers and Motivations Affecting Arts Attendance*, NEA research report 59

(Washington, DC: National Endowment for the Arts, January 2015), 21–22. See also NEA, *Decade of Arts Engagement*, 13.

10. Richard V. Reeves, *Dream Hoarders: How the American Upper Middle Class Is Leaving Everyone Else in the Dust, Why That Is a Problem, and What to Do about It* (Washington, DC: Brookings Institution Press, 2017), 32.

11. Carmen Morgan, *What Do We Mean by Diversity and Inclusion?* Theatre Communications Group Diversity and Inclusion Institute Field Reports (2013), 3, http://www.tcg.org/pdfs/advertise/whydiversity.pdf.

12. Marvin Carlson, *The Haunted Stage: The Theatre as Memory Machine* (Ann Arbor: University of Michigan Press, 2001), 5.

13. Melissa Hillman, "The Lies We Tell about Audience Engagement," in Svich, *Audience (R)Evolution*, 13–17, quotation on 16–17.

14. Carlson, *Haunted Stage*, 140.

15. Pierre Bourdieu, *Distinction: A Social Critique of the Judgement of Taste* (Cambridge, MA: Harvard University Press, 1984).

16. Harvey Young, *Embodying Black Experience: Stillness, Critical Memory, and the Black Body* (Ann Arbor: University of Michigan Press, 2010), 21–22.

17. For more on the "racing" of class, see Bryant Keith Alexander, "Black Skin/White Masks: The Performative Sustainability of Whiteness (with Apologies to Frantz Fanon)," *Qualitative Inquiry* 10, no. 5 (2004): 647–72, quotation on 650; and Daniel Rosenblatt, "Things the Professional-Managerial Class Likes: 'Distinction' for an Egalitarian Elite," *Anthropological Quarterly* 86, no. 2 (2013): 589–623.

18. Eduardo Bonilla-Silva, *Racism without Racists: Color-Blind Racism and the Persistence of Racial Inequality in America* (Lanham, MD: Rowman and Littlefield, 2003), 104.

19. For more on this manifestation of white habitus, see the discussion of *Broken Fences* in chapter 5; and Eduardo Bonilla-Silva, Carla Goar, and David G. Embrick, "When Whites Flock Together: The Social Psychology of White Habitus," *Critical Sociology* 32, nos. 2–3 (2006): 229–53.

20. Bourdieu quoted in Mustafa Emirbayer and Erik Schneiderhan, "Dewey and Bourdieu on Democracy," in *Bourdieu and Historical Analysis*, ed. P. S. Gorski (Durham, NC: Duke University Press, 2013), 148. See also Pierre Bourdieu and Loic J. D. Wacquant, *An Invitation to Reflexive Sociology* (Chicago: University of Chicago Press, 1992).

21. Judith Butler, *Gender Trouble: Feminism and the Subversion of Identity*, 2nd ed. (London: Routledge, 1999), xv.

22. Erving Goffman, *The Presentation of Self in Everyday Life* (Garden City, NY: Doubleday, 1959), 20.

23. Sullivan, *Good White People*, 4.

24. Butler quoted in Sullivan, *Good White People*, xiv.

25. Sullivan, *Good White People*, 7.

26. Reeves, *Dream Hoarders*, 3.

27. Reeves, *Dream Hoarders*, 32.

28. Sullivan, *Good White People*, 26.

29. Barbara Ehrenreich and John Ehrenreich, "The Professional-Managerial Class," *Radical America* 11, no. 2 (1977): 7–31.

30. Antonio Gramsci, *Selections from The Prison Notebooks* (New York: Columbia University Press, 1992); Michel Foucault, *Discipline and Punish: The*

*Birth of the Prison*, 2nd ed. (New York: Vintage Books, 1995); Michael de Certeau, *The Practice of Everyday Life* (Berkeley: University of California Press, 1984).

31. Jill Dolan, *The Feminist Spectator as Critic* (Ann Arbor: University of Michigan Press, 1988).

32. Dolan, *Feminist Spectator*, 2–3.

33. Susan Bennett, *Theatre Audiences: A Theory of Production and Reception*, 2nd ed. (London: Routledge, 1997), 2.

34. Roland Barthes, *The Pleasure of the Text*, trans. Richard Miller (New York: Hill and Wang, 1975), 6–7, emphasis in the original.

35. Louis Althusser, "Ideology and Ideological State Apparatuses (Notes towards an Investigation), trans Ben Brewster, in *Lenin and Philosophy and Other Essays* (New York: Monthly Review Press, 1971), 127–93.

36. Jacques Rancière, *The Emancipated Spectator*, trans. Gregory Elliott (London: Verso, 2009), 10.

37. Rancière, *Emancipated Spectator*, 13.

38. Rancière, *Emancipated Spectator*, 22.

39. Bertolt Brecht, *Brecht on Theatre: The Development of an Aesthetic*, ed. John Willett (1957; repr., New York: Hill and Wang, 1997), 71.

40. Augusto Boal, *Theatre of the Oppressed* (New York: Theatre Communications Group, 1985).

41. David Gillborn, "Rethinking White Supremacy: Who Counts in 'WhiteWorld,'" *Ethnicities* 6, no. 3 (2006): 318–40.

42. Joyce Bell and Douglas Hartmann, "Diversity in Everyday Discourse: The Cultural Ambiguities and Consequences of 'Happy Talk,'" *American Sociological Review* 72, no. 6 (2007): 895–914.

43. Robin DiAngelo, *White Fragility: Why It's So Hard for White People to Talk about Racism* (Boston: Beacon Press, 2018), 33.

44. Peggy McIntosh, "White Privilege: Unpacking the Invisible Knapsack," in *Privilege: A Reader*, ed. Michael S. Kimmel and Abby L. Ferber, 4th ed. (Boulder, Colo.: Westview Press, 2017), 28–40, quotation on 34.

45. Phoebe Maltz Bovy, *The Perils of "Privilege": Why Injustice Can't Be Solved by Accusing Others of Advantage* (New York: Saint Martin's Press, 2017), 17.

46. Bovy, *Perils of "Privilege,"* 8.

47. Bovy, *Perils of "Privilege,"* 8, emphasis in the original.

48. For more on privilege, see Allan G. Johnson, "Privilege as Paradox," in *White Privilege: Essential Readings on the Other Side of Racism*, ed. Paula Rothenberg (New York: Worth, 2005): 103–7.

49. Michael S. Kimmel, "Toward a Sociology of the Superordinate," in *Privilege: A Reader*, ed. Michael S. Kimmel and Abby L. Ferber, 4th ed. (Boulder, Colo.: Westview Press, 2017), 1–15, quotation on 10.

50. Richard Dyer, "The Matter of Whiteness," in *White Privilege: Essential Readings on the Other Side of Racism*, ed. Paula S. Rothenberg, 3rd ed. (New York: Worth Publishers, 2008), 9–14, quotation on 10.

51. DiAngelo, *White Fragility*, 9.

52. George Yancy, *Black Bodies, White Gazes: The Continuing Significance of Race in America*, 2nd ed. (Lanham, MD: Rowman and Littlefield, 2016), 19.

53. Joe Feagin, *The White Racial Frame: Centuries of Racial Framing and Counter-Framing*, 2nd ed. (New York: Routledge, 2013), 122.

54. DiAngelo, *White Fragility*, 103.

55. Matthew Frye Jacobson, *Whiteness of a Different Color: European Immigrants and the Alchemy of Race* (Cambridge, MA: Harvard University Press, 1998), 10.

56. Jacobson, *Whiteness of a Different Color*, 6.

57. Jacobson, *Whiteness of a Different Color*, 7–14.

58. Bryant Keith Alexander, *The Performative Sustainability of Race: Reflections on Black Culture and the Politics of Identity* (New York: Peter Lang, 2012), 30.

59. See Yancy, *Black Bodies, White Gazes*; and Claudia Rankine, *Citizen: An American Lyric* (Minneapolis: Graywolf Press, 2014).

60. For some examples, see Faedra Chatard Carpenter, *Coloring Whiteness: Acts of Critique in Black Performance* (Ann Arbor: University of Michigan Press, 2014).

61. James Thompson, *Performance Affects: Applied Theatre and the End of Effect* (Basingstoke, UK: Palgrave Macmillan, 2009).

62. Theatre Communications Group, *Audience (R)Evolution Case Studies Executive Summary* (New York: Theatre Communications Group, 2015), 9.

63. Kirsty Sedgman, *Locating the Audience: How People Found Value in National Theatre Wales* (Chicago: Intellect, 2016), 7.

64. Sedgman, *Locating the Audience*, 3.

65. Sedgman, *Locating the Audience*, 7–12.

66. Willmar Sauter, "Introducing the Theatrical Event," in *Theatrical Events: Borders, Dynamics, Frames*, ed. Vicki Ann Cremona et al. (Amsterdam: Rodopi, 2004), 1–14, quotation on 8–9.

67. Caroline Heim, *Audience as Performer: The Changing Role of Theatre Audiences in the Twenty-First Century* (London: Routledge, 2016), 1.

68. Heim, *Audience as Performer*, 24.

69. Heim, *Audience as Performer*, 22.

70. Alexander, *Performative Sustainability of Race*, 32.

71. For further reading on the pervasiveness of whiteness in theater audiences in theater contexts beyond the United States, see Josephine Fleming, Robyn Ewing, Michael Anderson, and Helen Klieve, "Reimagining the Wheel: The Implications of Cultural Diversity for Mainstream Theatre Programming in Australia," *Theatre Research International* 39, no. 2 (2014): 133–48.

## Chapter 1

1. The artistic team is full of high-profile US artists. Rankine's poetry collection *Citizen* has been honored with many awards and is the only book of poetry to be a *New York Times* best seller in the nonfiction category, Paulus is a Tony Award–winning director, and P. Carl is the founder of HowlRound and one of the most prominent public intellectuals of theater and community engagement in the United States.

2. The space is usually a 550-seat proscenium space, which about 2010 was restored to its original 1932 art deco splendor. This design fully transformed the space.

3. Script for act 2 facilitators, designed by P. Carl, dramaturg, in collaboration with Claudia Rankine and A.R.T. and ArtsEmerson community engagement staff.

4. Claudia Rankine and P. Carl, "A Note from Playwright Claudia Rankine and Dramaturg P. Carl," *ArtsEmerson Blog*, February 22, 2018,http://artsemersonblog.org/2018/02/22/a-note-from-playwright-claudia-rankine-and-dramaturg-p-carl/.

5. This study was funded by Northeastern University's College of Communication, Art, Music, and Design's Research Collaborative, as part of the Design + Human Experience working group, where I was appointed a Dean's Fellow for the duration of this study.

6. In total, we collected data on roughly 1,200 moments of audience performance, including speech acts and gestures; I learned how to handle NVivo data analysis software to manage a data set of this scale.

7. Initial unpublished script for act 2 facilitators, captured by research team members in field notes February 2018.

8. Claudia Rankine, "The White Card," unpublished script, 47. Subsequent page number citations are from this version of the play.

9. Divya Amladi, "The whole discussion/homework thing made it seem like the play was only for white audiences who need to #StayWoke," Twitter, March 6, 2018, 7:19 p.m., https://twitter.com/Divyamladi/status/971223806202269698.

10. Kelly Freebody and Michael Finneran, eds., *Drama and Social Justice: Theory, Research and Practice in International Contexts* (London: Routledge, 2016), 184.

11. Maureen White, telephone interview by the author, May 3, 2018.

12. Ashley Herring, personal email communication with author, May 11, 2018.

13. Judith Malina, in conversation with Hanon Reznikov and Josbeck Tameron, "What Do We Want to Achieve?" *Theater* 13, no. 3 (2001): 153–59, quotation on 154.

14. Brenna Nicely, postprogram focus group discussion at Northeastern University, Boston, April 25, 2018.

15. Rankine, *The White Card*, 42.

16. Sara Ahmed, *On Being Included: Racism and Diversity in Institutional Life* (Durham, NC: Duke University Press, 2012), 5.

17. Ahmed, *On Being Included*, 185.

18. Lauren Berlant, *Cruel Optimism* (Durham, NC: Duke University Press, 2011), 1.

19. P. Carl, in public conversation between P. Carl and Claudia Rankine, Emerson Majestic Theatre, Boston, March 4, 2018.

20. Claudia Rankine, in public conversation.

21. Rankine, *The White Card*, 54.

22. Claudia Rankine, "White Card," unpublished final production draft, 2018, 37.

23. Rankine, "White Card," 38.

24. Rankine, "White Card," 39.

25. Rankine, "White Card," 39.

26. Rankine, "White Card," 39.

27. Jared Sexton, "The Social Life of Social Death: On Afro-Pessimism and Black Optimism," in *Time, Temporality and Violence in International Relations:*

*(De) Fatalizing the Present, Forging Radical Alternatives*, ed. Anna M. Agathangelou and Kyle D. Killian (London: Routledge, 2016), 85–99. Quotation taken from pages 30–31 of earlier version viewed online April 4, 2018: Jared Sexton, "The Social Life of Social Death: On Afro-Pessimism and Black Optimism," *InTensions Journal*, no. 5 (Fall/Winter 2011), http://www.yorku.ca/intent/issue5/articles/pdfs/jaredsextonarticle.pdf. Subsequent citations of the work refer to the this version.

28. East Asian and South Asian audience members navigate white supremacy in racialized bodies, but their bodies are not, generally, overdetermined and misrecognized as dangerous. Neither the white people in the audience nor the Asian people in the audience appeared to fear for their lives as a result of such misrecognition. There is a racialized privilege in such freedom from fear. *Webster's* defines general regions of East Asia as including China, Japan, North and South Korea, Taiwan, and Mongolia, and South Asia as including some or all of India, Pakistan, Bangladesh, Nepal, Bhutan, Sri Lanka, and Maldives.

29. Amos Nasongo, field log, March 6, 2018, 13.

30. Rancière, *Emancipated Spectator*, 22.

31. Michael Finneran and Kelly Freebody, "Tensions and Mythologies in the Liminal Space between Drama and Social Justice," in Freebody and Finneran, *Drama and Social Justice*, 15–29, quotation on 26.

32. Ahmed, *On Being Included*, 13.

33. We documented 399 comments from act 2 discussions; 252 were spoken by audience members presenting as or self-identifying as white, 108 by audience members presenting as or self-identifying as black, and 39 by audience members presenting as or self-identifying as Asian, Latinx, Native American, or biracial.

34. Nicely, focus group.

35. Robert Duffley, postprogram focus group discussion at Northeastern University, Boston, April 25, 2018.

36. White, interview.

37. We heard 25 comments that these ideas are familiar and 63 comments using language in ways that indicate prior exposure to the ideas presented in the play, some of which overlap or are from the same speaker. We heard 37 comments that seem to provide evidence of learning or include a direct reference to learning something new.

38. Monica Prendergast, "Misperformance Ethnography," *Applied Theatre Research* 2, no. 1 (2014): 77–90, quotation on 79.

39. Saidiya Hartman, *Scenes of Subjection: Terror, Slavery, and Self-Making in Nineteenth-Century America* (New York: Oxford University Press, 1997), 22.

40. Hartman, *Scenes of Subjection*, 21.

41. Rankine, *White Card*, 56.

42. Hartman, *Scenes of Subjection*, 21.

43. Berlant, *Cruel Optimism*, 1.

44. Berlant, *Cruel Optimism*, 2.

45. Sexton, "Social Life of Social Death," 30–31.

46. Prendergast, "Misperformance Ethnography," 3–4.

47. *Citizen: An American Lyric* has also been adapted by Stephen Sachs into a play. It premiered to rave reviews at the Fountain Theatre in Los Angeles in 2015.

48. Rankine, *Citizen*, 41.

49. Rankine, *Citizen*, 60.
50. Rankine, *Citizen*, 76.
51. Aaron Coleman, "The History behind the Feeling: A Conversation with Claudia Rankine," *Spectacle*, no. 8 (2015), https://thespectacle.wustl.edu/?p=105.
52. Facilitators were billed with "Additional Staff" in the program, and there were no inserts or alterations to the program to indicate which facilitators were working on each night. American Repertory Theater, *The White Card*, theater program, February 24–April 1, 2018, https://issuu.com/americanrep/docs/the_white_card_program_final.
53. Nicely, focus group.

## Chapter 2

1. L. M. Bogad, *Tactical Performance: The Theory and Practice of Serious Play* (London: Routledge, 2016), 10.
2. Bogad, *Tactical Performance*, 9.
3. A.R.T also toured this production to sites in two low-income African American neighborhoods, Mattapan Teen Center and BCYF Perkins, in an effort to catalyze conversation beyond the performances in Cambridge. I did not see these performances and, as such, their impact is beyond the scope of this essay.
4. Young, *Embodying Black Experience*, 4.
5. Young, *Embodying Black Experience*, 3–4.
6. Keith Wallace, interview with the author at Tatte café in Cambridge, MA, September 11, 2017.
7. A number of white audience members self-identified as social justice activists in low-focus, informal conversation with me or in high-focus post-performance discussion.
8. Keith Wallace, "The Bitter Game" (unpublished manuscript, February 2, 2017), PDF, 9.
9. Bogad, *Tactical Performance*, 51.
10. Bogad, *Tactical Performance*, 51.
11. S. Jamil Ahmed, "When Theatre Practitioners Attempt Changing an Ever-Changing World: A Response to Tim Prentki's 'Save the Children? Change the World,'" *Research in Drama Education* 9, no. 1 (2004): 96–100.
12. Wallace, "Bitter Game," 13.
13. Wallace, "Bitter Game," 17.
14. Wallace, "Bitter Game," 19.
15. Wallace, "Bitter Game," 18.
16. Young, *Embodying Black Experience*, 11.
17. Wallace, "Bitter Game," 19.
18. Post-performance discussion, September 16, 2017. All direct citations from audience members in this chapter are taken verbatim from transcripts of archival recordings made of post-performance events.
19. Wallace, "Bitter Game," 26.
20. Kendrick Lamar, "Alright," track 7 on *To Pimp a Butterfly*, Aftermath Entertainment, 2015. *The Bitter Game* uses the BET/radio edit of the song.
21. Wallace, "Bitter Game," 2.
22. Wallace, "Bitter Game," 2.
23. Wallace, "Bitter Game," 47.

24. Bogad, *Tactical Performance*, 2.

25. *Oxford English Dictionary*, "safe, adj. (and int.)" accessed March 13, 2019, https://www-oed-com.ezproxy.neu.edu/view/Entry/169673?rskey=EvMPhn&result=2#eid.

26. Robert Duffley, email message to author, March 15, 2019.

27. The panel was approved by A.R.T. and by Wallace, who agreed to add Brooks to the panel, provided "the conversation could stay respectful, even if it was challenging." Duffley, email.

28. Post-performance discussion, September 14, 2017.

29. Rancière, *Emancipated Spectator*, 13.

30. Post-performance discussion, September 14, 2017.

31. Mo Barbosa, post-performance discussion, September 14, 2017.

32. Barbosa, post-performance discussion, September 14, 2017.

33. Liz O'Connor, post-performance discussion, September 14, 2017.

34. Post-performance discussion, September 14, 2017.

35. See Bonilla-Silva, *Racism without Racists*.

36. Robert Duffley, email message to author, October 17, 2017, based on notes Duffley took from a telephone call with Keith Wallace, July 26, 2017.

37. Wallace, "Bitter Game," 45.

38. McCarthy interviewed Wallace for a piece in the A.R.T. magazine, and they discussed McCarthy leading a postshow event at that time. Initially, McCarthy planned to facilitate a panel, but the panelists he invited were unavailable and so he adjusted the plan into the discussion format described in this chapter. Duffley, email, March 15, 2019.

39. Post-performance discussion, September 16, 2017.

40. Post-performance discussion, September 16, 2017.

41. Post-performance discussion, September 16, 2017.

42. Keith Wallace, conversation with stage manager Kamra Jacobs and author, Museum of Fine Arts, Boston, MA, September 22, 2017.

43. Wallace, post-performance discussion, September 16, 2017.

## Chapter 3

1. Soyica Diggs Colbert, *The African American Theatrical Body: Reception, Performance, and the Stage* (Cambridge: Cambridge University Press, 2011), 10.

2. Colbert, *African American Theatrical Body*, 7.

3. Colbert, *African American Theatrical Body*, 8.

4. Unless otherwise indicated, all quotations from James Scruggs are from an interview I conducted with him at the Boston Center for the Arts on November 3, 2017.

5. See Saidiya Hartman, *Scenes of Subjection*.

6. Jennifer Schlueter, "'How You Durrin?': Chuck Knipp, Shirley Q. Liquor, and Contemporary Blackface," *TDR/The Drama Review* 57, no. 2 (2013): 163–81, quotation on 164.

7. David Krasner, "The Real Thing," in *Beyond Blackface: African Americans and the Creation of American Popular Culture, 1890–1930*, ed. Fitzhugh Brundage (Chapel Hill: University of North Carolina Press, 2011), 99–123; and Yuval Taylor and Jake Austen, *Darkest America: Black Minstrelsy from Slavery to Hip-Hop* (New York: Norton, 2012).

8. Mike Sell, "Blackface and the Black Arts Movement," *TDR/The Drama Review* 57, no. 2 (2013): 143–62; see also the work of artists such as Dave Chappelle and Spike Lee, notably the latter's film that makes prominent use of blackface: Spike Lee, *Bamboozled* (2000; New York: Criterion Collection, 2020), DVD.

9. Catherine M. Cole and Tracy C. Davis, "Routes of Blackface," *TDR/The Drama Review* 57, no. 2 (2013): 7–12, quotation on 7.

10. Unless otherwise indicated, all quotations from Michael Bryan are from an interview I conducted with him at the Boston Center for the Arts on November 11, 2017.

11. Miwon Kwon, *One Place after Another: Site-Specific Art and Locational Identity* (Cambridge, MA: MIT Press, 2004).

12. Krasner, "Real Thing."

13. James Scruggs, post-performance discussion following matinee on November 11, 2017.

14. Eric Lott, *Love and Theft: Blackface Minstrelsy and the American Working Class* (New York: Oxford University Press, 2013), Adobe Digital Editions EPUB.

15. Post-performance discussion, matinee, November 11, 2017. I did not get to speak with this audience member and did not recognize him personally, but from his response I can only guess he's a scholar of blackface performance.

16. The man's raised hand bolsters my supposition from note 15. See Emily Badger and Quoctrung Bui, "Few Americans Say They've Worn Blackface: But Many Have Seen It," *New York Times*, February 10, 2019, in which the authors reveal that 20 percent of 2,026 American adults polled in February 2019 reported that they had seen someone wear blackface in person, and 5 percent admitted to wearing it. This statistic holds fairly consistent across age brackets, indicating that white people continue to dress in blackface. Blackface minstrel performances are rarely enacted in public, but these findings indicate that they continue in in semiprivate settings such as costume parties.

17. James Scruggs, "Trapped in a Traveling Minstrel Show" (unpublished manuscript, October 6, 2017), PDF, 7.

18. Scruggs, "Trapped in a Traveling Minstrel Show," 7.

19. Scruggs, "Trapped in a Traveling Minstrel Show," 7.

20. Scruggs, "Trapped in a Traveling Minstrel Show," 7.

21. Scruggs, "Trapped in a Traveling Minstrel Show," 8.

22. Scruggs, "Trapped in a Traveling Minstrel Show," 27.

23. Scruggs, "Trapped in a Traveling Minstrel Show," 27.

24. Carole Martin, *Theatre of the Real* (Basingstoke, UK: Palgrave Macmillan, 2013), 3.

25. Scruggs, "Trapped in a Traveling Minstrel Show," 28.

26. Sullivan, *Good White People*, 4.

27. Carson quoted in Scruggs, "Trapped in a Traveling Minstrel Show," , 28.

28. Scruggs, "Trapped in a Traveling Minstrel Show," 29.

29. Scruggs, "Trapped in a Traveling Minstrel Show," 28.

30. James Scruggs, telephone interview with the author, February 19, 2018.

31. Scruggs, telephone interview.

32. Sullivan, *Good White People*.

33. Sullivan, *Good White People*, 29.

34. Jacqueline O'Connor, *Documentary Trial Plays in Contemporary American Theatre* (Carbondale: Southern Illinois University Press, 2013), 2.

35. Scruggs, "Trapped in a Traveling Minstrel Show," 31.

36. Scruggs, "Trapped in a Traveling Minstrel Show," 31.

37. Scruggs, "Trapped in a Traveling Minstrel Show," 31.

38. O'Connor, *Documentary Trial Plays*, 6.

39. Scruggs, "Trapped in a Traveling Minstrel Show," 35.

40. Scruggs, telephone interview.

41. Post-performance discussion, November 9, 2017.

42. Post-performance discussion, evening performance, November 11, 2017.

43. Post-performance discussion, evening, November 11, 2017.

44. "The dozens" is an African American ritual game of quick-witted insults, in which players compete to improvise the most clever, elaborate put-downs of each other and their kin. The first player to lose their temper loses the game. John Russell Rickford and Russel John Rickford offer an example, "Yo mama so fat, instead of usin a beeper, she use a VCR," noting that some players draw the line at insults to mothers. For more on "playing the dozens," see John Russell Rickford and Russel John Rickford, *Spoken Soul: The Story of Black English* (New York: John Wiley and Sons, 2000), 68; Henry Louis Gates, Jr., *The Signifying Monkey: A Theory of African American Literary Criticism* (Oxford: Oxford University Press, 1988); and the TV comedy series *Yo Momma*, created by Wilmer Valderrama, aired April 6, 2006–December 27, 2007, on MTV, https://www.amazon.com/gp/video/detail/B000K3BC72/ref=atv_dp.

45. Colbert, *African American Theatrical Body*, 10.

46. Post-performance discussion, matinee, November 11, 2017.

47. For more on utopian performatives, see Jill Dolan, *Utopia in Performance: Finding Hope at the Theater* (Ann Arbor: University of Michigan Press, 2005).

48. Unless otherwise indicated, all quotations from Mark Rayment are from an interview I conducted with him at the Boston Center for the Arts on November 3, 2017.

49. NEA, *When the Going Gets Tough*.

50. Post-performance discussion, November 9, 2011.

51. Charlotte Meehan, informal conversation with author at Boston Center for the Arts, November 11, 2017.

52. The white woman audience member did not actually reference motherhood in her comment.

53. Bovy, *Perils of "Privilege,"* 19.

54. Hartman, *Scenes of Subjection*, 19.

55. Bovy, *Perils of "Privilege,"* 12.

56. Post-performance discussion, November 9, 2017.

57. Scruggs, "Trapped in a Traveling Minstrel Show," 29.

## Chapter 4

1. Berlant, *Cruel Optimism*, 5.

2. Both the *Chicago Tribune* and the *Chicago Sun-Times* will allow a non-subscriber to access a few articles for free, but beyond that, all content is locked behind a digital paywall.

3. Neil Blackadder, *Performing Opposition: Modern Theater and the Scandalized Audience* (Westport, CT: Praeger, 2003), x.

4. Blackadder, *Performing Opposition*, xi.

5. John Fletcher, "Denouement: Notes on the End(s) of Activism," in *Theatre, Performance and Change*, ed. Stephani Etheridge Woodson and Tamara Underiner (London: Palgrave Macmillan, 2018), 71–80, quotation on 74.

6. Fletcher, "Denouement," 74–75. For more on *moral revolution*, see Kwame Anthony Appiah, *The Honor Code: How Moral Revolutions Happen* (New York: Norton, 2010).

7. Ernesto Laclau and Chantal Mouffe, *Hegemony and Socialist Strategy: Towards a Radical Democratic Politics*, 2nd ed. (London: Verso, 2001), 112.

8. Anthony P. Cohen, *The Symbolic Construction of Community* (Chichester, UK: Ellis Horwood, 1985), 21.

9. Cohen, *Symbolic Construction of Community*, 12.

10. Victor Turner, *The Ritual Process: Structure and Anti-Structure* (Chicago: Aldine, 1969), 154.

11. Laclau and Mouffe, *Hegemony and Socialist Strategy*, 98–100.

12. Sara Ahmed, *Cultural Politics of Emotion*, 2nd ed. (London: Routledge, 2014), 49, emphasis in the original.

13. Ernesto Laclau, *On Populist Reason* (London: Verso, 2005), 70.

14. "The racial bias on display in her reviews are dangerous and disgusting. The Chicago community that makes art and consumes art deserves better." Krista D'Agostino, comment on change.org petition "Stop Inviting Hedy Weiss To Your Productions," June 2017, https://www.change.org/p/the-chicago-theater-community-stop-inviting-hedy-weiss-to-your-productions.

15. Ahmed, *Cultural Politics of Emotion*, 82.

16. Ahmed, *Cultural Politics of Emotion*, 85.

17. Ahmed, *Cultural Politics of Emotion*, 98.

18. Audre Lorde, "The Uses of Anger," *Women's Studies Quarterly* 9, no. 3 (1981): 9.

19. Donatella Galella, "Feeling Yellow: Responding to Contemporary Yellowface in Musical Performance," *Journal of Dramatic Theory and Criticism* 32, no. 2 (2018): 67–77. In *yellowface* performance an actor who is not East Asian dons makeup to play an Asian character. The practice caricatures people of Asian ancestry just as blackface caricatures people of African ancestry. The term can also refer to performances in which people who are not East Asian appropriate aspects of Asian racial identity or play Asian roles without makeup.

20. Meghan Sutherland, "Populism and Spectacle," *Cultural Studies* 26, no. 2–3 (2012): 330–45, quotation on 339.

21. For more detailed discussion of online shaming culture and the ways social justice activist virtual communities police their boundaries, see Bovy, *Perils of "Privilege."*

22. Cass R. Sunstein, *#Republic: Divided Democracy in the Age of Social Media* (Princeton, NJ: Princeton University Press, 2017), 72–73.

23. Sunstein, *#Republic*, 99.

24. Kevin Coval and Idris Goodwin, *This Is Modern Art* (Chicago: Haymarket Books, 2016), 59.

25. Coval and Goodwin, *This Is Modern Art*, 45.

26. Chris Jones, review of *This Is Modern Art*, by Kevin Coval and Idris Goodwin, directed by Lisa Portes, Steppenwolf Theatre, *Chicago Tribune*, March 1, 2015, https://www.chicagotribune.com/entertainment/theater/ct-steppenwolf-show-says-graffiti-is-art-not-vandalism-20150301-column.html.

27. Hedy Weiss, "Steppenwolf's Deeply Misguided 'This Is Modern Art' Spray Paints All the Wrong Messages," review of *This Is Modern Art*, by Kevin Coval and Idris Goodwin, directed by Lisa Portes, Steppenwolf Theatre, *Chicago Sun Times*, March 1, 2015, https://chicago.suntimes.com/2015/3/1/18449609/steppenwolf-s-deeply-misguided-this-is-modern-art-spray-paints-all-the-wrong-messages.

28. Bear Bellinger, "Graffiti makes people like you feel unsafe, but for those of us who grew up surrounded by it, it makes us feel at home and that is who the show is talking to," Facebook, March 3, 2015, https://www.facebook.com/BlackBear710 (content no longer available).

29. Jones, review of *This Is Modern Art*.

30. Weiss, review of *This Is Modern Art*.

31. Sara Ahmed, *Living a Feminist Life* (Durham, NC: Duke University Press, 2017), 37.

32. Mica Cole, "Chris, the frustration that I have with your review is that it is NOT daring. If you wanted to be daring you might have actually reviewed this play based on its own ambitions . . . ," Facebook, March 2, 2015, , https://www.facebook.com/profile.php?id=715118853 (content no longer available).

33. Ellen Chambers (@EllenChambers41), "@HedyWeissCritic Just read your review of THIS IS MODERN ART. Did you really call them URBAN TERRORISTS? Are you that bigoted? #racism," Twitter, March 1, 2015, 9:15 p.m., https://twitter.com/EllenChambers41/status/572264446493507584.

34. Lisa Portes, "Friends—clearly I don't mind engaging in public debate, but I don't support the personal attacks on Hedy Weiss or Chris Jones. Name-calling shuts the conversation down . . . ," Facebook, March 2, 2015, https://www.facebook.com/profile.php?id=715118853&lst=834356%3A715118853%3A1545151789.

35. Chris Jones, "Truly, I don't want to justify my review. I had my say and alternate views are fair enough, assuming they aren't libelous or insulting. To be a critic—one who was young once but has aged . . . ," Facebook, March 2, 2015, https://www.facebook.com/profile.php?id=715118853 (content no longer available).

36. Chris Jones, review of *Native Son* at Court Theatre, *Chicago Tribune*, September 23, 2014, https://www.chicagotribune.com/entertainment/theater/ct-ent-0922-native-son-review-20140923-story.html. See also Chris Jones, "So Why Doesn't Chicago Have a Major African-American Theatre Company?" *Chicago Tribune*, July 18, 1999, https://www.chicagotribune.com/news/ct-xpm-1999-07-18-9907200123-story.html.

37. Keith Jackewicz, "Truly great art, however, extends beyond the borders of personal experience and captures deeper, more enduring angles of reality. When I first saw Othello at the Chicago Shakespeare Theatre," Facebook, March 2, 2015, https://www.facebook.com/BlackBear710 (content no longer available).

38. Jackson Hawley, "I agree that most professional critics lack perspective, which is why I do my best to take in art from all over the world, in all styles.

I've seen tons of graffiti and listened to the artists' defenses of it." Comment on review of *This Is Modern Art* at Steppenwolf Theatre, *Chicago Tribune*, March 2, 2015, https://www.chicagotribune.com/entertainment/theater/ct-steppenwolf-show-says-graffiti-is-art-not-vandalism-20150301-column.html (content no longer available).

39. Alex Huntsberger, "We would absolutely NOT be seeing these kinds of hand-wringings expressed by major theatre critics if it was a show about, say, Shepard Fairey or Banksey." Facebook, March 1, 2015, https://www.facebook.com/alex.huntsberger/timeline?lst=834356%3A4303838%3A1584344299.

40. Mia McCullough (@brazenhussyrant), "If you see a Shakespeare or McDonagh drama, do you criticize the artists for glorifying/condoning murder?" Twitter, March 3, 2015, 6:49 a.m., https://twitter.com/brazenhussyrant/status/572740669028089856.

41. Lisa Yun Lee (@Doclisayunlee), "@hedyweisscritic unable to grasp how criminality functions as a component to black political consciousness in graffiti—read Frantz Fanon," Twitter, March 2, 2015, 12:58 p.m., https://twitter.com/Doclisayunlee/status/572471070063796224.

42. Paul Biasco, "Playwrights Rip *Tribune* and *Sun-Times* Critics of Graffiti-Themed Work," DNAinfo.com, March 2, 2015, https://www.dnainfo.com/chicago/20150302/lincoln-park/graffiti-hating-critics-rip-new-steppenwolf-play-by-city-youth/.

43. Halle Gordon, "Create a Movement: The ART of a Revolution," *HowlRound*, March 8, 2015, https://howlround.com/create-movement.

44. Frank B. Wilderson III, *Red, White and Black: Cinema and the Structure of US Antagonisms* (Durham, NC: Duke University Press, 2010), 5.

45. Transcribed by the author from Spike Lee's filmed adaptation of the Steppenwolf production of *Pass Over* (Amazon Studios, 2018). Quotations of the play are from this transcript; I use "n*****" and "n*****s" in place of the racially offensive words. Lee's film of the Steppenwolf production foregrounds itself in the experience of black audience members taking a bus from the South Side to Steppenwolf in Chicago's upscale Lincoln Park neighborhood. Lee intercuts moments of their reactions into the film, showing, for example, responses of black men and boys to the sound of gunshots on the block. Implicit in this framing is the haunting whiteness of Steppenwolf as a mainstream institutional theatre in an affluent North Side neighborhood whose default audience is predominantly white.

46. Hedy Weiss, "Pass Over' Envisions a Godot-like Endgame for Young Black Men," *Chicago Sun Times*, June 13, 2017, https://chicago.suntimes.com/entertainment/pass-over-envisions-a-godot-like-endgame-for-young-black-men/.

47. Weiss, "'Pass Over' Envisions Godot-like Endgame."

48. ChiTAC did not name Walsh directly; when she recognized her review had been referenced as problematic, she apologized publicly and edited the review to omit the offensive language.

49. Ike Holter, Kevin Matthew Reyes, Tony Santiago, Sydney Charles, and Sasha Smith, "Freedom of Speech Does Not Give License to Racism: The Call to Eliminate Hate Speech from Theater Critics," *Chicago Theater Accountability Coalition*, June 14, 2017, https://www.chitac.org/news/.

50. Holter et al., "Freedom of Speech Does Not Give License to Racism."

51. Bear Bellinger, "Dear Goodman Theatre: I Will Not Perform for Hedy Weiss," *Medium*, June 16, 2017, https://medium.com/@bearbellinger/dear-goodman-theatre-i-will-not-perform-for-hedy-weiss-5b86d972eb68.

52. Kelly Ann Parker (@elle_parks), "I'm begging everyone, please stop inviting @HedyWeissCritic to your shows. Chicago doesn't need anymore racists and she must be stopped," Twitter, June 13, 2017, 6:10 a.m. https://twitter.com/elle_parks/status/874615010131144704.

53. Mark Schreppe, "We Need to Talk about Hedy Weiss," *Hawk Chicago* (blog), June 14, 2017, http://www.thehawkchicago.com/articles/we-need-to-talk-about-hedy-weiss.

54. Maddie Martin, "I'm signing this petition, because I believe in a safe positive theatre world in which all artists regardless of race, sexual orientation, appearance, etc. can create and collaborate without the fear of being judged unfairly," comment on change.org petition "Stop Inviting Hedy Weiss to Your Productions," June 2017, https://www.change.org/p/the-chicago-theater-community-stop-inviting-hedy-weiss-to-your-productions.

55. Jay Easton, "Racism is not acceptable—not in theatre; not anywhere else," comment on change.org petition "Stop Inviting Hedy Weiss to Your Productions," June 2017, https://www.change.org/p/the-chicago-theater-community-stop-inviting-hedy-weiss-to-your-productions.

56. Nic Park, "Hedy Weiss is a racist dinosaur," comment on change.org petition "Stop Inviting Hedy Weiss to Your Productions," June 2017, https://www.change.org/p/the-chicago-theater-community-stop-inviting-hedy-weiss-to-your-productions.

57. Tracy Swartz, "Steppenwolf Denounces 'Bigotry' in *Sun-Times* Critic's Review," *Chicago Tribune*, June 15, 2017. http://digitaledition.chicagotribune.com/tribune/article_popover.aspx?guid=a56a3acd-cbf1-45e3-acbb-fb7fbb08586a.

58. Editorial, "Hey Steppenwolf, Critics Gonna Critique," *Chicago Tribune*, June 19, 2017. https://www.chicagotribune.com/opinion/editorials/ct-critic-weiss-sun-times-pass-over-edit-0620-md-20170619-story.html.

59. Chicago Tribune Editorial Board, "Statement of Principles," *Chicago Tribune*, February 23, 2016, https://www.chicagotribune.com/news/opinion/editorials/ct-tribune-statement-of-principles-20160223-story.html.

60. Chicago Tribune Editorial Board, "Statement of Principles."

61. Fletcher, "Denouement."

62. Chicago Tribune Editorial Board via Chicago Tribune Opinion (@chitribopinions), "Complain too much, theater people and you look like crybabies, especially if you also accept praise," Twitter, June 20, 2017 10:18 a.m., https://twitter.com/Trib_ed_board/status/877213959836717057.

63. Chicago Sun-Times Editorial Board, "We Stand by Our Critic and a Vital Chicago Theater Scene," *Chicago Sun-Times*, June 23, 2017.

64. Sun-Times Editorial Board, "We Stand by Our Critic."

65. Joseph Sikora (@JosephSikora4), "I support @HedyWeissCritic," Twitter, June 16, 2017 7:18 a.m., https://twitter.com/JosephSikora4/status/875719330117320704.

66. Elizabeth Johnson, "So disappointed in Steppenwolf's over-the-top response to the review. Not exactly the way to foster open dialogue. There was a way to address your concerns. This wasn't it. Shameful to malign Hedy in the

way you did," Facebook, June 23, 2017, https://www.facebook.com/search/top/?q=Steppenwolf%20Theatre%20Company&epa=FILTERS&filters=eyJycF9jcmVhdGlvbl90aW1lIjoie1wibmFtZVwiOlwiY3JlYXRpb25fdGltZVwiLFwiYXJnc1wiOlwie1xcXCJzdGFydF9tb250aFxcXCI6XFxcIjIwMTctMDZcXFwiLFxcXCJlbmRfbW9udGhcXFwiOlxcXCIyMDE3LTA2XFxcIn1cIn0iLCJpbnRlcmFjdGVkX3Bvc3RzIjoie1wibmFtZVwiOlwiaW50ZXJhY3RlZF9wb3N0c1wiLFwiYXJnc1wiOlwiXCJ9In0%3D.

67. Ahmed, *Cultural Politics of Emotion*, 10.

68. The Chicago Theatre Standards are in part based on the workplace safety rules and communication pathways required by Actors Equity Association. For more information or to access the standards, see #NotInOurHouse: A Chicago Theatre Community (website), https://www.notinourhouse.org/.

69. Kevin Coval quoted in Rick Kogan and Tracy Swartz, "Some Theaters Say They Will No Longer Invite *Sun-Times* Critic Hedy Weiss to Openings," *Chicago Tribune*, June 23, 2017, www.chicagotribune.com/entertainment/theater/ct-hedy-weiss-coalition-ent-0623-20170622-story.html.

70. Hedy Weiss, "Generations Meet in Joyful Song," *Chicago Sun-Times*, October 2, 2007, https://www.pressreader.com/usa/chicago-sun-times/20071002/282333970535465. This is Weiss' review of Black Ensemble Theatre's 2007 production of the world premiere musical *Sounds so Good, Makes You Wanna Holler*, written by Rueben Echoles and Dawn Bless and directed and choreographed by Echoles. The production ran from September 30 to November 20, 2007.

71. Sianne Ngai, *Ugly Feelings* (Cambridge, MA: Harvard University Press, 2007), 3.

72. Sullivan, *Good White People*.

### Chapter 5

1. In this capacity, I attended each of the productions I describe in this chapter only once. Following each performance, I immediately wrote detailed field notes capturing the event. I took detailed notes during the *Forgotten Future* town hall and interviewed Sarah Moeller.

2. Rancière, *Emancipated Spectator*, 75.

3. Meghan A. Burke, *Racial Ambivalence in Diverse Communities: Whiteness and the Power of Color-Blind Ideologies* (Lanham, MD: Lexington Books, 2012), 97–99.

4. John W. Meyer and Ronald L. Jepperson, "The 'Actors' of Modern Society: The Cultural Construction of Social Agency," *Sociological Theory* 18, no. 1 (2000): 100–120, quotation on 100.

5. Meyer and Jepperson, "'Actors' of Modern Society," 101.

6. For more information on Collaboraction, see its website, https://www.collaboraction.org.

7. Sarah Moeller, interview by the author, Chicago, November 7, 2014. Unless otherwise indicated, all quotations from Sarah Moeller are from this interview.

8. Snowball sampling is a process in which a researcher asks participants in their study to recommend or help recruit other prospective participants with whom they share key traits, accessing the social networks and expertise of the people participating in the study.

9. Turner, *Ritual Process*.
10. C. Martin, *Theatre of the Real*, 10.
11. Sonja Arsham Kuftinec, "'Do You Need Help?': Dialogics of Change in Community-Based Theatre," *Theatre Survey* 57, no. 3 (2016): 419–23.
12. Sarah Moeller, telephone interview with the author, March 2, 2016.
13. Moeller, telephone interview.
14. C. Martin, *Theatre of the Real*, 12.
15. Rancière, *Emancipated Spectator*, 103.
16. For more on color-blind racism, see Eduardo Bonilla-Silva, *Racism without Racists: Color-Blind Racism and the Persistence of Racial Inequality in America*, 5th ed. (Lanham, MD: Rowman and Littlefield, 2018).
17. Lara Nielsen and Patricia Ybarra, eds., *Neoliberalism and Global Theatres: Performance Permutations* (New York: Palgrave Macmillan, 2012), ix–x.
18. For the review I reference, see Dani Snyder-Young, "Race and Real Estate in Next Theatre's *Luck of the Irish* by Kirsten Greenidge," *HowlRound*, March 25, 2014, https://howlround.com/race-real-estate-next-theatres-luck-irish-kirsten-greenidge.
19. Alexander, *Performative Sustainability of Race*, 29. Alexander critiques the way he is accused of "acting White" when enacting performances common to upper-middle class people, as if such actions are "presumably relegated exclusively to White people."
20. Sullivan, *Good White People*, 5.
21. Bell and Hartmann, "Diversity in Everyday Discourse," 907.
22. Feagin, *White Racial Frame*, 137.
23. For more on "dog whistle politics," see Ian Haney López, *Dog Whistle Politics: How Coded Racial Appeals Have Reinvented Racism and Wrecked the Middle Class* (Oxford: Oxford University Press, 2014).
24. Bridget Kiger Lee and Patricia Enciso, "Testing the Waters of Change in the Classroom: The Case for Incremental Transformation in Teacher Practice," in Woodson and Underiner, *Theatre, Performance and Change*, 183–91, quotation on 189.

## Chapter 6

1. Caridad Svich, "De Troya" (unpublished manuscript), PDF, 67.
2. Halcyon Theatre, "Mission, Values, and Vision," accessed June 18, 2018, https://halcyontheatre.org/missionvaluesandvision.
3. Moon-Kie Jung, *Beneath the Surface of White Supremacy: Denaturalizing US Racisms Past and Present* (Stanford, Calif.: Stanford University Press, 2015), 59.
4. Svich's *De Troya* does not specify the family's origins as Puerto Rican in the text; it is written in a manner open to pan-Latinx casting. The Halcyon production made this culturally specific choice.
5. Tony Adams, email to the author, October 1, 2018.
6. Heim, *Audience as Performer*.
7. Halcyon does not routinely collect information on how its audience heard about its productions, and so I cannot provide specific figures on the percentage of its audience comprised of friends and family of artists. Adams estimates that friends and family compose 25 to 30 percent of Halcyon's audience.

8. For more information about the details of this study, see Dani Snyder-Young, "Ownership, Expertise, and Audience Research: Developing Collaborative, Artist-Centric Methods for Studying Reception," *Theatre Topics* 30, no. 1 (March 2020), 31–40.

9. Jenn Adams, who is white, house managed and researched all three productions. The *American Hwangap* team also included Hayana Kim, who is Korean, and Maggie Patchett, who is white; the *River Bride* team included Victoria Apodaca, who is Latinx, deZane Rouse, who is black, and Jamie Kreppein, who is white and whose work on this project was supported by an Illinois Wesleyan University Eckley Fellowship. The *De Troya* research team also included Rouse and Gelyssa Rankin, who is Caribbean, front of house, along with the full ensemble of Latinx actors.

10. Heim, *Audience as Performer*, 22.

11. Gloria Anzaldúa, *Borderlands/La Frontera: The New Mestiza*, 4th ed. (San Francisco: Aunt Lute Books, 2007), 25.

12. Barry Freeman, *Staging Strangers: Theatre and Global Ethics* (Montreal: McGill-Queen's University Press, 2017), xix.

13. Ahmed, *Living a Feminist Life*, 34.

14. Gillian Sandstrom and Elizabeth Dunn, "Social Interactions and Well-Being: The Surprising Power of Weak Ties," *Personality and Social Psychology Bulletin* 40, no. 7 (2014): 910–22.

15. Lewis Hyde, *The Gift: Creativity and the Artist in the Modern World*, 2nd ed. (New York: Vintage Books, 2007), 73.

16. Hyde, *Gift*, 73.

17. Jamie Kreppein, "Where does the spectatorship of theatrical events and current events intersect?," unpublished final paper for Eckley Fellowship, Illinois Wesleyan University, August 2017, 12.

18. Lloyd Suh, *American Hwangap* (New York: Samuel French, 2010), 14–15.

19. Suh, *American Hwangap*, 31. A *ah-joo-mah* is a married woman.

20. Lindsay Cummings, *Empathy as Dialogue in Theatre and Performance* (Basingstoke, UK: Palgrave Macmillan, 2016), 7.

21. Irene Hsiao, "A True American Family: A Review of American Hwangap at Halcyon Theatre," *New City Stage*, March 4, 2017, https://www.newcitystage.com/2017/03/04/a-true-american-family-a-review-of-american-hwangap-at-halcyon-theatre/.

22. Rancière, *Emancipated Spectator*, 22.

23. Marvin Carlson, *Speaking in Tongues: Languages at Play in the Theatre* (Ann Arbor: University of Michigan Press, 2006), 9.

24. Anzaldúa, *Borderlands/La Frontera*, 77.

25. Carlson, *Speaking in Tongues*, 17.

26. Caridad Svich, "De Troya," 2.

27. Anzaldúa, *Borderlands/La Frontera*, 81.

28. Caridad Svich, "De Troya," 61.

29. Lisa Jackson-Schebetta, "In the Heights at the University of Pittsburgh: Failures, Successes and Change," in Woodson and Underiner, *Theatre, Performance and Change*, 145–54, quotation on 153.

30. Jorge Huerta, "Fifty Years of Chicano Theatre: Mapping the Face(s) of the New American Theatre," in Woodson and Underiner, *Theatre, Performance and Change*, 133–43, quotation on 136.

31. Robin DiAngelo, "White Fragility," *International Journal of Critical Pedagogy* 3, no. 3 (2011): 54–70, quotation on 54.

32. This exchange was relayed to me both by Jenn Adams and Flavia Pallozzi in informal interviews on June 9, 2017, and documented in detail by Jenn Adams in field notes dated June 14, 2017.

33. Anzaldúa, *Borderlands/La Frontera*, 81.

34. Brian Eugenio Herrera, *Latin Numbers: Playing Latino in Twentieth-Century U.S. Popular Performance* (Ann Arbor: University of Michigan Press, 2015), 75.

35. Herrera, *Latin Numbers*, 74.

36. Angela C. Pao, *No Safe Spaces: Re-casting Race, Ethnicity, and Nationality in American Theater* (Ann Arbor: University of Michigan Press, 2010), 11.

37. Herrera, *Latin Numbers*, 80.

38. Pao, *No Safe Spaces*, 13.

39. Ju Yon Kim, *The Racial Mundane: Asian American Performance and the Embodied Everyday* (New York: New York University Press, 2015), 5.

40. Brian Eugenio Herrera, "'But Do We Have the Actors for That?': Some Principles of Practice for Staging Latinx Plays in a University Theatre Context," *Theatre Topics* 27, no. 1 (2017): 23–35, 33.

41. Hans Abbing, *Why Are Artists Poor? The Exceptional Economy of the Arts* (Amsterdam: Amsterdam University Press, 2002), 31.

42. Abbing, *Why Are Artists Poor?* 46.

43. Danielle Rosvally, "Letting the Love Love You: Navigating the Gray Areas of a Love or Money Industry; Part One: Finding Love." *HowlRound*, October 3, 2013, http://howlround.com/letting-the-love-love-you-navigating-the-gray-areas-of-a-love-or-money-industry-part-one-finding.

44. Jesse Green, "How Chicago Is Changing Theater, One Storefront at a Time," *New York Times*, October 8, 2018, https://www.nytimes.com/2018/10/08/theater/chicago-theater-scene.html.

45. With the notable exception of Fin Coe, who served as the company's associate artistic director in 2015–17.

46. Collaboraction, "Summary of *Gender Breakdown* 2015–16 Chicago Theater Data," news release, accessed July 27, 2018, http://www.windycitymediagroup.com/pdf/Collab_GenderBreakdown%20data%20summary_2.8.17.pdf.

47. My experience working with Halcyon as a midcareer white scholar-artist largely fit this description.

48. The company created a prototype program to give ensemble artists space to drive developmental projects. It was conceived as a way to develop projects for eventual mainstage production. However, Halcyon typically produces two full mainstage productions each year, and these productions are helmed by experienced directors and written by playwrights with national or international reputations. Prototype processes driven by early-career artists provided developmental opportunities but did not, in practice, result in mainstage productions.

49. Quiara Alegría Hudes, "High Tide of Heartbreak," *American Theatre*, October 2018, https://www.americantheatre.org/2018/09/27/high-tide-of-heartbreak/.

### Conclusion

1. Wallace, interview.

2. See Brecht, *Brecht on Theatre*; Boal, *Theatre of the Oppressed.*

3. Martine Kei Green-Rogers, "Talkbacks for 'Sensitive Subject Matter' Productions: The Theory and Practice," in *The Routledge Companion to Dramaturgy*, ed. Magda Romanska (London: Routledge, 2015), 490–94, quotation on 491.

4. Maurya Wickstrom, *Performance in the Blockades of Neoliberalism: Thinking the Political Anew* (Basingstoke, UK: Palgrave Macmillan, 2012), 97.

5. Scruggs, telephone interview.

6. Talkback following a performance of *3/Fifths Trapped in a Traveling Minstrel Show*, Boston Center for the Arts, November 9, 2017.

7. Talkback.

8. Green-Rogers, "Talkbacks for 'Sensitive Subject Matter' Productions," 491.

9. ArtEquity offers facilitator trainings, webinars, and additional resources for equity, diversity, and inclusion specifically focused on the needs of theater artists and institutions. For more information, see the organization's website, https://www.Artequity.org.

10. Matthew Reason, "Watching Dance, Drawing the Experience and Visual Knowledge," *Forum for Modern Language Studies* 46, no. 4 (October 2010): 391–414.

11. Laurie Brooks, "Put a Little Boal in Your Talkback," *American Theatre*, December 2005, 58–60.

12. Cummings, *Empathy as Dialogue*, 33.

13. Augusto Boal, *Games for Actors and Non-Actors* (London: Routledge, 1992), xxxi.

# INDEX

Page numbers in italic refer to figures.